I0612741

THE YEGGMAN'S
APPRENTICE

C.K. CRIGGER

WOLFPACK
PUBLISHING
— EST 2013 —

WOLFPACK
PUBLISHING
— EST 2013 —

Paperback Edition
Copyright © 2019 C.K. Crigger

Published in the United States by Wolfpack Publishing, Las
Vegas

Wolfpack Publishing
6032 Wheat Penny Avenue
Las Vegas, NV 89122

wolfpackpublishing.com

Paperback ISBN 978-1-64119-828-8
eBook ISBN 978-1-64119-827-1

Library of Congress Control Number: 2019944492

THE YEGGMAN'S APPRENTICE

Chapter One

"Take your time. You've got all night. Pay attention to the job."

One area of Wilkie's mind heard this oft-repeated advice as if it were a part of her heartbeat, which, although she hated to admit it, tripped along at a terrific rate. At the same time, another area, the real physical one, heard something else, the *snick* as the lock's tumblers caught and registered. Finally. This was the second of those sounds she needed to hear. One more to go. The last should be the easiest; the middle number always being the hardest to catch.

Not much longer now, she thought.

Better not be. Her internal time clock told her that much. She'd already been here too long, knees cramped from crouching in front of the biggest safe she'd ever seen. Let alone attempted to open.

Not attempt. She *had* to open it.

Wilkie, short for Wilhelmina, Van Slyke wished she dared light a lamp and look at the watch pinned under the lapel of the man's coat she wore. She also wished she could shed the coat since she was sweating like a stevedore on a San Diego dock. Although, since she'd never been to San Diego, let alone met a stevedore, the point was moot. Combine a closed room where the summer heat lingered even into the night with a heavy coat, add a whole wad of nervous stress, and she felt likely to faint. But she couldn't and wouldn't. She had a job to finish.

Slowly, ever so slowly, she twisted the dial to the left, counting down the spaces. Eight-one, eighty, seventy-nine... And then she had it. The final click sounded, and relief flooded in.

The door to the Spooner Bank and Trust of Butte's massive Mosler safe swung open at last, revealing stacks of cash and several boxes of folders held closed by a thin string wound around an affixed cardboard button. These were her target. Or the ones marked Burke, Boothe & Venig, anyway. Now she had to spark a light.

One candle is all she allowed herself. No battery operated doohickies for her. No lamps or lanterns. Just the single candle set in a holder that kept light from sneaking out the back.

Her hands trembled as, steadfastly ignoring the money, she searched through the folders. At least they were all readily identifiable and filed alphabetically by last name. The folders she needed were at the back of one box. In opposite alphabetical order she found Sylvester first, then Banks, and finally, Badrac. Relieved and anxious to be away, she snatched up the folder. Only by accident, as she started to put the others back in order, did she notice two files crammed in the same folder. Both bore the same name. Magdalena Badrac, no mistake. But why were there two? There couldn't be two women of the same name, at the same bank, could there? An unusual name like that?

The folders appeared to match, so at first, she thought she was simply looking at a duplicate. But then she spotted a monetary total at the bottom of the fifth page in the second file and gasped. Fingers flying, she found an almost identical page in the first file and compared them. *Almost identical.* Those were the important words because the totals differed by several thousand dollars. Several? Make that many thousand dollars.

Enough for fraud, probably enough for murder. It cast doubt into Wilkie's mind about the honesty of their client. But that wasn't part of the job. None of her business.

Fiddle dee dee! Now she had to go back and check about the other two. Had she gotten everything the client demanded? Time was not on her side.

A slight sound from beyond the vault room registered on her danger scale. Most people wouldn't have noticed it, but Wilkie's hearing, honed and polished over the years, was more sensitive than average. She heard the metallic rattle of a key in a lock. The shift of feet on the floor. Sensed the rustle of clothing. And then a sound like that of a revolver's cylinder turning over as the hammer was eased back.

They were on to her. Or not her, specifically, but someone.

She shoved all the folders she'd found into specially made pockets in the coat lining, where they settled along her ribs. A blown-out candle allowed the odor of burned wax to spread and linger. Instead, she licked her fingers and pinched the wick to extinguish the flame, then stowed the holder in an asbestos-lined side pocket. Last of all, she closed the safe door with a soft 'snick' and spun the dial.

There. All locked up tight and, she trusted, nothing to show she'd broken in. Another name added to her uncle Jameson's satisfied customer file. Heart thundering like the power-driven wheels on a steam locomotive, Wilkie slipped from the vault room and shut the heavy door behind her. Padding silently on moccasin-clad feet, she made her way down the hall toward the back entrance. If whoever had entered the building had only known, she'd left this door not just open, but the slightest fraction ajar, after she picked the lock.

A dim amount of outside light entered the hall through a small transom window. Wilkie's heart almost failed her when a coat hanging from a hook just inside the door appeared to be a person. She hadn't even noticed it, particularly when she entered. A bench maybe five-feet long sat under the coat, with some overshoes sitting on top. Both were there for the poor unfortunate who had to bring in wood or coal from outside and needed to keep his or her clothing from becoming soiled.

Hurrying now, she grabbed at the knob, ready to pull the door wider when something, a sense of wrongness, struck and halted the motion.

Behind her, a lantern's light slashed from side-to-side as footsteps drew closer, a man's shadow leading the way. She imagined she could see a gun, although maybe that was impossible. Ahead of her, through the door, the wrongness coalesced into danger.

Trapped.

Breath coming short, Wilkie did the only thing she could see to do. She dropped to the floor and rolled under the bench, careful to keep knees, feet, and arms locked close to her crunched body.

Scant seconds later, a man walked past as she held her breath. He tugged the knob, stumbling as the door flew open without resistance.

He spoke. "Did you catch him?"

"Catch him? Nobody came out this way." A man answered from outside. His voice was deep, and he spoke with an accent she had never heard before.

Wilkie couldn't help feeling proud of her instincts, just then. They'd saved her from walking right into an ambush. But she'd best not be too proud. Her mission wasn't yet complete. She still had to get out of here and deliver the documents.

"No one? Are you certain? I thought I heard someone. And why is this door unlocked?"

"I don't know, but I'm telling you, no one came through it. Maybe you heard a rat."

"There are no rats in here." It had been an insult.

Teeth gnashing down on her lip, Wilkie tasted blood. Good God. She hoped he was right. Rats gave her the horrors.

The outside man entered. Two sets of feet became visible. One set wore highly polished dress shoes, pant legs just covering the high tops. The other was clad in high laced boots; his trousers tucked in. The night watchman, she supposed.

Wilkie thought she recognized the laced boots, oddly enough. She'd met someone who wore similar ones in the hotel tonight, after dinner when she'd been mounting the stairs to her room on the second story. Or not met him, exactly, but come face-to-face with him as he'd been coming down. She shuddered, remembering pale, cold eyes.

Fortunately, neither man saw the slight movement under the bench because the dress shoe man, whom she figured was the manager here, said, "Well, come on, then. He must still be inside. We'll search the building."

"One of us should stay here. Make sure he doesn't double back." The English was fluent, but his accent thick.

The dress shoes stepped forward. A key rattled in the lock. "There. Nobody will be leaving through this door. Not unless he has the key. And Hoerner is at the front. If the thief tries to escape through there, Hoerner will hear him. We'll catch the intruder in a pincher."

"You're the boss," the other man said, a shrug easily imagined.

The two pairs of feet moved beyond Wilkie's sight, and she dared to take a small breath.

"I'll search the upper floor," the manager said as the two went down the hall, toward the public part of the building. "You check the rooms down here."

"Yes. Don't worry. If he's still here, I'll get him."

The manager's voice turned icy. "You'd better. That's what I'm paying you for."

The other man didn't answer.

The sound of their fading footsteps galvanized Wilkie into action. Her picks were out of one of the coat's special pockets before she'd gotten to her feet. This kind of lock, no matter what the manager thought, proved easy for her tools. Once outside, she paused.

Normally, in a situation like this, she'd simply scurry away as fast as her legs could carry her. But this case seemed a little different. Best, she thought, a small smile touching her lips, to lock up after herself. Hard for anyone to claim a break-in when the door remained locked.

In less than a minute, she'd skipped around the corner onto the deserted main street. Slinking from storefront to storefront like a wraith, it didn't take long for her to reach the hotel. To avoid the entrance with its open lobby, she went around to the side overlooking a stable for their guests' horses, which stood mostly empty. The majority of visitors to the hotel arrived by train or, nowadays, occasionally in a dashing motorcar.

Stopping out of sight, she waited a few moments to make certain she was alone before approaching. A rope ladder, barely visible, dangled from an open second-story window. Wilkie swarmed up the ladder as lithely as any circus performer and climbed in.

She landed almost on top of her uncle, narrowly avoiding knocking him over. He slept, sitting propped against the wall, snoring his head off.

Wilkie stifled a grin. Sure as the world, he'd be complaining of a stiff neck tomorrow. Her fault, the caper having taken longer than either of them expected. Her inexperience showing up.

Jameson wouldn't blame her, though. It had, after all, been his voice echoing in her brain telling her to take the time she needed. To not get careless. To do it all by the careful training he'd provided in the years since he'd begun teaching her. Anyway, it had paid off. The object of the theft retrieved, she'd gotten away clean with no one the wiser. Only her second job on her own, and she'd done it.

Imagining rockets bursting overhead, euphoria claimed her, and she laughed out loud.

"Hey, Uncle Jameson," she said. "Wake up. I'm home free."

Chapter Two

"Jameson? Uncle Jameson?"

Beginning to think her uncle had been hitting the sauce, concern touched Wilkie when she received no response to either her laughter or to her greeting. In fact, he didn't so much as twitch a muscle. Just kept right on snoring.

Grimacing, she gave his arm a quick shake. A quick, careful shake, before smartly stepping back. A man easily startled; Jameson had hair-trigger reflexes. She'd once seen his little hide-out gun appear in a blink, holding an importunate person in shocked silence with his mouth hanging open. Seen something similar more than once, to tell the truth.

But nothing so precipitous happened this time. Apparently, Jameson hadn't felt her touch, let alone heard her speak. Shocked by his lack of reaction, Wilkie's breath drew in.

She'd never forget a certain poker game in a logging town over the line into Montana they'd visited once. Jameson had begun taking her along on nearby jobs, using a girl's presence as a cover for his activities. He told everybody she was his daughter. A lie. A little white one, as he treated her like a daughter. And sometimes lately, she'd wondered—Well. Enough speculating.

She disremembered exactly which town they'd visited, but not what happened. A poker game went awry, and Jameson's sleeve pistol snapped into his fist. He'd backed out of the room with her scooting along in front of him. She'd been shaking with fear; he'd been laughing. Still, even he admitted they'd been lucky to escape the card players' wrath without getting lynched. Him, anyway. She didn't really figure they would've have hanged her. Maybe.

They'd skipped town in a tearing hurry, although the very next night Jameson went back without her and finished the job he'd been hired to do. He'd been embarrassed and angry, at himself most of all. But true to his calling.

"Jameson?" This time her voice must've penetrated because he stirred, and his eyes opened. Just for a moment, Wilkie didn't think he even saw her standing beside him. But then he did.

"There you are," he said, the words slow, and a trifle slurred. "Took you long enough. You're late." Staggering a little as he rose, he clutched the chair back. "Everything go all right?"

His skin had turned a peculiar gray color. Sweat beaded his forehead. Wilkie stared hard at him and sniffed. No, he didn't smell of liquor. So. Not drunk then. What was she thinking, anyhow? He'd never touch the stuff with her out on what was only her second solo job. Especially one so important as the retrieval of these files. Was he sick? He'd only admitted to feeling shaky, which is why she'd gone to the bank alone.

If he *was* sick, he'd never say.

"Well?" he demanded. "Did you manage the Mosler all right? Those are tricky. Safest safe in the business for bankers. Not the easiest for people in our line of work." He managed a chuckle that to Wilkie's ears didn't sound quite right.

The euphoria that had accompanied her on the way to the hotel and while climbing the rope ladder vanished without a trace. With only an illusion of her previous glee, she dug the folders from the coat's lining and made a show of flourishing them.

"Of course, I handled the Mosler — eventually. Took a bit longer than we estimated, is all. I'm sorry. Anyway, I had no trouble with the safe, but something else happened." She handed Jameson the stack of folders.

Staring down at six when he'd expected only three folders, he scowled. "What's this?"

"Take a look. You'll see," she said.

Wilkie shrugged out of the coat, sighing her relief at being rid of its twenty-pound weight and the heat it imbued. "Missus —" she started, but his quick "Shh. No names." stopped her from saying the client names out loud.

The walls have ears. They hear all our secrets. One of Jameson's favorite sayings and she thought it must be true. Impossible not to suspect it was why the bank manager and two security guards showed up tonight without apparent cause, an act definitely outside their usual routine. Only who'd said what to whom, and where? Whose walls had supplied the ears?

If Uncle Jameson was sick, should she even mention her close call? Especially since he asked no questions? Probably not. He'd only be worried.

Which reminded her. Turning back to the window, she began hauling the rope ladder into the room.

Her uncle ambled over to the bed with the folders, sinking down onto the mattress edge. Sank down heavily, as though exhausted. He opened the first folder and scanned the top page before opening the second file and reading it. "Aren't these the same?"

Wilkie, folding the ladder rung by rung and

tying a final loop around the hemp to secure it, shook her head. "Is that the Badrac file? Wait until you get to page five, both copies. Check the expense column, then the bottom line on each."

She stowed the ladder in a special compartment concealed in the top of Jameson's dome-lidded steamer trunk. It always seemed a little more caution than necessary to hide the rope, an item easily explained as many hotels in the small towns didn't sport fire escapes, but her uncle said it'd be better to avoid questions in the first place. She supposed he was right.

Jameson seemed to perk up as he read, holding the documents at arm's length and squinting. He had reading spectacles somewhere, but hated for anyone, even her, to see him wearing them. She sighed, her mouth quirking at the corner. He was almost as vain as a tony high society lady — or maybe her mother.

Closing the window, Wilkie sat in the chair Jameson had vacated, waiting and watching as he examined the financial documents. All of them.

An uncle of uncertain provenance, Jameson *may* have been her *father's* brother. That's what her mother said anyway, and he went along with the story. Wilkie wasn't so sure. For one thing, Jameson had very blond hair. Almost white, same now as it had been when he first came to live in her mother's boarding house a good many years ago. His eyes were the color of a cloudy sky, surrounded by dark lashes and eyebrows. She always thought his coloring odd and distinctive. Her father, on the other hand, or so her mother said, had light brown hair and blue eyes. Wilkie had never seen him in person. Dead before his time, not that Esther had cried any crocodile tears when she told Wilkie about it.

Anyway, Wilkie had seen photographs of some of her mother's kin, too. Never any of her father's. When pressed about him, Mother produced a worn photograph of the man she said was Wilkie's father. It always worried her that she didn't resemble anyone on either side. How could all those blue-eyed blonds have produced a black-haired, brown-eyed girl like her?

Paper rustled. Jameson's piercing whistle made her jump.

"Well done, Wilkie my girl. You make this old man's heart proud. If we're lucky, this might even earn us a bonus."

"Shall I write a report for this Mrs. Badrac and the other two women?" Wilkie asked. "Let them know what I've found?"

"Not at this time. I'm told she's an intelligent woman, but I'm to talk to her lawyer, and he'll relay everything she needs to know." Pausing, his brows drew together. "What's his name again?"

"The lawyer? Boothe, with an E. Of Burke, Boothe, and Venig, Attorneys at Law." The names tripped off Wilkie's tongue even as her own brow puckered. How could Jameson not have remembered? They'd laughed about it on the way to the hotel when they arrived in Butte late yesterday afternoon.

"Yeah. Them," he said. "I'll meet with Boothe first thing in the morning. Soon as I'm done, we'll be on the train out of here."

"All right. I'll pack everything up tonight and be ready to leave."

Jameson hated sticking around after a job. He was always jumpy as a fly on pudding until they left the site far behind. Wilkie often wondered if he'd just gotten nervous because she'd come with him or if he was always like this. She thought not. As she remembered, the habit dated from some years back when he'd disappeared from the rooming house and was gone for eleven whole months. Then one day, he showed up on their doorstep. That night, when she was supposed to be asleep, she'd sneaked downstairs and heard him and her mother talking. To Wilkie's shock, he admitted to serving a stretch in Walla Walla State Penitentiary. He told her mother he'd mistakenly trusted a client to keep his name quiet while he dallied in the vicinity.

"Something I'll never do again," he'd said then. "A hard lesson learned."

Adamant they get out of town the minute they were paid, he certainly conducted business differently now.

Jameson set the files aside. "I'm tired, girl."

Concerned, she saw his eyelids drooping, his mouth a little slack. As she watched, he swiped the back of his hand across it.

"You must be tired, too," he said, the slur more pronounced. "Scoot on over to your own room and get some sleep. You've earned it."

Wilkie couldn't argue with that. Her bed drew her although she doubted sleep would come easily. The excitement, the satisfaction of a job well done, and yes, even the surging fear she'd felt as those men closed in on her, all seemed likely to keep her awake. She'd meant to report the whole episode to her uncle, tell him how suspicious she was, but now—

How could he have forgotten the lawyer's name? He always demanded every detail, even on her training runs. Not this time, even after she said something had happened. Something that might be important. Was he ill? A simple, passing thing?

What should she do?

Undecided, she glanced over at him before she headed for her room next door. He was sweating again. What did that mean?

Not now, Wilkie. Any fool could see it wasn't a good time. They'd just have to deal with the situation in the morning—but definitely before Jameson met with the attorney.

***

Except the next morning, admitting he didn't feel up to snuff, Jameson bowed out of the meeting. And in truth, he looked like death warmed over. Worse than last night for sure, and that had been bad enough.

"Sorry, Wilkie." Eyes looking like darkened windows, it seemed as if he couldn't quite focus on her face. "You'll have to meet with Burke by yourself and finish the deal."

"Boothe," she said. "Not Burke. Are you sure, Uncle Jameson? I've never even sat in on one of your client meetings. I won't know how to conduct myself." How many times had he told her the secret to making a good deal and assuring further employment was to be professional and confident? To act as if nothing, at least to the potential client, was impossible.

"Sure, you will. I've told you often enough

what goes on. What people say. What *I* say. How I handle the client." Brushing aside her wide-eyed astonishment, he picked up a cup of the coffee a bellhop had brought to his room and took a sip. His hands shook. The cup rattled against his teeth and a bit of liquid trickled from the corner of his mouth.

"Confound it!" He blotted the trickle on the sleeve of his shirt. "Yes, I'm sure this one is up to you. Look at me. I'm..." But then he seemed to think better of what he'd meant to say and began outlining a plan to see her through the meeting. "You'll have to do something with your appearance. You're too young and too pretty. You need to look tough and show the know-how to be my partner. He won't believe you capable, otherwise. I got a notion he's the kind of man who thinks only plain women can do things. Plain older women."

Wilkie, unaccustomed to praise—if that's what it had been—from anyone, couldn't help being touched that her uncle thought she was pretty. "If he thinks I'm your secretary or something, that's fine by me," she said.

"Is it?"

"Yes. Better, in fact. I'm less likely to end up in jail." She grinned.

The mention of jail had Jameson recite a whole

list of instructions. Some of them hardly made sense, although she agreed to every one. "Most importantly," he said, "always act in a ladylike manner."

"I will," she promised. Then, forgoing a breakfast she was too nervous to consider eating anyway, Wilkie went back to her own room and spent the short amount of time until the meeting making herself appear older.

The transformation wasn't easy for a fresh-faced girl of eighteen. Not that Wilkie *felt* eighteen; however, that was supposed to feel. No one who'd lived her whole life in Esther Van Slyke's boarding house could remain innocent of what went on in the world. Especially when the male residents—and the residents were mostly male—began taking an interest in her at an early age.

Standing in front of the small mirror above the washstand, Wilkie braided her black hair into a thick rope and swirled it around her head. It made her look top heavy and larger, exactly her intention. A small hat perched on top increased the effect. The hat's dark veil draped over her face and helped obscure already altered features. Pale-colored powder dulled her creamy complexion and, when scrubbed over her eyelids, lightened thick black lashes. She practiced a sour expression until her lips fell into a downturned line and a crease formed between her brows. Brows which she'd filled-in using a dark pencil to make thicker and to obscure their fine arches. Padding wrapped around her chest, waist, and hips put ten or more pounds onto her slender frame.

Lastly, Wilkie stepped into some shoes she'd found in a second-hand store that added three inches to her height. The rusty black suit she wore was second-hand, too, and a little smelly. And truly ugly. Wilkie had a notion it had been a widow's cast-off.

Taking a moment, she studied herself in the mirror.

"Perfect," she breathed. *Perfectly awful.*

Jameson had demanded an inspection and made sure she complied by holding onto the folders until she was ready to leave. Shoes clomping, she stepped into his room where she found him lying in bed with his arm over his eyes.

"Still feeling poorly?"

"Yes."

"Well," she demanded, "what do you think of my outfit?"

He lowered his arm, eyed her as she made a slow twirl, and laughed himself into a coughing fit. "You'll do. If your mother could only see you now."

"My mother would think my attire just fine —
as long as she's not the one wearing it."

He didn't even try to deny the accusation. "You
don't look like you, sweetheart, and that's what
we're aiming for. All to the good. I don't want the
clients getting a handle on you." Locking the se-
date brown leather briefcase containing the folders, Jameson handed it to her. "You remember the
combination?"

"Of course."

"That's my girl. Now don't forget. I don't ac-
cept payment in checks, and Boot knows it. Cash
only, the agreement is for gold. Don't you leave
without collecting every penny."

Boot? He'd forgotten —or misspoken— the attorney's name again. "I know," she said, concern
once more jangling her nerves. "I won't."

Wilkie thought there might've been other
things he wanted to talk about, but time had run
out. Only a few minutes remained for her to reach
the Burke, Boothe, & Venig office on time, which,
from a previous scout, she knew to be situated
on the floor above a corner dry goods store three
blocks from the hotel. The shoes, though. She felt
sure she'd need the whole time allotment due to
the awkward high-heels slowing her down.

"Be careful," Jameson adjured as she closed the
door behind her.

The shoes pinched her toes even as they slipped on her heels, but she was glad of them as she hustled down the street. They managed to alter her stance from a free-striding young lady to a sore-hipped, middle-aged woman, one whose shoulders rose up toward her ears.

A separate closed staircase on the side of the dry-goods building led to the attorneys' office on the second floor. Wilkie took the set of steep stairs, clinging to the rail with her free hand. The office she sought lay at the very end of the hall, making it necessary to pass two other, less ostentatious offices. A little breathless, she'd drawn even with the second when, without warning, a man flung it open and stepped out, knocking into her.

"Watch it, lady," he said. "Get out of my way."

Wilkie, who scrambled to do just that, bit down the words on the tip of her tongue. Certainly not to answer like she wanted to, which would've been to lay into him with muleskinner's language. He'd run into her, after all, not the other way around.

"Sorry," she muttered, but he wasn't listening to her. He focused on a man behind him.

The thing is, she recognized his voice, deep and dark and accented, having heard it just last night. Moreover, considering she felt it wise to keep her head down, she recognized those laced-up boots he wore. She should having stared at them at eye level while cowering under the bench in the bank. The right one had a discoloration across the toe whose mottled appearance reminded her of a bacon strip.

What was he doing here? That's what she wanted to know. It seemed too far-fetched to be by accident.

Another man had come out of the room behind him, saying, "You'd better go before anyone sees you here. You know what to do."

Mr. Laced Boots nodded. "Same terms?"

"Same terms," the other replied. "Only no mistakes this time." His voice sounded fretful as he added, "I can't imagine why the manager showed up right then. Or how Van Slyke got past you. It should've been easy."

"No," Laced Boots growled, "bad timing all around. But I'll take care of it. There'll be no foul-ups this time."

"Better not be." It was a warning. "We don't want witnesses."

So far as Wilkie could tell, she might've been invisible.

Which, she decided a few seconds later, was a very good thing. That's because when she went through the imposing carved mahogany door with signage stating *Burke, Boothe & Venig, Attorneys at Law,* the first item to catch her eye was a series of photographs depicting said Burke, Boothe, and Venig. One of the three was the man she'd seen in the hall.

Not Laced Boots. The one who'd been giving the orders.

Chapter Three

A young man attired in a snappy tan-colored tweed suit, his starched round collar tilting his chin in what looked an uncomfortable angle, came through a door from an inner hallway as Wilkie studied the photographs. His pleated-front jacket was open to show a vest embroidered with, of all things, bumblebees, and he bore a flower-strewn china coffee service. Placing it on a massive desk barring the way into the inner sanctum, he gave her the fisheye.

"Yes?" he drawled, thin nose pointing higher than the collar accounted for.

"Yes," she drawled in return. *Ass.* "I..." she began.

At the same time, apparently noticing the briefcase she carried, he said, "Give me that. I'll hand it over to the correct attorney. I suppose you don't know who requested it?"

It seemed evident he took her for a courier.

Wilkie kept firm hold of the briefcase, stowed under her arm. "I'm here to see Mr. Boothe. I'm his eight o'clock appointment."

He didn't so much as glance at what she took for an engagement calendar lying open on the desk. "Nonsense. Who do you think you're trying to fool? Mr. Boothe has a *gentleman*—" he put an emphasis on the word "—client due in this time slot. If you're just delivering papers, do so. If not, leave."

Her costume and disguise, Wilkie thought, her mouth twisting, must lend her a more disreputable aspect than she appreciated. Or maybe it was the smell of sweat emanating from the woolen fabric and seeming to grow stronger every moment.

"Are you the receptionist? If so, you're very rude," she said, gratified to see his fair, if slightly bumpy, complexion turn crimson.

"I'm Mr. Boothe's assistant."

Wilkie gathered from his stiff tone that an assistant was more important than a receptionist. Even so, they were at a standoff, until a man's resonant voice carried through from an inner room. "Mr. Avery. Is that Mr. Van Slyke you're speaking with? If so, please show him in."

"Huh." Moving faster than Avery could block her, Wilkie darted past him into the hall. Spotting a middle-aged gentleman standing in a doorway, she tripped toward him with her hand outstretched. She recognized him from one of the photos, mostly because of the round-lensed glasses perched on his high-bridged nose. Otherwise, he appeared considerably older and thinner than in the photograph, his jacket hanging loosely from narrow shoulders.

"I am Wilhelmina Van Slyke," she announced, avoiding Avery's grab at her arm by a mere gnat's nose as she barreled past him. "I'm here in Jameson's place."

"Are you his daughter? I believe he mentioned you. Ah..." Mr. Boothe seemed not to know what else to say, but with a shushing motion at Avery, he stepped aside for her to enter his office.

Mentioned her? Taken by surprise, Wilkie nodded, storing the idea away to think about later.

Pointedly, she turned back to make certain the door latched behind them before taking the chair he held for her. The office, she observed, was quite opulent, all beautifully finished wood paneling, flocked wallpaper and velvet draperies. A thick carpet caught at the heels of her shoes. The floral pattern reminded her of a high-class bordello—or what she imagined one might be like. The one she'd been in had not been the epitome of elegance, she feared, although the carpet had been an identical deep burgundy shade. The lingering odor of cigars was the same, too.

"May I ask why Mr. Van Slyke himself isn't here?" Stiff-kneed, Boothe dropped into his seat as though exhausted.

"I'm afraid he isn't feeling well today. Something he ate last night, I believe." The fib slipped from her mouth without so much as a second thought.

Leaning back in his chair, Boothe sighed. "I'm sorry to hear that. Was he able to complete the... ah... undertaking? If not, you know, I'm afraid the client will refuse to be responsible for reimbursing his travel expenses. I don't wish to sound insulting, but she is not the most generous or trusting of women."

Wilkie, from her position of reading through two very different records of the same account, wondered why he'd even mention the word 'trust.' From what she'd discovered, Mrs. Badrac had plenty of reason for a lack of confidence in her bankers. And in her attorneys, too, if she only knew. Them, most of all.

"The mission went well, without problems. I have the requested item right here." She patted the briefcase.

"Did it?" he said as if surprised.

"Oh, yes. And I'm authorized to take the agreed upon payment."

"Good. Ah... excellent. Now, I believe the

standard fee is—" He got out a checkbook and, uncapping a pen, filled in an amount and scribbled his signature. Pushing it across the desk to her, he kept his forefinger on the check, pinning it down. "There, all taken care of, and when the client signs off, I'll mail the expense account reimbursement to Mr. Van Slyke, as well. As long as she does sign off, that is," he added. "The firm can't be responsible for monies owed. Now, I'll take the... ah... items."

"What is this?" Wilkie leaned a few inches forward and peered at the check. Her heart beat a little faster as she sat back. *Trust.* A joke, indeed. Certainly not a word to be used in connection with this outfit.

Her tongue clicked as though reproving a dog for piddling on her mother's second-best carpet. Her lips turned down in the practiced scowl. "For shame, Mr. Boothe. You know very well this," a wave of her hand showed disdain for the check, "does not meet the terms of the agreement."

"I suppose," she added, drawing in a deep breath, "you do remember the agreed-upon method of payment? And the amount? If not, I can refresh your memory."

He stared at her over the tops of his spectacles. "Excuse me? I don't know what you're talking about."

"And I'm equally sure you do. Let me remind you. Payment is due in gold coin and in full. You put the money on this desk, and I'll put the folders beside it. I pick up the money, and you take the folders. I walk away and forget this meeting ever happened; the deal completed. If you don't pay as promised, well, I walk out of here then, too, only with the documents. As to what I'll do with them, you must agree several options are open."

Had Jameson known Boothe would pull this stunt or another like it? Was the enterprise a test to see how she'd handle herself? If so, there might be a few surprised men. A few surprised men sniveling about being bested by a girl.

Boothe's pale cheeks took on a peculiar kind of waxen hardness. It appeared unhandsome young women wearing odorous second-hand suits were not in the habit of speaking so plainly and so insultingly to him. His appearance indicated a lack of appreciation for her implicit warning.

With a serene expression, although her stomach roiled as though filled with live fish, Wilkie waited him out. After a moment, Boothe tried getting tough, no more than she'd expected. What a good thing Uncle Jameson preached a constant sermon of preparedness.

"You do realize, young woman, that you're outnumbered here. If you persist in these threats,

I'll be forced to call in help to oust you. We'll simply take the documents, and you will forego any kind of payment."

"I don't make *threats,* Mr. Boothe. Mr. Van Slyke has taught me better than that. Do you really think you can get away with using any kind of force?"

"Oh, indeed I do." The timbre of his voice had changed, become higher and thinner.

Wilkie thought for a moment. A window, open a little at the bottom, let in sound from the street below. She'd heard the murmur of a woman's voice as she went toward Boothe's office. In fact, she heard one there now. And the receptionist, honest or in on the scam? How many other people might be within this warren of rooms? And would they all be crooks?

She settled back into her chair and rolled the dice. "Well then, let's just see. You see, I have several items in here that will prove incriminatory to this firm should they come to light."

"Forgeries," he said on a note of scorn.

"Are they?" The downturned smile came again, no matter that she had a hard time maintaining it. "I'll have quite a tale to tell to the proper audience, I assure you. An audience I'll have the moment I claim assault." Drawing a deep breath, she looked him in the eyes, opened her mouth, and prepared to scream.

He rose to his feet, seeming a little tottery. "All right," he said. "All right. It's not... you're not worth the trouble. Be quiet. Gold it is."

Although he sounded beaten, Wilkie felt the anger rising off him. Hot anger. But he most definitely wasn't prepared for anyone to hear her story. Not anyone.

Releasing her pent air, she stood up, too, matching him, and prepared to open the locked briefcase.

"I hope you realize you've ruined Van Slyke's chances of doing repeat business with Burke, Boothe, and Venig," he said. "And I shall put out the word that he is unreliable. Your fault."

Pausing over the tiny lock, Wilkie looked up. "Unwise, I should think."

A cold smile creased his lips. "But you're a young girl wearing a hideous disguise. What do you know about unwise? Not much, I should say."

By this time, he'd key-opened a desk drawer and lifted out a pouch imprinted with the Spooner Bank and Trust logo. It appeared of adequate weight to contain the required number of twenty-dollar gold pieces. With an almost careless gesture, he dumped the coins onto the desk where they spun and clattered.

"Satisfied?" he said.

Wilkie counted with a glance. "I am. Please restore them to the bag."

He huffed but did so as she unlocked the brief-case and withdrew the folders, placing the stack beside the money on the desk. The name on the topmost folder stood out prominently.

Boothe nodded and grabbed the folders as though afraid she'd reclaim them. Wilkie picked up the bag and made a show of stowing it in the briefcase and closing it as the attorney opened one of the folders.

She pivoted toward the door and, before he could say another word, slipped through the narrowest of openings and ran down the hall to the front. Two people, one a woman in tears, occupied the waiting room chairs as Mr. Avery hovered about them. These clients seemed to be the recipients of the elaborate coffee service he'd brought out earlier. They all watched as she rushed through the reception room and down the hall. A hall that seemed strangely elongated.

Regretting the high-heeled shoes, Wilkie made it to the exit and clattered down the stair-well, stumbling in her haste. But then, just as she made to push through to the street, another of her premonitions stopped her. At the same time, voices rumbled from overhead. Angry voices.

"Stop her," someone said.

Trapped.

A moment later, her brain started working again. They'd no doubt expect her to head directly toward the hotel, it being obvious they knew where she and Jameson were staying. They'd count on her running straight into their waiting clutches. Most likely, they'd prefer not to cause a commotion right outside the law offices. Stood to reason, anyway. They'd try to grab her at the street corner, where Burke, Boothe, & Venig would not be involved.

Most probably.

And then what? Wilkie didn't think she wanted to find out.

Hurrying footsteps sounded from the top of the stairwell.

"... or get off the pot," she thought and pushed out onto the sidewalk, made an immediate turn and entered the dry goods emporium. Visible only bare seconds, she hoped she'd not been detected at all. Moving quickly between tables laden with bolts of fabric, ribbons, lace, and a plethora of other items both necessary and luxurious, she headed for the back of the store. In a busy town like Butte with its steep, narrow streets, stores moved their stock in through the back so not block the front entrance. Which meant she had a chance of escaping by the same route.

As long as she could evade the person hurrying toward her, that is. Pretending not to see the clerk, a female with an eager expression, Wilkie dodged around a table piled high with some kind of felted stuff that appeared to be sheep wool batting and kept going.

"Good day, madam," the woman called, her own impetus curbed because of the crowded conditions. "How may I assist you?"

Stay out of my way. Wilkie didn't say it out loud. She had the rear door in sight, with only the hall leading to the outside dock to traverse. Once there, she'd be home free.

She hadn't counted on a hand reaching out from within a dark storeroom and nabbing the briefcase as she passed.

Chapter Four

Wilkie took pride in her fast reflexes and steadfast refusal to be intimidated. By anyone, bigger or stronger, male or female. Excepting only her mother. Esther could freeze her with a look. It just so happened the man who snatched the briefcase was no Esther Van Slyke and Wilkie, in a tearing hurry, had no time to fiddle with explanations, excuses, or bribes. Barely noticing his face, she fought back.

Her knee jerked upward into the area she'd once heard Jameson call a man's soft spot, landing with satisfying force. The briefcase sailed through the air, freed as the man's grip on it spasmed, and his hands reached elsewhere.

Wilkie hardly broke stride. She made a smooth catch of the case and pushed outside onto the loading dock behind the store. The platform was only three feet tall, a comfortable height for a man unloading a wagon. No problem for a girl to jump, either. She bounded forward.

One problem. She forgot about the twice-damned, high-heeled, too-large shoes. Until she landed, that is, and her left ankle rolled over.

Wilkie gasped aloud at the sharp pain.

It wasn't broken. She knew that, but, mercy, did it ever hurt. And would hurt worse when she ran, which came next.

Hobbling down the alley, she barely managed an odd sort of half-run. Or, considering the strange lurch, did she mean running on only one side with a hippity-hop motion?

But not in the direction of the hotel, where they'd expect her to flee. She prided herself on being smarter than that. Crossing behind the mercantile, and consequently, the lawyers' offices, she went up a block before doubling around to Park Street. But even then, she didn't head toward the hotel. Not just yet. Jameson would have to take care of himself, which she had no doubt he could do, sick or not. She had a different destination in mind.

Wilkie knew where to find Copper Street in general, it being in an established area of some of Butte's older family homes. She spotted the address she sought without too much trouble, backtracking only once. Her ankle, complaining at the recent abuse, had swollen drastically in ten minutes as she walked. Swearing under her breath, she stopped, straightened her sad little hat, brushed dust from her skirt, and limped first up a steep hillside, then an even steeper set of steps. The steps ended on a recently swept stoop.

Setting herself, she rapped on the plain slab door and waited. A full minute later, having met with no reply, she knocked again. This time, a tiny woman wearing a black, polished cotton dress and a perky red cap peered out. Though no longer young, the woman's complexion was smooth, and her thick white hair coiffed into an upswept hairdo to rival Wilkie's own in height.

"'Allo," the woman said. She studied her visitor up and down and sideways before her gaze caught on the briefcase under Wilkie's arm.

"Good day." Casting a glance behind her toward the street, Wilkie saw a man striding their way. Something in the way he walked, sort of crouched forward, gave her an uneasy feeling. "Are you Mrs. Badrac? If so, I have information I need to discuss with you. I assure you, you will be interested. It is to your advantage."

"My advantage?" Mrs. Badrac, if this were indeed she, pressed her lips together. She, too, kept an eye on the man chugging their direction. "Who are you?" Her bright dark eyes narrowed. "Do you know who that is?" A nod indicated the man.

"My name is Wilhelmina Van Slyke." She felt

sure it would mean nothing to the woman, whose blank look proved her right. "And I don't know exactly who he is, but I think he may be a crook."

"A crook?" The woman's eyes lit.

She nodded. Feeling uncomfortably exposed standing outside in broad view from the street, Wilkie shifted, aggravating the pain in her ankle. A small grunt escaped, causing the woman to peer at her.

"Is something wrong?"

"Yes," Wilkie said. "I'm afraid I've sprained my ankle. Please, may I come in? I promise, I mean you no harm."

"Harrumph." Even though she didn't appear particularly trusting, the woman allowed the door to open wider and beckoned to her. "You may come in and sit down. Put the briefcase on your lap and your hands on the briefcase. We will talk, yes?"

"Yes." Wilkie thought she may have shown more relief than she intended. Especially since, as she followed the woman into the house, she spotted the derringer Mrs. Badrac held in the folds of her skirt. Was Butte a city where women carried a gun to their door as a general practice?

They passed through a rather dark foyer that contained hooks for coats and hats although it was bare of either at the moment, a small table with a chair on each side, a couple of seascapes on the wall, and an elephant's foot umbrella stand by the door.

The woman didn't show Wilkie into the spacious formal parlor she spotted off to the side. Instead, they continued down a hall past an elaborate dining room to the kitchen where a Majestic cookstove released enticing scents from the oven. Pulling a chair forward, Mrs. Badrac gestured. "Sit. Do you wish coffee? It is still hot from breakfast."

Wilkie collapsed onto the chair. "Yes, please. I would love some coffee." As a matter of fact, she smelled yeast bread and cinnamon, too, which made her mouth water.

She hoped the aroma hadn't made her drool, but if so, the *faux pas* paid off when the woman piled several puffy rolls on a plate and set it within Wilkie's reach.

"Eat," Mrs. Badrac said. "Then talk."

It took Herculean effort, but Wilkie passed on the rolls, although she gulped half of her coffee. She hadn't forgotten the man who appeared to be following her. "I think we'd best do it the other way around," she said. "Talk, then eat—if the invitation still stands."

A smile drifted over the older woman's face. "Then speak."

Still, Wilkie hesitated. "I'm not sure how to explain this, but perhaps I can just say that my uncle — Jameson Van Slyke — is experienced in opening safes and bank vaults, locks of all sorts, without benefit of keys or combinations. He—"

The woman nodded. An eyebrow rose. "A safe-cracker, yes?"

Wilkie drew in a breath. Was it odd for her to say safecracker and not locksmith? "Um, yes. I guess. In certain circumstances, I suppose. And so am I. He's teaching me the trade. But I hope you'll understand that he doesn't *rob* banks and such."

Or not much. The qualification rose in her mind, unbidden and unspoken.

"Two weeks ago a well-known attorney from Butte contacted him about a job," she went on. "The attorney said a clerk had inadvertently transferred a few of his clients' account folders to a prominent bank's secure vault without their knowledge. The attorney's that is. He wanted to get them back without upsetting the client by informing them of what had happened. However, the bank wouldn't release the files without the client being present. He told a fine story, one of innocence and goodwill. My uncle agreed to the job."

"What attorney? What clients?" Mrs. Badrac's

eyes narrowed. She leaned across the table. "What bank?"

"Burke, Boothe, and Venig are the attorneys. Spooner Bank and Trust is the bank." Wilkie paused. "I believe you are one of the clients. Shall I go on?"

"Oh, yes. I think so."

"I came here with my uncle. He likes me to take care of acquiring train tickets or renting buggies, of transporting his tools, of checking into hotels. Helping him out in general. He's going to have me taught to drive a motor car one of these days."

When Mrs. Badrac appeared unmoved by this proud statement, Wilkie cleared her throat and continued. "We arrived here the afternoon before last. My uncle—"

"From where. You came from where?"

Wilkie waved the question away. It was one Jameson told her never to answer. "That's not important. What is, is that my uncle met with the attorney and later, scouted access to the bank. Last night he chose to complete the task. He likes to get in, get the job done, and leave town as quickly as possible."

"Wise, I'm sure," the woman said, the observation sounding dry.

Here Wilkie felt herself faltering over the tale. Should she admit she was the one who'd actually taken the folders, or should she let Jameson bear the blame. Or credit. She supposed — hoped—the proper word might be credit. From Mrs. Badrac's viewpoint, at least.

She sighed. "But yesterday he got sick. Last night, he sent me in his stead."

Mrs. Badrac's mouth rounded in an O. "You? A woman safecracker?" Her mouth pursed. "A girl?"

Wilkie had forgotten her disguise, which apparently hadn't fooled this woman at all. Nor, she remembered wryly, had it fooled Mr. Boothe.

"*Not* a safecracker. But yes, me. I had no real difficulty opening the locks, but when it came time to secure the client folders, I found they all had copies in a sub-folder, which I hadn't been expecting. There were three clients in all, each with an original and a copy, which made rather thick files. And then I discovered they weren't actual duplicates. The accounts had different sums listed in the expense columns. In your case, the sum is considerably different."

At this, the woman jumped to her feet and ran twice around the kitchen, all the while crying out a lengthy, and very loud, spate of words. Wilkie, staring open-mouthed, figured she was cussing. Since she'd never heard the language before, she couldn't be sure. She just knew it sounded impressive. And angry.

"How much?" Mrs. Badrac dropped heavily onto her chair and followed the cursing with the explosive question. "How much have they stolen?"

The woman had caught the implication right away.

"May I show you?" Wilkie suddenly remembered she never had gotten around to obeying the woman's demand she keep her hands on top of the briefcase. It appeared Mrs. Badrac had forgotten as well.

At the older woman's nod, she twirled the combination lock and in a matter of seconds, opened the briefcase. Inside, the double eagles made a faint clinking sound as she withdrew the second folder, the one she'd withheld from Mr. Boothe, as well as the separate sheet of paper her uncle had painstakingly copied of the original document.

She passed the file across the table. "I had to give one folder to Mr. Boothe but see for yourself. This file is one of the originals from the attorney's office. The single page is a copy of the last page from the other file."

The little woman stared hard at the paperwork. "I knew," she whispered fiercely. "Yes, I knew."

Wilkie, giving in to temptation, reached for a cinnamon bun. "That you were being robbed?"

Mrs. Badrac's lip curled in disdain. "He told me times were bad. That everyone was losing money. I wondered even then."

Just as Wilkie's mouth closed around a warm, succulent bite, a man spoke from the doorway. She jumped, banged her sore ankle on a table leg and, to make matters worse, choked on a crumb.

Mrs. Badrac didn't even look up.

What had the man said? Too busy coughing to make sense of anything, the next thing Wilkie knew, someone was patting her on the back. It didn't help.

"Water," Mrs. Badrac ordered, and the man, who seemed to know his way around the kitchen, moved to obey.

Through teary eyes, Wilkie saw he was the same man who'd tried to take the briefcase from her at the dry goods store. The same man who'd felt the force of her knee. How long had he been standing there? How much had he heard? Merciful heavens, what had she gotten herself into? Should she be frightened? Maybe not, she decided, seeing what seemed to be concern on his face, along with a twitch of amusement. Unless what she saw was a pained grimace.

She knew Uncle Jameson would be worrying about her by now. He'd be wondering what was taking so long. Deliver the goods, collect their pay, and get out of town. That was the way he conducted business. Simple.

Only not this time. The deal hadn't worked out as planned. Her fault.

A brimming glass of water thumped down on the table in front of her, spilling over the side. Wilkie grabbed it, took a sip, then another. Gradually, her coughing died away.

"Thank you," she said when she had breath.

"At Burke, Boothe, and Venig, they call what they do *creative bookkeeping.*" The man repeated what he'd said earlier, and added, "Or double-entry. That always draws a laugh."

Yes. That's what he'd said before, more or less, when he'd startled her into a coughing fit. Only this time she noticed the bitterness in his tone when he said it. Where had he even come from, to walk into this house without knocking?

He looked a little pale as he leaned against Mrs. Badrac's chair and put his hand on her shoulder. "Come right down to it, it's nothing but plain, old-fashioned stealing. I figured you were in on the scheme when I saw you in Boothe's office handing over the folders. Right up until I followed you here, in fact. I lagged behind some due to a certain unfortunate incident I don't wish to explain." He shifted his stance, as though seeking a more comfortable position. "Sorry to be late."

"And I thought you were one of them," Wilkie retorted. He had a sore "soft spot," she had a sore ankle. In her book, that made them even. But maybe not enemies. She frowned. "You saw me in Boothe's office?"

"Yes. I'm Venig. The present Venig in that office full of scoundrels. My father was the Venig listed in the corporate name. He's dead, now. Died in a so-called accident three months ago. I've taken over his desk in the office but haven't met with any of my father's clients yet. Burke and Boothe, they want to buy me out. Their offer," he added somewhat dryly, "strikes me as hurried and in-appropriate."

"You should tell her the rest." Mrs. Badrac, thumbing through the file pages, appeared fully involved in the paperwork.

"The rest?" Wilkie wondered what all this had to do with her. She didn't want to know anything more.

The man, Venig, sat down, then promptly stood back up, at which Wilkie stifled a smirk. "Later, perhaps, Aunt Magdalena. For now, what have you discovered so far?"

Aunt Magdalena?

Mrs. Badrac looked up from the pages she'd been examining and shook her head. "You are right, Eldon. Creative bookkeeping indeed. When

Joseph was alive, they would not have dared do such a thing. And they will not get away with it now. You—" She pointed at Wilkie. "Forgive me. I have forgotten your name. What can you tell us about the others who have been robbed? Who they are? Where they are? How much was stolen from them?"

Wilkie was a little reluctant to repeat her name. The less these people knew about her or Jameson, the better. But regarding the other victims, well, that put her in a quandary. Unsure if speaking of them would be ethical, not that any of this was ethical or legal or anything else, she pondered the other questions posed. Mrs. Badrac's was the only affected account here in Butte. But maybe a clue?

"All three are women. Widows, I think," she said at last. "One lives in Anaconda; one lives in Clinton."

"Mrs. Banks," Mrs. Badrac said, as though it were a foregone conclusion. "I am not certain of the other."

The one from Anaconda. She was right.

Wilkie blinked a tell-tale semaphore message just as one of her strange premonitions swept over her. Gasping, she jumped to her feet, nearly toppling as her ankle protested. "I need to get back to the hotel. Right now. My uncle... my uncle will want to leave immediately."

Jameson. Something is wrong. I know it.

"Wait," Venig said. "You have to tell us more."

Wilkie hesitated. "I'm just a delivery person, my job is done. What you do with the information is up to you. Please, leave me out of it." She moved to retrace her way to the front door, gripping the briefcase under her arm.

"But..." Venig started until Magdalena cut in. "She is right, Eldon. We must let her go. You know it was dangerous for her to come here. We owe her for this."

"No. Nothing. Not a thing." What would Jameson have to say about she'd done? He'd say she should've demanded pay, that's what, but she'd rather stay out of whatever happened next. Could these people be sworn to secrecy about where they'd gotten their information?

No time. No time to negotiate. Worry pulsed along her veins.

"Do wait." Mrs. Badrac followed her, looking anxious. "Get Hixson," she said over her shoulder to Eldon. "He can give her a ride to the hotel with his machine. She shouldn't be walking on that ankle."

"Hix is here?"

"Yes. In the barn loft room, still asleep, I imagine. He came in late." And to Wilkie, as Eldon moved toward the back door, "Hixson will have you at the hotel in half the time. Most certainly faster than you can walk."

Wilkie stopped in mid-flight, hoping. Mrs. Badrac had said *machine*. "In a motorcar?"

"I'm afraid not. Aboard a motorcycle. It looks dangerous to me, but perhaps you, a modern girl, will find it of no matter."

Wilkie had seen one or two flitting around Butte, making a fearful racket and spewing an awful stench into the air. "I think I'd rather ride a horse," she said.

"Yes." Mrs. Badrac nodded approval. "So would I."

But in the end, the pain in Wilkie's ankle decided her. Anyway, she'd never ridden on a motorcycle. It would be something new to experience.

Chapter Five

Hixson Forry, better known as just plain Hix, rolled over and blinked his eyes open at the first creak of the stairs. For a moment, he forgot where he was and automatically reached for the Smith & Wesson revolver on the bedside table. But then a familiar voice called out, and he stopped in mid-reach. Sinking into the thin mattress once more, he ignored the hail and prepared to go back to sleep.

From the sound of things, other folks had a different idea.

"Hix. Hix, wake up. Aunt Magdalena needs a favor from you."

Hix growled under his breath. Truth be told, he had a hangover and wasn't in the mood for one of Magdalena's chores. They'd been known to encompass everything from digging a hole to plant a tree, to escorting a married lady running away from her husband all the way to Fargo, North Dakota. Turned out it hadn't been just an escort. It had been the bodyguard. The lady was now a widow and happy as a meadowlark in spring mating season.

"Hix, right now. This is important." The shout came again. The voice belonged to his cousin Eldon, and if he'd had his druthers, he would've ignored it.

"I know you're there," Eldon said. "I'm standing right beside your motorcycle. When did you get it?"

Grunting, Hix sat up. At least Eldon wasn't climbing up to dump cold water on him or play some other infantile trick. Although it would be just like him to put sugar in the Triumph's gas tank.

"What do you want? What does *she* want?" His feet thumped to the floor. He pulled on pants and boots, slipped a shirt over his head, and stowed the S&W in a shoulder holster before covering it up with his jacket. Still a little dizzy, he made his way down the steep set of steps from the loft room to the floor of the barn. His aunt didn't keep horses in the barn anymore, depending on a hired driver for her transportation around town, but the cavernous space still smelled of animals and manure.

He found Eldon Venig, a cousin, either first or second, Hix wasn't sure which, poking around the motorcycle, fingering the switches.

"Hands off." Hix strode toward him. "I want this machine to run the next time I need it."

Eldon took a step away from the bike. "I'm just looking. Why didn't you buy a motorcar, while you were at it? It would be more practical than this thing."

"I like this 'thing.' It goes over roads and into places you can't get a motorcar. Not that I have money for one of them anyway."

Eldon waved the money aspect aside. One way or another, he'd never had a problem acquiring it. A situation Hix knew all too well.

"Magdalena has use for you and your machine," Eldon said. "She needs you to give a woman, a girl, a lift downtown on it to her hotel."

"What girl? Why don't you take her? Don't look like you're doing anything else."

"I don't have transportation."

Hix scratched his head, wishing a nagging ache away. "How'd you get here, then? How'd the girl get here?"

"We walked. Separately, of course."

"Walked?" Hix couldn't keep his astonishment at bay. Eldon wasn't the kind to walk anywhere.

His cousin avoided the question. "The girl brought Magdalena some papers. I'm going to help Auntie look them over and try to explain them to her. It's about an investment account, I believe."

He spoke as if it were the most important thing in the world. Of course, it might've been. Hix wasn't exactly up on accounts, investment or otherwise. But Eldon made it seem as if their aunt couldn't figure the paperwork out herself, which Hix knew was far from the truth. The old gal was sharp as an obsidian blade.

"Besides," Eldon said, "Now I'll have to walk back the office. And..." he grew louder, "... I'm in pain. The little bitch kneed me."

"Kneed you?"

"In the balls," Eldon explained as if Hix hadn't already grasped the idea.

He choked back a laugh. "Why'd she do that?"

"Why? Well, at first, I thought she was a thief, and I was trying to get the goods back."

"So she isn't a thief?"

"No. Yes. Maybe. There's no need to discuss it. Hurry up. Magdalena is waiting for you. So is the girl."

Doing his aunt a favor wouldn't hurt him any, Hix decided. Except for his aching head. Especially since Magdalena gave him a place to stay on the rare occasion, he visited Butte, even if it was just a room in the barn loft. And maybe he wanted to meet this woman, or girl, with the guts to sink a knee into his cousin's groin.

Regretting the lack of coffee, Hix donned a

pair of goggles — good for more than keeping the
dust and bugs out of his eyes, the darkened lenses
helped hide his features — and jammed a cloth
hat down over his hair. Nobody in Butte would
ever expect to see Hix Forry wear anything but
ranch-hand duds. He'd already found that when
garbed in his motorcycle gear friends passed him
by without a second look. Although, he reflected,
that might be because the Triumph interested
them more than the rider did.

First making sure the Triumph had gas in the
tank, he fired it up, gratified when the machine
started after only the fifth or sixth kick. It didn't
always. He followed Eldon, the bike wobbling
only a little as his cousin limped back to the
house. Hix figured the limp was mostly for show,
something he'd done from the first time they'd
met and Hix got blamed for a hooligan trick of
Eldon's that had gone awry.

He was prepared to like a girl who dared put
up a fight against his cousin.

***

With Mrs. Badrac at her side, Wilkie hooked
the arm unfettered by her briefcase around a
porch post, standing on her one good foot. She
fretted some as they waited, her sense of urgen-

cy aggravated by worry, but soon the pop and sputter of an engine announced the arrival of her transportation. Crouching over the motorcycle's handlebars, a man wearing a short coat, high boots, and dark-lensed goggles planted his feet on the ground as he came to a stop in a shower of dust. The machine's engine continued to roar, breaking the quiet neighborhood silence.

"This is another of my nephews, Miss Wilhelmina. He will see you safely to your hotel." Mrs. Badrac's gaze seemed almost disapproving as she eyed the man. "Won't you, Hixson?"

His reply growled like part of the motorcycle's rumble. "As you say, ma'am." His glance at Wilkie through the goggles seemed appraising. "Mount up, little lady."

Mount up? She studied the noisy machine. Maybe she'd as soon walk, after all, sore ankle notwithstanding. Nevertheless, she moved toward the machine.

A flat metal platform no more than six inches wide and maybe eighteen-inches long protruded over the rear fender. Eldon Venig escorted her down the steps and, grunting as though it hurt him, lifted her onto the platform. Side-saddle, like riding a horse on a jaunt around a park. Wilkie had seen that once, in Spokane.

"Oh." She didn't think she cared for the way

the machine vibrated beneath her. "What do I hang onto?"

The man, Hixson, chuckled. "Me. Fold your skirt away from the chain. We wouldn't want it ripped off, would we?"

"My skirt, or the chain?" Wilkie had seen chain-driven machinery before. She'd been warned of danger then, and this seemed even more dangerous.

"Either. Both." He twisted around to check her position, noting the briefcase hanging from her arm. "Try to keep that centered, so it doesn't pull you off kilter. Hold your feet and legs up and well away from the road. Do not attempt to put your feet down."

"I won't." He must've thought her an idiot. Settling her bottom on the platform, she balanced herself and took firm hold of his coat. "I'm ready to go."

He revved the engine, making it whine even louder. "Where to? You're the one calling the shots."

Wilkie knew her face turned red, a revealing habit of hers. Of course, he didn't know. "The Finlen Hotel on Broadway," she said.

"The Finlen it is."

The resulting jerk nearly knocked her loose, so she caught only the tail-end of Mrs. Badrac's called thanks. They zipped from the back yard to an alley, and then onto the main road. Once there, she got the hang of riding, swaying over the ruts and around corners as Hixson instructed her to lean into them with him. At first, she thought she'd either fall off, or they'd roll all the way over, but they never did. Almost as bad were the steep hills where she feared she'd slide off the back. Sooner than she believed possible, they swept around a corner and pulled up at the rear of the hotel, stopping with a jerk that thrust her forward into his back.

How had he known to go around back? But she was glad he had.

The thrill, if that's what one called it, faded as her stomach settled down.

"Okay?" Hixson turned and grinned at her, raising the goggles onto the top of his head. His eyes were hazel with the whites reddened, she guessed, by a night on the town. The smell of whiskey clung to him. He was young and basically clean-shaven, though dark whiskers had sprouted.

"Sure." Glancing about, Wilkie released his coat and put her feet on the ground, gasping as a stone rolled beneath her as she tried to stand. She grabbed onto Hixson to steady herself. "Ouch. No."

He looked at her, eyebrow cocked, and although aware, she paid no attention. Her gaze fixed elsewhere with what she saw enough to make her skin crawl. They were in the same area where last night her ladder had dangled from Jameson's window. She distinctly remembered closing the window when she returned, but it was wide open now, and a rope, not the ladder, dangled with the end about eight feet above her head.

The sense of wrongness plaguing her, stifled during the harrowing motorcycle ride, returned in force.

Hixson followed her line of sight, turning to stare at the hotel wall. "The rope?"

"Yes." Even Wilkie heard the tightness of her answer.

"Not yours for a quick getaway?"

Why had he even thought of that? "No." Her voice trembled. Just a little, but enough to reveal the trepidation she felt. Perhaps the Van Slyke family business was no longer as secret as it should've been.

Hixson fiddled with a switch, killing the motorcycle engine. The resulting silence allowed them to hear a cat meowing near some overflowing garbage cans alongside the stable. Some wise head had placed them distantly enough to keep most of the odor away. They heard the ticking of the cooling engine, and most oddly of all, at least to Wilkie, the total silence from the open window.

If Jameson had been there, the sound of the motorcycle would've drawn him to the window for a look. Something, Wilkie thought, had happened. Something major that boded ill. "I hate to ask," she said, hesitating, "but will you come upstairs with me. Please. I — I'm afraid something has happened to my uncle."

She hadn't a thought for the way the plea sounded.

Hix may have had a nose for trouble, too, because his short nod answered. "Come on," he said, hardly waiting for her as he headed toward the kitchen entrance.

There they found a route to the hotel guest rooms via a narrow set of steps separated from the kitchen. The steep stairway, one intended for tradesmen or perhaps clandestine visitors, led up. They passed inside without interference and climbed the first flight of stairs. Here Wilkie had to stop a moment for the pain in her ankle to subside.

"Going to make it?" Hixson asked.

"Of course." Wilkie's chin tilted. But when she would've charged ahead, he stopped her with a hand on her elbow.

Hixson put a forefinger over his lips. They stood immobile, once again listening. After a few moments, he nodded and let her lead again, only stepping ahead when she reached Jameson's door.

A door that hung agape.

Wilkie's heart pounded.

Hixson produced a small revolver from inside his coat. Useless, as it happened, since there was no one to shoot.

Or only Jameson, except he was already dead, the room silent and empty of spirit.

Wilkie surged past Hix' outstretched arm. "Jameson? Uncle Jameson?" She sank down beside the bed where Jameson lay. Unchanged in position, he appeared just as when she left him more than an hour earlier. She shook his shoulder, trying to rouse him, even though she knew it useless. No amount of shaking could bring a man back from where he'd gone.

"Oh, no. Oh, no, no." She couldn't seem to find words for anything else, until finally she looked up at Hixson, still standing at the room entrance and said blankly, "He's dead," as though Hixson needed telling.

"Yes. I see he is."

"What should I do?" She continued to stare at him.

Hixson, who, when Wilkie thought about his reaction later, appeared a little bewildered and wild-eyed at this turn of events, shook himself. "I think you'd better take a look around and see if everything else seems right."

"What?" But even as she spoke, Wilkie regained enough presence of mind to observe her surroundings. Yes, her uncle was certainly dead, but she didn't see a single out-of-the-way mark on him. He'd been sick, and she knew it. He'd died right there in his bed, most probably immediately after she left. His coffee cup still sat on the bedside table with an inch of liquid in it. She recalled him setting it there as she left.

None of which justified the state of the room. "Oh."

"Somehow, I doubt your uncle did this." Hixson's gesture encompassed the trunk standing open with the contents scattered in a mad circle around it. The next irregularity, Jameson's satchel containing his extra clothing, with every article dropped on the floor and trod upon, the bag's taffeta lining ripped out. His shaving mug lay in pieces atop the commode, the straight-edge razor hammered into the wall beside the mirror, which bore a crack it'd lacked earlier when Wilkie had examined her disguise. Signs of someone in a fit of pique.

Someone not Jameson.

She shook her head and finally answered Hix's comment. "No. He certainly not."

More telling, whoever had done the damage must have been looking for her, too. The door between his room and a smaller, adjoining one, which she knew had been locked, was broken open, it's bottom panel kicked through. The room had been occupied the night they arrived, and she'd been assigned a room across the hall and a couple doors down.

Had they found that? She was afraid to find out.

Hixson paced the cramped area, peering into the now empty trunk and eyeing some of the tools of Jameson's trade. "What were they looking for?"

"The papers I delivered to Mrs. Badrac, I imagine. And the fee for our work." Wilkie felt as if all her blood had been sucked out and her hulk left to dry. She fought back a sob. "I broke the contract when I did it. But the attorney, he tried to cheat not only his clients but me —us—, and it made me angry. Just ask Mr. Venig. He'll tell you."

"Yeah, he mentioned something." The muscles beside Hixson's mouth twitched. "And he calls me an outlaw," he muttered so softly that, if not for her sharply tuned hearing, Wilkie would've missed.

Outlaw? She decided to ignore it. "Your aunt, she's apt to need protection from them."

"Eldon is with her. He'll call for help if needed." He chuffed. "The family doesn't lack for relatives. Or resources."

Hix didn't appear too worried, although Wilkie thought she saw a tightness around his mouth she hadn't noticed before.

"Resources?" she asked.

"Favors to call in. People to fight for her. Like you, she doesn't appreciate being cheated."

Wilkie stared down at Jameson's body, the only person who'd ever fought for her. He looked peaceful enough, lying there. Not scared or pained or anything horrible. But, unlike how people always said, "Oh, how natural he seems. As if he's only asleep," well, it just wasn't so. He looked waxen, pale, and most certainly, lifeless. And she, well, Wilkie had no clue what she should do. They'd discussed sometimes what her steps would be if he were arrested. And Jameson had joked about getting lynched, not meaning it. Or not after that one time, anyway, but this— They never discussed the possibility of him just up and dying while out on a job. Never.

Tears welled over and leaked toward her cheeks. Angry at her weakness, she scrubbed them away, unaware that at the same time, she scrubbed off the powder she'd used to alter her appearance.

Hixson studied her, a frown forming between his brows, not that she paid him any mind. "Miss," he said, hesitating before adding, "I don't know your name. Magdalena called you..." He shrugged. "I've forgotten."

She didn't see any point in keeping her identity a secret. Didn't he deserve to know who he was helping? "Wilkie. My name is Wilhelmina Van Slyke." Grunting a little, she got to her feet. She didn't propose to dilly dally here much longer. Jameson would never approve of doing nothing. If only she were certain what it was, she ought to be doing.

"Wilhelmina? Huh. Well, Wilkie, what do you have in the way of resources?"

She eyed him. "I'm not sure what you mean."

"Money, for starters. Do you have any money?" He honed in on her obvious uncertainty. "Because if your uncle carried the money, you can be sure it's gone now. Whoever turned this place over was thorough. And I suspect we ought to hurry and get you out of here. From what Eldon said, Boothe or Burke will be siccing the law on you pretty soon. If not the law, then somebody worse. Depends on who they've bribed."

"Oh. But what about my uncle? I can't just leave him like this." She hardly heard him as she viewed the ransacked room with dismay.

"Sorry, Wilkie, but I think you're going to have to. I know somebody. Maybe he can do something for him later."

Later. If only all of this could be later.

She needed to sort through the stuff. And, much as it distressed her, check over Jameson's body. It didn't look as though he had been disturbed. But then what she should do? What should she do with *him?* Was this man... was Hixson, right? Just leave him? After all, he'd done for her?

Swallowing a lump in her throat that felt like a hot cannonball, she flung back the blankets covering her uncle. Best not to delay this next part.

"What are you doing?" Hix started forward like maybe he thought she'd lost her mind.

Though she hesitated to touch her uncle, it had to be done. First, his money. He kept it with him at all times when they were away from home, including when he went to bed. And there it was, his wallet tucked between the sheet and the blanket down by his feet. Intact. Wilkie held it up for Hix to see. "Jameson says most people don't sleep with their money," she said. "But he always did."

Aware of Hix's watchful gaze, she replaced the blanket, tucking it around Jameson's body before fetching his boots, which had been shoved under the bed. A twist of the heel in one brought forth his set of lockpicks. Tools of the trade, he called them. They'd been made in England of the finest steel, and he was proud of them. Proud of his special hardened-steel drill bits, too, still in their canvas bag and kicked under a chair.

Wilkie retrieved them.

At least they hadn't gotten hold of his little black book, the thin, leather-bound journal where he kept track of clients' names and dates and jobs. Wilkie had a hunch, more than money, that's what they'd ransacked the room to find. It had become Jameson's habit, when they were on a job together, to give it to her for safekeeping.

"I should see if they found my room."

Hix stared at her as she went about her business. "You had your own room?"

"Yes. Of course. My goodness! You don't think—" But she could tell what he had thought by the way his ears turned blood red. "Oh."

He recovered before she did. "I hope you're done here. We need to get out."

Speechless, she led the way. Two doors down and across the hall, she stopped. "The door is closed, at least."

He tried the knob. "And locked. I'll need the key."

Wilkie handed it over without argument, wondering all the while if she was doing the right thing. Wouldn't Jameson expect more toughness out of her? More independence? But it was a relief when Hix entered the room first, his body a shield at the front. And found, this time, nothing out of place. Nothing added, and nothing taken away.

***

"Pack up." Hix leaned beside the door, left an inch ajar, his arms folded across his chest. He kept a lookout as Wilkie discarded the ridiculous shoes she'd been wearing and wiggled her toes in relief. The small motion suited her good foot fine but made her swollen sprained ankle howl with pain. He heard her pained inhalation.

"Hope you got something to wrap that ankle with," he said, seeing her wince. "In case—"

"In case I have to run," she finished for him.

"Make sure it's tight."

As though she needed telling.

The only thing she found suitable for use as a bandage was one of the strips. She bound her breasts with when she wore boy clothes. Not that she thought Hix would recognize the long strip for what it was, but even so she turned from him while she wrapped her ankle. Finished, it felt bulky and cumbersome, but the ankle more stable. Good enough to bear her full weight in a pinch. She slipped on boots, hardly aware of the incongruous sight her mixed attire and the smeared blobs of powder made of her.

One of Jameson's first lessons had taught her that when staying in hotels, it meant they always had to be ready to run. And also, "Never spread your belongings about," adding it was too easy for the housemaids to steal and say any missing items had simply been lost or misplaced. But the most important reason, Wilkie figured, was the ability to make a quick getaway without leaving everything behind. Too bad it hadn't worked for him this time.

His lessons meant it took only moments for Wilkie to pack. She left the shoes beside the bed, abandoning the sorry things with glee. Anyone who wanted them could have them with her blessing. Not more than three minutes later, she turned to face Hix. "I'm ready."

"You might want to—" Hix, flummoxed by the girl's efficiency in light of his experience with ladies, jerked erect as voices sounded in the hall. Loud voices. Unfriendly voices and they ended up right outside Jameson Van Slyke's room.

"This is it," a man said, and a heavy fist pounded as though to beat the door down.

They heard the door creak as it swung open.

Men muttered, then went silent.

Chapter Six

The girl's eyes opened wide as she stared at him. "Oh," she said, more an escape of pent breath than an actual word. "Who is that?"

He shrugged. "You'd know better than me." It struck Hix that she wasn't as old as he'd thought at first, having seen through her flimsy disguise. In fact, if they hadn't been in what he suspected was a bad spot, he might've been amused by the attempted obscuring of her features. She'd managed to muddle the thick coating of powder she'd layered on her face in an obvious attempt to hide her youth. Now, instead of an older lady, she looked like a mottled clown trying to draw laughs. And not much more than a kid.

But there wasn't anything funny about the way they'd found her uncle if that's what the dead man truly was. And Hix couldn't help rethinking his agreement to give the girl a lift from one place to another. What began as a simple favor to his aunt had turned into something else. Something beginning to look dangerous. To the girl and most probably, anybody associated with her. Meaning yours truly, good ole Hixson Forry.

Had Eldon known? Considering his cousin and the way he operated, Hix figured he probably had. The short explanation Eldon had given as to why Hix needed to do this favor had sounded off at the time, more so as he remembered it now.

Damn, but a man wasn't as sharp as he oughta be when abruptly awakened after a night of drinking whiskey and playing cards. Anyone dealing with Eldon needed to be alert and on their game. He should know that better than anyone.

After what seemed like a prolonged silence, although it probably wasn't more than a half a minute, Hix stuck his head into the hall and took a long look around. At that point, thuds and bumps arose from the dead man's room, along with a great deal of cursing. Ducking back, he beckoned the girl forward.

"They're busy tearing that room to pieces. This is your best chance to get out of here. Do you have someplace to go?"

She kind of settled herself. "Train station, I guess. But... my uncle. I can't just leave him."

Hix felt for her. He'd had to leave a friend behind once, and it haunted him to this day.

His voice hardened. "You'd better rethink that.

Did he have any family except you?" He picked up her tapestry valise, finding it deceptively heavy. A sense of urgency drove him.

Little lines formed between her eyes, then cleared. "I don't know. I think just me. Otherwise, why would he—" She broke off.

"It doesn't matter. For now, let's just go."

"My luggage. How will I manage..."

"Forget it," he advised. "Send a telegram to the hotel asking them to send on. C'mon, darlin'. Let's get out of here while we still can."

At least her preoccupation allowed him to usher her, both of them silent as two cautious people can be, along to the opposite end the hall, on to the main stairwell, and down the two flights. At the landing, he lowered the goggles over his eyes before entering the lobby.

"Don't stop. You won't be checking out." Hix guided her toward the entrance, staying between her and the desk clerk. Fortunately, he was busy answering a richly-clad matron's question about mid-morning tea service and ignored them as they passed.

"Our rooms were paid. I wasn't going to stop," she said when they'd passed outside without incident.

Hix halfway expected someone to recognize him and set up an outcry, but they didn't. He and the girl might've been anybody out for a stroll and taking in the sights of Butte. Except they weren't.

He nodded toward a store on the corner across the street. Mildred's Dress Shoppe. "Think you can get over there and wait for me?"

Her dark eyes flashed upward. "Wait for you?"

"I've got to get the motorcycle. And with it being parked right under your uncle's window, I might be in a hurry." He didn't pull his punches. "If I have to run for it, you'd slow me down."

Nodding, she wrinkled her nose and reached for her valise, grunting a little under its weight as she took it from him. What the hell did she have in there? Cannonballs?

"All right." She started off, then turned back to him. "Thank you."

He hadn't been expecting thanks. He'd been the thankful one, up to now. Thankful the girl hadn't started bawling, and thankful nobody had recognized him. So far.

Just before he turned the corner to go around the back of the hotel, Hix noted she was also somewhat wily. Either that or no novice at evading unwanted scrutiny. Instead of crossing Broadway by the closest route, which meant straight across, she walked all the way up to the next cross street and darted through the heavier traffic, dodging horses, dogs, some children, and even a motorcar in order to reach the other side. No one paid her any notice. So, old man Boothe, or maybe it was Burke, hadn't pointed her out as yet. Or maybe her disguise had actually worked. But they'd obviously gotten somebody, either a henchman or the law, which pretty much amounted to the same thing, after her uncle.

Whoever had gone in Jameson Van What'shisname's room, he hoped they'd been surprised, and dealt a setback, by what they'd found.

Satisfied Wilkie would be at Mildred's when— or if— he succeeded in retrieving his motorcycle, he went on, pausing to survey the area before he stepped into the open where he'd left the vehicle.

The last step didn't get taken.

A man stood under the back entrance overhang. In deep shadow, so it took a keen eye to spot him right off. But then the guy flipped a cigarette butt into the yard, seemed to think better of his action when the butt landed in a clump of tall, dry grass, and he broke cover to come out and stomp on it.

Sunlight flashed off the badge he wore, gleaming against his uniform.

Well, hell. Now what?

A bellow came from overhead. "Richards. Get your ass up here."

The policeman, caught rubbing his smoke into

the dirt, looked up. "What do you want?"

"Need your help," the man sticking his head out the second-story window said. "Got a body to move."

The copper, presumably Richards, stood with his hands on his hips. "Who killed him?"

"Don't look like anybody did. *What* kilt him is the question, and we'll find that out sooner when we get the body over to the morgue. Let the doc figure it out. Get a move on, Richards, ya lazy bugger."

"Standish said to stay down here," Richards said stubbornly. "He said to watch for anybody trying to make a getaway."

"This is the one you were supposed to be watching for, stupid. And he ain't makin' any getaways except to hell." The window slammed shut.

After a moment, Richards stuck up his middle finger in a universal gesture. Then, moving without apparent haste, he made his way into the hotel, turning toward the staff stairway just as Hix and Wilkie had earlier.

Hix grinned. When he was sure the police were busy upstairs, he wasted no time in getting to the motorcycle where it leaned against a sturdy old hitching rack. Not to start the engine and mount it, though. No, sir. Grunting a little, he pulled in the clutch and took off pushing. No sense in alerting the cops. Maybe they wouldn't even notice it was gone. Or not until he'd picked up Wilkie and they were well away. Away to where, he didn't know.

***

He hardly recognized Wilkie when he rolled up in front of Mildred's Dress Shoppe. Arriving from the direction opposite he could be expected, her head was turned the other way. She no longer wore the hideous brown suit and had donned a tan-colored split riding skirt, a pale green blouse, wide leather belt, and laced boots much like ones he favored. Her lustrous black hair was tied at the nape with a green ribbon before tumbling in waves down her back.

Still, he knew her by the way she stood; shoulders thrust back and something ever watchful in the tilt of her head. It didn't hurt that the tapestry valise sat at her feet.

Amused, he saw that while she'd managed to scrub most of the powder off her face, she'd missed a spot along her left jawbone.

The clatter of his Triumph's engine brought her head around to face him. Hix was pretty sure that was relief he saw.

"Hop on." He eyed the valise doubtfully, but,

in a common sense kind of way, she straddled the fender platform and stowed the bag between their bodies. She'd either abandoned the briefcase somewhere or put it in the valise. "Smart girl. Did you decide on a destination?"

"The train depot, please."

"Good enough. Hang on."

Hix made sure their progress to the station was circumspect. No revving the Triumph's engine, no quick maneuvers, no speeding or scaring horses or pedestrians. Nothing to call attention to them, except maybe for the way Wilkie held her legs apart from the machine's moving parts. At another time, he might've laughed at the picture they made. He with his dark goggles and his cap pulled low; her with what had to be an uncomfortable position and her arms wrapped around his middle until he could barely breathe.

They stopped once. Hix braked outside a quiet saloon and shut off the motorcycle. "Wait here," he told Wilkie. "I'll only be a couple minutes."

Her arms tightened. "I'd rather go with you."

"It's a saloon. And not a..."

"I know what it is. I'd rather not sit out here, that's all. It's too... exposed."

It sounded to him as if she had experience and hadn't found it pleasant. He shrugged. "Your choice. Don't say I didn't warn you."

She packed her valise with her, holding it close to her chest as she followed him through the warped and scarred plank door into a cavernous dark and evil-smelling room. A flush of embarrassment colored Hix's cheekbones when a voice called out, "Hix, you no-good S.O.B., what're you doing back here so soon. Thought we got all your money last night."

The girl stopped when Hix did, bumping her nose on his back.

"You did," he said. "But I got a customer for little job employing Henry if you think he'll take it on,"

A man loomed out of the darkness, emerging from behind the bar. He wore a white shirt with the sleeves rolled to his elbows, and a porkpie hat that added a couple inches to his already extraordinary height. "It's nothin' that'll scare him, is it?"

"Shouldn't. Not as long as he isn't afraid of the undertaker. I've never known Henry to be superstitious." Behind him, at the word *undertaker,* Hix felt the girl give a jerk. He put out a hand to steady her.

"Superstitious? Henry? Hell no. He used to be a doctor, ya know."

"So he says," Hix said. "I've even known him to appear respectable when he's halfway sober. That's why I'm asking if he can take on a job."

"He'll take it," the big man said. "He owes me money. If I get in fast enough, I reckon I can persuade him to pay a little something on account."

Hix laughed. "Yeah, as long as you're in at the exchange. Just don't take it all, Tom."

Tom lifted massive shoulders in a shrug. "Goes without saying. I don't cheat him. Hell, he's my brother. Hang on a minute. I'll wake him up." He headed over to the darkest corner of the room where a man, visible only when attention was called to him, sat at a table with his head resting on his folded arms. His snores resounded even to where Hix and Wilkie stood.

"You've got some money, don't you?" Hix whispered to Wilkie. He hoped so since Tom hadn't been joking — not much, anyway — when he talked about taking all Hix's money last night. Hix's pockets were pretty light right now.

"Y-Yes. A little." Wilkie's agreement sounded cautious. "Why?"

Hix approved of her caution. "I can have Henry collect your uncle from the undertaker when the coroner is done. The undertaker can put his coffin on the train to wherever you want it to go. It'll take some money."

She made a quiet sobbing sound. "How much?"

"Fifty ought to cover it. The coffin, the undertaker, the train, and Henry."

"All right," she said, then hesitated. "Can I trust them."

Hix snorted. "As much as you can trust anybody." Hell, she didn't really know she could trust *him.*

Wilkie stepped around to the back of the bar. Hix heard the rustle of clothing and the rasp of metal. A few moments later, she appeared beside him again and thrust two double eagles and a ten in gold toward him.

He chuckled. "Gold. Henry will like this."

"Apparently Tom will, too."

Their business concluded quickly, after that. Wilkie, the cagey little minx, wrote a shipping address of general delivery, to be called for, in Spokane. He found it interesting that she showed signs of knowing how to cover her tracks, even to shipping a body by rail.

He thought they were both beginning to relax when they drew up behind the Butte Northern Pacific Depot. Wilkie slid to the ground, and Hix propped the motorcycle against a tree. He picked up her valise, figuring to carry it around to the boarding area for her.

Wilkie led the way, mingling with a half-dozen other people as they started up the steps to the ticket window.

Hix thought later they spotted trouble at the

same time. His breath hissed out. "Stop," he said, at the very moment, she turned on her heel and ran face first into him.

Chapter Seven

Wilkie realized she'd made a mistake a second too late. She'd been too forward, too previous. By that time, she'd already drawn attention to herself — and to Hix—by slamming into him hard enough to cause him to stagger. More than one person standing on the platform turned to look. That included the attorney, Burke, and his hired henchman, Mr. Laced-up Boots.

Hix uttered a soft curse even as his arms closed around her. He swept her into a no-doubt passionate looking embrace.

"Sweetheart," he said, louder than necessary if he'd meant it for her ears only, "please say you'll stay. You won't be sorry. I promise."

Wilkie's eyelashes fluttered like butterfly wings. "I... I—" She guessed what he was trying to do. He was trying to take away any appearance of trying to escape this town by playing the part of a lover about to be separated from his girl. But like a dumbstruck fool, she couldn't think of the proper words to answer.

Two older ladies tittered behind their hands.

A young man dressed like a cowboy and toting a saddle spoke up. "Why don't you just kiss her?"

She almost thought he would, but he didn't. Wilkie didn't know if she was glad or sorry about that. Instead, he twirled her around the way they'd come, pushing past a doddering Leonard Boothe on the way up who glared venomously at Hix. Wilkie, after a first worried glance, kept her eyes down. Their dark color was entirely too distinctive, and Boothe had looked piercingly at her during their meeting earlier.

Meanwhile, Hix had a ready excuse for their sudden turn. "I like privacy when I kiss my girl," he tossed back over his shoulder to the cowboy.

They rounded the corner toward Hix's motorcycle, with Hix pulling her by the hand. Somehow, he'd taken her valise, too, making it easier for her to ignore the pain in her ankle and run.

Someone, she thought she recognized Laced Boots' deep voice and odd accent bellowing something that ordinarily would've given her pause.

"That's Hixson Forry. He's wanted in Jefferson county," he said. He didn't say wanted for what.

Boothe's voice joined the commotion. "The woman stole papers from me. Catch them. There's a reward."

Footsteps pounded on the wooden train platform as men headed their way.

But there was no time to think about any of it. Hix had the motorcycle on its wheels and the engine firing before she could swing her leg over the back. The valise stuck out more on one side than the other as they started off with a jolt, providing a sense of imbalance. Wilkie knew that if she'd been riding sideways, she'd have landed on her rear in the road. As it was, she clung to Hix as if her life depended on it.

But then, she guessed it did. A shot sounded from behind them, and Wilkie saw the corner trim of the station sort of explode, splinter and break off. It hadn't missed them by much. Her back stung as though expecting to fly apart like the station.

Hix's trick riding had them skidding around the corner with the building between them and the shooter. She figured it was Laced Boots with the gun.

Once on the road, Hix opened the throttle full on. They barreled along so fast the wind whipped tears from her eyes. No wonder Hix wore those dark goggles, she thought, finally able to straighten her valise between them. To save her vision, she buried her face in his back and held on.

Wilkie had no idea how long or how far they

traveled. A long time, or so it seemed, all the time as fast as if they were racing the wind. The road changed from a graded surface to ruts and bumps, and finally to a trail more suitable for horses and in some cases, a wagon than two-wheeled bike. Neither of them tried to speak. She was aware of tall mountains rising around them, snowcapped though the calendar said it was June. She wasn't even certain which direction they were going. West, she thought. Or south and then west. How did he know which way to go? Why not east?

After some time, hours, most certainly, the motorcycle sputtered and died. The quiet held them both silent for another moment as Hix put his feet on the ground to balance them. Then he cursed, and Wilkie dismounted. At least, she guessed that's what you called it. Her legs shook as she stood.

"What happened?" she asked.

"Ran out of gas." Hix pushed the cycle off the trail into the shelter of some bushes and rocks "You up to walking? I know a place not far from here where we can maybe get a couple horses. Doubt he'll have any fuel, though."

"How far is 'not far?'" Wilkie set the valise at her feet. "Oh, never mind. It doesn't matter. I'll manage. It's not as though I have a choice." The ribbon holding her hair had slipped almost off.

She retied it with angry jerks. "How did those men know to ambush us at the depot, Mr. Forry?"

"Call me Hix." He picked up her valise. "That's a good question. One I've been asking myself. Maybe somebody is just a good guesser. I suppose it's logical you'd be heading out on the train. That's how you and your uncle got here, isn't it?"

She nodded, noting Hix looked grim and thoughtful at the same time. He took off walking, the dark goggles pushed up on his forehead. Limping, Wilkie followed, dreading every step.

"On the other hand," he said, "it strikes me they were waiting there for you to arrive, mighty sure you would. And me. But I don't know why they'd be looking for me."

The very thing that had been running through Wilkie's mind during their flight. "Don't you? But I distinctly heard Laced Boots saying you were wanted. Wanted for what, Mr. Forry?"

His silence lasted a couple heartbeats too long before his grin flashed. "Don't know, Miss Van Slyke. Maybe for my handsome looks and debonair attitude?"

Wilkie snorted. She recognized a sidestepping fib when she heard one. "They give rewards for that in this part of the country, do they?"

He had the grace to blink before going back to the would-be ambush. "What I can't figure is how they had time to set their trap."

Wilkie had a suspicion. "I can guess. They knew my uncle was dead and thought I'd be an easier target. Remember, someone had searched his room and found him, but evidently not what they were looking for. It wasn't the police who did it since they showed up later. But someone tipped them off. Someone with connections."

Hix nodded. "Figure so. Boothe or Burke most likely."

"Or Venig."

A frown gathered between his brows as he stopped, blocking her. "You mean Eldon? Why would he do that? Now, it's for damn sure Eldon ain't the most admirable man in Butte, Montana, but it's his... our... Aunt Magdalena being swindled, which I understand is how you and your uncle got involved. Right?"

"Right. And the funny part is that the person who hired my uncle... hired us... is the same one committing the crime." She walked around him and struck out ahead. "Anyway, your aunt is not the only one being swindled. There are a couple others that I know of. And who better to put a bit of skullduggery in motion than a relative with active knowledge of the process?"

"He's gonna inherit her holdings one of these days, anyway. He's her favorite." It was apparent

Hix didn't agree with her idea. "I don't imagine he'd want to queer that."

"Does he know he'll inherit?" Wilkie couldn't help thinking of her own mother. Always so secretive that Wilkie often wondered if they truly shared a bloodline, or if the faeries had left her on Esther's doorstep and she'd only ever been tolerated because Jameson insisted. Esther's brother had a son. Wilkie was pretty sure he was the one named as heir in her mother's will. If her mother even had a will.

"Plain as the nose on your face," Hix said.

"To you. Maybe not to him."

"Well, that's just wrong."

Wilkie, sensing him gaining on her, turned to face him. "Then there's you."

"Me?"

"You could've told those men that I'd soon be arriving at the station. Hand delivered, so to speak. I had to wait for you an awfully long time in front of the dress shop."

She wasn't prepared for Hix's show of temper. The way he threw the valise down at her feet, glared daggers and said in a dangerously quiet and disgusted voice, "The hell! If you aren't the most ungrateful little—"

She blinked and spoke over him. "Not that I think you did. I just mean you *could* have. If you'd... um... been... uh..." She floundered to a stop.

"Bribed? Well, I wasn't, or believe me, lady, you wouldn't be walkin' down this road right now, free as a bird. You'd either be behind bars or sitting in a room somewhere being slapped around by Burke's hired muscle." His voice pitched high, mimicking her as he said, "Mr. Laced Boots," before returning to normal. "That is if you hadn't already been murdered and your body tossed down some abandoned mine shaft."

Wilkie gulped. "I'm sorry. I didn't mean to insult you. I'm just trying to figure out what happened. Truly, I'm grateful to you for everything. I don't know what I'd have done if you hadn't helped me. With my uncle. With this escape. With *everything*."

He wasn't mollified. Not by a long shot, not that she blamed him. She glanced sideways at him from under her lashes. Maybe she'd been too blunt. Spoken without thinking. But it was true. He could've been working for the crooked attorneys. She just didn't believe so. Not really.

But she still had some concern over that "wanted" comment and the mention of a reward. And his evasive answer.

"I'll see you into Deer Lodge where you can catch the train to Spokane. Or wherever you're going. It don't matter to me. After that, you're on your own." The frost in his voice chilled her.

They walked in silence for the next mile, when they came to a side road leading off to the left through a dip in the landscape. A half-hidden post with a flat board nailed to it announced the Jacksons lived somewhere in that direction.

"We'll take this side road," Hix said. "I'll see if we can borrow a horse or two from this Jackson feller."

Wilkie nodded, a little breathless from exertion as Hix kept up a fast pace. In fierce pain, she'd begun limping badly. She was also sweating like a horse and so thirsty her tongue felt like a flap of cardboard in her mouth. The sun's position in the sky indicated it was getting on for mid-afternoon. Sourly, she felt more like it should've been midnight. She found it hard to fathom all that had already happened today. The meeting with those crooks. Another with Mrs. Badrac. The discovery of Uncle Jameson's body. Her flight — and fight—with Hix. What more could be crammed into such an awful day?

A job begun as a lucrative adventure had turned into a disaster. When, or if, she ever got home, what would be her mother's reaction? She would confiscate the money, and that would be the last Wilkie ever saw of it. No surprise there

even if it wasn't fair. Or right. But without Jameson to take her part—

She must've made a sound because Hix turned
to look at her. Really look at her. Did she only
imagine his expression softened a smidgeon?
Unless that was just exasperation turning his lips
down.

Her head lifted. "What?"

They'd only come a hundred yards down the
Jackson's road or, more accurately, trail. To call it
a road stretched the facts as it was only two narrow bare tracks split by a grass and weed covered
strip down the middle. Not easy footing at best.
Wilkie thought maybe the Jackson's didn't go out
much.

Hix nodded off to the side where a few trees
shaded an outcropping of rocks. Birds flitting
about in the scraggly limber pine kept up an in-
cessant racket.

"You want to stop and wait for me here? Seems
like a good place to sit and rest your ankle. Might
be best if nobody sees you with me."

The idea made sense. Her glance followed his
to the area. It did look tempting, and she was so
tired. And her bag was heavy. "You'll come back
for me?"

"Only one road in and out of here that I know
of," he said. "Don't see how I can avoid it."

Not the most flattering summation. She drew herself up. It wasn't flattery she needed anyway. Just help to the next train station. That's all. And she'd pay Hix one of those twenty-dollar gold pieces stashed in her briefcase. Or maybe a ten-dollar. She wouldn't stiff him. She paid her debts.

"All right." She made her way to the nearest seat-high boulder, dropped her valise, and collapsed onto the sun-warmed rock surface with a soft sigh.

Hix grinned at that and strode quickly out of sight.

The birds, left undisturbed by the girl sitting immobile in the sun, soon toned their noise down to a soft chatter. Even when Wilkie, deciding the stone was hard on a heinie already pummeled and possibly bruised by riding a motorcycle over rough ground, eased herself onto the grass, removed her boot, and stretched out. She wished she'd asked Hix to bring back some water.

After a while, the pain in her ankle eased, and she may even have slept a few minutes. Men's voices, loud in the overall silence, startled her awake.

Hix, she thought before realizing the sounds came from the wrong direction. Men, at least two, were having a discussion, a very carrying discussion, down on the main road. Or were they quarreling? If she'd been a dog, her ears would've pricked as she listened. She didn't even have to strain her ears.

"This is the first side road since we found his motorcycle," one said. "If he's smart, he'll get rid of the girl as quickly as possible. If he hasn't already."

"I say he was smart enough to dump her somewhere and take off on his own. After that fiasco at the train station, isn't that what you'd do?"

"Yes. Still means he'll try for the nearest place he can find a horse. Or hope for a rancher who runs gas machinery to beg some fuel for his motorcycle. When we catch up to him, I can persuade him to tell us about the girl."

The coldness of the last voice indicated Hix wouldn't enjoy the method.

This argument seemed to find favor, even as Wilkie's blood ran cold and she felt like crying. She took no pleasure in discovering she'd been right and Hix wrong in their guessing game. Except it hadn't been a game.

"Tell you what," the first voice said, "I'll keep going into Deer Lodge. You follow this trail and talk to the rancher. Maybe you'll be lucky, and you'll find Forry there."

"Won't do any good if I do. He's wise to what's

going on by now. The girl will have told him, and he isn't stupid by any means. Stubborn, too."

"So shoot him. What do you think you're carrying that pistol for?"

"I don't shoot." Frost coated this one's statement. "I talk."

"So talk. I'll do the shooting when the time comes."

After a short pause, this same man called, "Hyah," and she heard the creak of harness and the clomp of a horse's hooves.

No more than a minute later a man walked past Wilkie's hiding spot where she sprawled full length on the ground behind the boulder.

The man, as she'd already known it would be, was Eldon Venig. He no longer walked bent over, which she thought was too bad. She wished she'd kneed him with more lasting force.

Chapter Eight

Hix whistled as he walked into the rancher's yard. Not because his spirits were so high the tune burst out of its own accord. Nope. He'd found it paid to give a man or, more likely, a woman a bit of warning before knocking on the front door. Some folks didn't take to being startled.

Although in this case, the door was open to the air and nobody answered either his whistle or his knock.

"Anyone home?" he called into the empty front room. "Mr. Jackson?"

Nothing there but silence.

Grumping a little, he went past a recently hoed garden showing the rough leaves of potato tops, beans, and spiked shoots of corn as well as some things he didn't recognize and headed toward a barn sitting off a little way. A couple big mules drowsed in a pasture that backed up to the barn. A watering trough kept filled by a constant trickle of water from a narrow pipe was surrounded by a well-trampled mess of mud, reminding Hix that his throat was arid as an Arizona desert. He expected little Miss Wilkie's must be in like condition.

It occurred to him that she hadn't complained once. Not even when he made her carry her own valise, though he figured the dang-blasted thing must weigh thirty pounds with all the stuff she'd crammed into it.

Sticking his head into the barn, he called out again. Again, no answer. But did he hear something down toward a small creek? It sounded almost like a hiccuping sob. Hix decided he'd best investigate.

He found the Jacksons down by a little springhouse. Them and a dog so old its black muzzle had turned white as the stripe down a skunk's back. The dog, head on its paws, lay next to an old woman who also lay on the ground. Her arms were crossed over her flat chest. A weatherbeaten man sat next to her. He glanced up when Hix's shadow passed over him but didn't move. Neither did the dog.

Hix had the queasy feeling he'd come upon a tragedy. The old woman looked dead to him. He gulped. Two corpses in one day. It set a new record for him.

He squatted down next to the trio. "Sir? Can I be of help?"

The dog's tail thumped, and he whimpered once. Hix lay a soothing hand on his head. He wished he could do the same for the man who, he discovered, had tears coursing over wrinkled cheeks. He hadn't been mistaken. It had been a sob that guided him here.

"I don't reckon there's anything you can do," the old feller said. Hix assumed he was Jackson. "She's been took. Been feeling poorly the last few days. She washed up after dinner and said she felt like resting here in the cool by the spring. Her and the dog. I found them a bit ago. Dog don't want to leave her."

"I see." Hix shifted uncomfortably. He didn't feel right asking to borrow a horse. Not now. Or even to inquire about gas. He doubted the old man stocked fuel anyway. Looked to him most things got done around here same as they had for the last thirty years. He cleared his throat. "Can I help you get her into the house? Maybe lay her on a bed?"

"That'd be real thoughtful of you." Jackson swiped the moisture from his cheeks and tried to rise to his feet. Finally, Hix gave him a boost, lifting under his arms. He'd noticed Jackson talked with a deep south accent. Probably moved here sometime in the bad years after the war between the states, he thought, seeking to escape the carpetbaggers. The dog stood, too, his hindquarters struggling for traction.

Eyeing the corpse, Hix figured Mrs. Jackson had probably had a cancer eating at her, as she seemed too diminished for her clothing. He picked her up with no problem, grateful she hadn't yet started to stiffen. "I got her," he said. "Just show me where you want her if you would."

Nodding, Jackson shuffled toward the house, while the dog trailed Hix and his burden. The house, when they entered, was close and hot, even with the door open. But spotlessly clean and tidy, as though the old lady's pride dictated, she'd leave her home in apple pie order for her own funeral.

She'd evidently taught her husband well, too, as he fussed around in the bedroom and had Hix wait while he unfolded an old blanket over the white crocheted bedspread. Hix put the body down, relieved when the old man ushered him and the dog out and closed the door.

"Thankee, son," he told Hix. "I appreciate you comin' by. I'd've had to drag her, and my old woman wouldn't've like that, trailing her skirt in the dirt and scuffing her shoes."

Hix didn't know what to say. "No. I expect not."

"Sit down at the table. I believe this occasion calls for a libation." Jackson poked around in a pantry off the kitchen, emerging finally with a brown bottle. It had a label, too, although one so worn as to be unreadable. He found a couple small glasses and set them on the table. The whiskey smelled like the good stuff when he pulled the cork, although Hix wondered if it was a product of Jackson's own making. The old man poured, filling the glasses to the brim, with the whiskey showing a fine amber color.

Collapsing onto a chair across from Hix, Jackson lifted his glass in a toast. "To my wife, Clara June Jackson. She was a good woman, a good wife, and a good mother, though all our children died young. May she rest in peace."

Hix, still trying to think of a way to ask about a horse, raised his glass and clinked it with Jackson's. "To Mrs. Jackson, may she rest in peace."

The dog, who'd been lying flat on the floor, raised onto his haunches and placed a paw on the old man's knee.

"Well, who is it?" Jackson asked the dog, and then to Hix, "It ain't often we get more than one visitor in a day. Ma will..." He bit off what he he'd started to say and gulped the last of his whiskey as footsteps sounded on the stoop outside.

Hix expected it'd be little Miss Wilkie Van Somethingoranother darkening the doorway, but it was a man's long shadow cast into the room. Somehow, when his cousin Eldon walked through the open door, Hix wasn't even surprised.

"Here you are," Eldon said to Hix. "I wondered where you'd got to."

"Wondered about me? What for?" As if Hix didn't have strong suspicions. Didn't hurt to play a part, though, same as Eldon. He shrugged. "It's not any of your business, as far as I know."

Eldon had walked in without invitation, which caused the old man to scowl and the dog to rumble a complaint.

"You know this yahoo?" Jackson looked at Hix. "Kinda pushy, ain't he? Most folks ask for an invite before they barge into another man's house. A stranger's house."

"University education." Hix shook his head. "Puts him ahead of other people, or so he thinks. But they didn't teach him any manners."

Eldon's face turned red. "What do you know about manners, you uncouth son of..."

Hix spoke over him. "Why are you're chasing me?"

"I'm not chasing you. Or not in particular. I want that girl."

Seemed kind of fruitless to act like he didn't know what girl. "You mean the girl Magdalena had me take to the hotel? When all was said and done, due to a small problem, I dropped her off on the outskirts of Butte." The lie came easily to him. "She didn't much care for riding on my motorcycle."

Head cocked, Eldon glared at him. "That I can believe, but I doubt you dropped her off anywhere. Where is she?"

Hix, eyes narrowed, studied his cousin. Something strange was going on. "Why? What do you want with her? Last I heard she just wanted to go home."

Eldon ignored this. He started forward, aiming for the closed bedroom door. "In here?"

"You stay outta there." The old man's chair clattered sideways onto the floor, which set the dog to howling.

By this time, Hix was up and charging toward his cousin. He came to an abrupt halt when Eldon hauled out a big old Colt .45 Peacemaker that Hix remembered had belonged to Magdalena's husband.

Eldon pointed the revolver first at him, then the dog, then Jackson, and back at him. "Shut that dog up," he snapped at Jackson. "I'm not adverse to shooting it."

The old man stepped in front of his dog. "The hell."

"The dog *or* me, from the looks of things," Hix

said. "Or any of us, for that matter. Eldon, what do you think you're doing?"

"Finishing some important business, cousin. Don't get in my way." Eldon backed up until he managed to fling open the bedroom door and yell, "I know you're in there. Come out, right now."

When the woman on the bed, naturally, didn't stir, he demanded, "What's the matter with her?"

"She's dead." A second later Hix thought maybe he should've softened that, the bald statement sounding cold. But Jackson was still occupied guarding his dog and didn't seem to hear the exchange. The dog's ears were pricked as he pawed the old man's knee.

"Uh-huh," Jackson said.

Eldon's patience had about run out. "Where is the Van Slyke girl?" His Peacemaker waved a circle before centering on Hix's chest in a wobbly kind of way.

Hix couldn't help but see the pistol was cocked. The only thing needed was for Eldon to touch the trigger for it to go off, whether by accident or by intent.

He guessed the only ones not surprised were Jackson and the dog when Eldon's question received an answer.

"I'm right here, Mr. Venig."

Eldon whirled around to face the doorway where Wilkie, looking hot, her face red, stood glaring. "You!" Eldon said. "You've led us on a merry chase."

Us? Hix wondered who else was out there. Someone who could be expected to show up at any minute, guns blazing? Burke's henchman, the fellow from Bulgaria, or some such Slavic country, seemed a likely candidate. And for all of Eldon's proclaimed search for Wilkie, he didn't really seem that pleased to see her.

Come to think of it, neither was he. What had possessed her to announce herself?

***

Wilkie stood just outside the ranch house door. Having followed Eldon almost from the moment he passed her hiding spot out by the main road, she'd been in time to hear him yammering at Hix, the old man, and the dog. On the way here, he'd never once looked behind him, not even when she'd stepped on a small, dry branch. It popped like a gunshot when it broke, or so it had seemed. He hadn't noticed.

Not a good conspirator, in her estimation. But he *had* managed to sneak up on Hix and the ranch owner, whose name, she assumed, was Jackson,

like on the sign posted at the end of the trail leading to the house If she got the chance, she figured
on punishing Venig again via his 'soft spots.' It
would serve the silly booger right. And this time,
given she wore a split riding skirt, she'd be able to
put a lot more force behind her knee.

What did he mean, anyway, when he said she'd
led them on a merry chase? Merry had nothing
to do with it.

"I've done my best to avoid you," she said,
"while trying to do what's right." She forced a
smile. Jameson always said her smile was sure
to disarm a man, but right now she had some
doubts. "Maybe you should turn over a new leaf
and do the same."

Hix barked a laugh, which probably didn't do
any good. In fact, she was sure of it when Eldon
turned the gun on him again. Although that may
have been Hix's intention.

The old man stood there, bleary-eyed with his
hand on the dog.

Wilkie took a step forward. Coming in from
the sunlight made it hard to see. Just enough to
tell the way Eldon waved the gun about as if it
were some kind of child's toy was worrisome.
Not safe at all for those on the wrong end of it.

Another step into the room, and her eyes grew
more accustomed to the dim light. Hix drew his

cousin's attention by saying something about Eldon bamboozling his own relatives, then asking if he had been in on the murder of his own father.

Eldon shouted some reply, a denial of any such thing while telling Hix he was a poor excuse of a cousin who chased anything in skirts and was taking the little whore's part over his own cousin.

Whore? Just who did he think... Outraged, Wilkie's breath caught. How dare he! If that weren't the outside of enough, Wilkie didn't know what was. She'd been trying to make up her mind what to do, but now she knew.

As the two men continued their argument, she reached in her boot, retrieved the .32 pocket pistol stowed there, and almost casually shot the Peacemaker out of Eldon's hand.

He hollered worse than a bee-stung toddler as the pistol dropped to the floor.

And, since he'd had it cocked, the gun went off, firing a shot that caromed into space.

Not quite what she'd planned.

Unlike Eldon, she managed not to scream when the bullet, taking a bite of flesh with it, scraped her arm on the way out the door open behind her. For a moment she didn't feel any pain, just a shock.

Then she did. Both legs went right out from under her, and she sank to her knees on the floor.

"Wilkie!" Hix lunged toward her, halted mid-way, and turned to shove Eldon aside.

"Well, bull-snot," the old man said to his dog. "Clara June sure will be sorry to have missed the excitement."

Chapter Nine

Wilkie, feeling a little light-headed, watched in fascination as Hix bundled Eldon onto a chair in a most uncousinly fashion, and told him to sit there and shut up.

"You're not hardly even bleeding," he said in disgust. Reaching into Eldon's pocket, he withdrew a sparkling white handkerchief and pressed it into his cousin's good hand. "Here, wrap this around that little gash. It's barely a scratch."

Eldon blubbered.

What would Hix have to say about her wound? Wilkie wondered, finally working up her nerve to look at the damage. The sleeve of her pretty green blouse bore a gaping hole. The furrow along the outside edge of her arm appeared a bit more than a scratch. It bled copiously, the spreading stickiness running all the way down to her hand and onto the floor.

In the first instant, she'd figured herself a goner. Her arm still felt as if it'd been set on fire. But she wasn't dead, and the arm wasn't really burning.

Jameson always said to show no weakness. Good advice, especially now.

Grunting, she worked herself into a position to use the table as a prop and got onto her feet.

The old man stared at her. "Well, ain't you something?" he said in an admiring tone of voice.

"Something," she replied, only in a disgusted sort of way, embarrassed to have let herself be knocked off her feet.

Hix interrupted before she could think what 'something' that might be. "Got a piece of rope long enough to corral this idiot?" he asked Jackson. "I'll tie him to a chair. Keep him out of our way."

"I'll make you sorry, Hix," Eldon said.

"I'm already sorry." Hix sounded put upon. "Sorry I didn't shoot you years ago. I wouldn't have aimed for your hand. But it's too late now. I've picked my side."

Wilkie shook her head, intensifying the disconnected feeling between her body and her brain. What did he mean by that?

Mr. Jackson, listening avidly as he searched out a length of rope, found some behind the stove and handed it to Hix. "This do?" A thought seemed to strike him. "What are you folks? Outlaws? A new Wild Bunch? Inheritors of the Henry Plummer gang?"

Hix laughed. "Not me. Ask him." He indicated his cousin, still sitting and nursing his wounded hand. "He might be."

"Nonsense," Eldon said, slapping at Hix as he approached with the rope. The slaps, not surprisingly, were ineffective.

Wilkie guessed that made her the one to blame for revealing a criminal plot and causing this whole sleazy shebang. It made her dizzy just to think about it.

The next thing she knew, she sat slumped at the table with the old man washing blood off her bare arm while the dog watched. The hot water stung like the dickens, although she knew it was necessary. Mr. Jackson had cut off the sleeve of her blouse to disclose the wound, so at least she wasn't sitting there in her shift amongst three men. A small blessing. On the other hand, her shirtwaist was ruined.

"I know it pains, but I'll be done in a minute," the old fellow told her. "Ma has some bandages here rolled ready to use. You'll be fine. Have a scar, I expect, but those don't hurt none. I'll put some of Clara June's special salve on. She swears by it."

Wilkie, as the hot water washed through the gash, thought she'd just plain like to swear, loud and long.

Hix, with Eldon secured, leaned over to peer at Jackson's work, nodding in approval. "I don't suppose you know how to sew. Looks like she could use a stitch or two."

Barely suppressing a moan, Wilkie shook her head, grateful when the old man said, "I'll just bind'er up good. Couple days and she won't even notice it ever happened."

Wilkie took his opinion with a grain of salt. Commiserating, the dog lay his head in her lap and licked her good hand.

Apparently, Hix and Mr. Jackson had come to some sort of deal while she'd been... indisposed... because after being plied with fresh, cold water and hot, strong coffee to build up her blood, her vision cleared, and she looked outside to see a tall bay mule tied at the post in front of the house.

"I'll leave the mule at the livery in Deer Lodge." Hix went over and checked the rope fixing Eldon to the chair. His cousin's mouth had a cloth tied around it now, and although words were not discernible, Eldon still managed a loud, angry buzzing sound.

"Maybe you can let him go after me, and Miss Van Slyke take our leave. Or do whatever you want. The sheriff might ought to take a look at his activities."

Eldon yowled a protest behind the gag, which

Hix and Mr. Jackson both professed not to hear.

"Maybe calling in the sheriff could wait." Wilkie, having been privy to Jameson's tales of near escape from the law, had a different idea. She wanted well away from here first, preferring not to explain how she got involved.

Hix paid her no heed. "Whatever you decide to do," he said to Jackson. "I'll let someone know about your wife when we reach town."

The old man nodded. "Tell the storekeeper. He'll send out the undertaker and notify the womenfolk about arrangements. Time out of mind, my Clara June worked with the other ladies. Now it's her turn." He seemed puzzled, as though he couldn't believe how such a thing came to be.

Wilkie knew how he felt. She couldn't believe Jameson lay on some cold table back in a Butte mortuary, either. Alone and unidentified. Her stomach knotted.

Hix touched the old man's arm. "We'll be on our way, sir. You ready?" This last was aimed at Wilkie.

"Yes." More than ready. She thanked Mr. Jackson kindly and patted the dog one last time.

***

The mule, a big fellow with a draft horse in his background, posed a problem when it came time to mount. Between her sore ankle and an arm that felt useless, Wilkie didn't see how she'd make it to the top of him.

Hix wore a frown, too. "How're we gonna work this? You want to ride in front of me or in back? Best maybe in front in case you pass out." He studied her and nodded. "Yep. In front."

Wilkie wondered why he even posed the question since he'd already made up his mind. But truthfully, that was her choice, too. He'd put his arms around her and —and what in the world was she thinking?

He brought the mule in close to the porch, facing the direction enabling her to stand on her good side while he helped her get her other leg over the animal's back. Then he mounted behind her and situated them both. "All right?" he breathed in her ear, his arms snug around her.

Wilkie shivered. "Yes."

A last wave from Mr. Jackson saw them down the road. At the rock where he'd left her when he went to look for horses, Hix dismounted long enough to scoop up her valise, tying it behind the old-fashioned cantle with the worn saddle-strings.

From there, it didn't take so awfully long to reach town, a matter of about four miles. Not long enough, maybe, considering the first person they spotted as they trotted down the main street. The prison loomed over every other building.

"'Blame it!" Sawing on the reins, Hix spun the mule off into a side street even though the livery beckoned from just ahead.

"What?" Then Wilkie saw him too.

Their nemesis, Mr. Laced Boots, was lounging on a bench outside a saloon called The Patch. His feet stuck out onto the porch, causing customers to go around, and he appeared as relaxed as a hunting cat. Which meant he'd likely be ready to leap into motion, claws bared, at the slightest indication of trouble.

Jameson had been like that, too, sometimes. Deceptive. Disingenuous. Downright sneaky. All necessary in their profession. Wilkie had been practicing, but she didn't think those character-istics quite fit her. Yet. Although she'd certainly escaped the bank last night, right under this same man's nose, so she might someday learn.

As long as she survived today.

"What shall we do?" She turned in Hix's arms to look up at him. He didn't appear scared, nor even especially worried—a relief. There was something, though, in his set jaw that worried her a little. Maybe just aggravation his plans weren't working out. His scheme to be rid of her might not be so straightforward as he'd hoped.

"I'm thinking," he said.

"Do you know where the depot is?" she asked.

"Tracks are up ahead, but on the other side of town." His head jerked, indicating the direction. "The train is due any minute if I'm not mistaken. But it only stops if the stationmaster puts out the signal."

Wilkie didn't know if he heard anything, but she did. The train was nearing town already, its rumble more a feeling in the pit of her stomach than an actual sound. Until its whistle blew. Instead of slowing down, she thought it was gaining speed.

"I'm afraid we're too late." Her voice squeaked.

His arm felt like a chain pinched around her middle. "That tears it. Now there isn't any way out of here until tomorrow."

"No more trains?"

"Nope. Not today. Next one headed west will be tomorrow morning, early."

The mule moved beneath them, seeming of a mind to walk right out into the street where Laced Boots would spot them. Hix pulled the animal's head around until it pointed the other way. "We'd best stay out of sight. There's a back way into the livery. We'll go down a street, cut in behind the corral, and I'll drop off Mr. Jackson's mule there.

Then... huh."

"Then huh what?" If her question didn't exact-ly make sense, Wilkie didn't care. Her arm hurt, and she was of no mind to sit around and wait for Laced Boots to find her.

Hix huffed and puffed for a minute and got the mule going in the right direction. "Changed my mind. I doubt you're going to like this, but I figure our best bet is to stash you someplace safe where you can't be seen. I'll buy some gas at the drug store and ride the mule back to Jackson's, then walk to where I left the motorcycle. After that, I'll come back, pick you up and we'll go on to the next town. Maybe all the way to Missoula."

"Stash me?" Offended, Wilkie's voice rose.

"Shh." He stared around, looking to see if any-one might have heard. "I just mean for you to stay out of sight. No parading up or down the street. Rest up. You're not in any condition to be dodging that son of a gun. I'll be back by evening."

He made it sound easy.

"Somewhere where, exactly?" Wilkie viewed Hix's plan with a full-sized dose of skepticism. Sounded dubious, to her. And what did he mean, parade up and down the street? As if she ever would.

They pulled up at the rear of the livery and Hix swung down to stand at the mule's head. "Dunno.

I'll ask the hostler if he knows a nice private spot a lady could rest a bit. If he doesn't know, I'll ask at the pharmacy. Or maybe the store, when I pass on the message about Jackson's missus."

He had a lot of meetings lined up for someone who needed to keep to the shadows and evade a bad man's notice. Plus, all this meandering took time. Did he think they'd travel west, to Missoula or anywhere else, in the dark on his motorcycle?

She shuddered at the thought. If Hix was any-where near as tired as she was, he might not even notice if she bounced off into the night. "Maybe we both should stay out of sight and catch the train in the morning. Follow the first plan."

But her suggestion didn't meet with his ap-proval. Not at all. "I'm not leaving my motorcycle laying in the bushes to rust or get stolen. If it hasn't been already." His mind was clearly made up.

She understood. Even saw his point. Motorcy-cles were a huge expense to a man who did... what? She didn't even know. Here she was, putting her trust in someone she knew nothing about. His cousin Eldon had implied he was a bit of an outlaw. But then, Eldon hadn't proved the most reliable of witnesses.

And no matter what, they were stuck here until they thought of a way out, whether by train or by motor, or even shank's mare.

Chapter Ten

The idea Wilkie put forth finally prevailed, one that struck her as a fine solution though it took a lot of arguing. Hix had only to drop her off at the depot while he went to collect his motorcycle.

Hix being Hix, he identified what he saw as a major flaw in her reasoning.

"The depot?" He pushed his cap back and scratched his head. "What for? The train's gone, and there won't be anyone there. Stationmaster will have locked it up until tomorrow."

"That's what I'm counting on," Wilkie said.

"You are?"

"Yes." She eyed him as if he were something less than the tallest tree in the forest. "You said you intend on stashing me somewhere. Somewhere safe. Well, what could be safer than an empty train depot? There will be water, a bench to lie on, and nobody poking around."

Hix had to concede she had a point. Except for one little thing. "The stationmaster has the key. I'm pretty sure he doesn't leave it under the doormat for any old hobo to find."

"I don't need a key." She brushed his objection, for that's what it was, aside as if it meant nothing.

"Lady, even the stationmaster needs a key."

She shook her head and smiled faintly. "Not me."

Hix tried to think. Was she, by any chance, trying to ditch him on the premise she'd be better on her own? If so, he should just shut up. He'd go his way; she'd go hers. He'd given her a ride to the hotel, which is all his aunt had asked him to do. Then, when that went sideways, he'd gotten her out of Butte. He'd done his duty if that's what you wanted to call it. More than.

He gave in. "All right. Whatever you say."

Swinging aboard the mule again, Hix guided them into the alley and, keeping a close lookout for the lawyer's henchman, took the back way across town. It didn't take long, Deer Lodge being of no great size.

The station sat only a few feet off the tracks, with its back to the town. They had to ride around the building to reach the front where, sure enough, they found the place deserted. A sign had been stuck on the door with a tack. Hix dismounted in order to read it.

"Next train tomorrow at 8:17 a.m. Open at 8:00 sharp." He tried the door and shook his head, then

jumped forward barely in time to catch Wilkie as she slid from the tall mule.

"Thank you," Wilkie murmured, those big dark eyes of hers lifting to meet his for just a moment. Digging in a pocket of her split skirt, she came forth holding a small, thin metal pick with a hook on the end and funny little L-shaped wrench.

To Hix's wonder, she poked them into the door lock, and about fifteen seconds later had the door open.

She noticed his reaction. Couldn't help it probably, since he stood there with his eyes bugged out.

"What the hell?" he said. "How'd you learn to do that?" Moreover, how'd she come to have the *means* to do it right there in her pocket?

"I guess your cousin didn't mention how I came to meet with Mrs. Badrac, or why she asked you to give me a ride?" She looked around, as though to make certain no one was watching or could overhear.

"No." Hix rubbed the scowl line on his forehead. "Are you going to? All I know for sure is Eldon is mixed up with some bad men, and between you and him, I'm in trouble, too. Yeah. And my aunt seemed to think she owed you for something."

Wilkie snorted. "If she thought she owed me before, you can be sure the debt is growing. And I've still got—" Whatever she'd intended on saying, she cut it off.

"Still got what?"

"Never mind." She held out her right hand as though expecting him to shake it. "Thank you for your help, Mr.... Hix. If we don't meet again, I want you to know I'm very grateful."

Her oddly formal little speech struck him to the heart. He took her hand, small, but strong, and gently shook it. She had a firm grip.

"If I can get back here tonight, I will." He made the promise almost against his will. "Keep you company if nothing else, and make sure you catch the train tomorrow." Not to mention he'd need an out of the way place to stay overnight as much as she did.

She nodded and forced a smile, the mere up-curving of her lips. "All right. I'll see you later, then." After a final glance around, she went into the station and closed the door.

Hix mounted the mule, planning a route to avoid Burke's man until he left the town behind. He figured Wilkie watched until he was out of sight. He just had that feeling.

A short detour for gas and a stop at the store to announce Mrs. Jackson's demise drew more attention than he liked. Especially the part about Mrs. Jackson. One old lady kept asking him if he was a nephew or another long lost relative; one wanted every detail of her last illness and got angry when Hix didn't know; one man thought they should call the sheriff in case foul play was involved. Hix didn't much care for the way the feller eyed him as he said it.

Other than that, Hix took advantage of the cautious one's suggestion to bring in the sheriff. He told the feller that Mr. Jackson had caught someone snooping around and might need help, at which the feller trotted off toward city hall where a small sign indicated the sheriff had an office.

Finally, duty done, he was free to leave, kept so long answering questions that he was afraid the sheriff would beat him to Jackson's place. Not an idea he liked. But if necessary, he'd just turn the mule into Jackson's pasture and slip away unseen. Let the sheriff deal with Eldon.

Riding east gave him plenty of time to reflect on little Miss Wilkie Van Slyke and how she figured in his aunt's business. For instance, how she had gotten crosswise with Eldon and the thug. The bits and pieces he'd learned didn't add up to a whole lot of anything. More puzzling, the relationship with her dead uncle. What were they even doing here, to be in so much trouble? Or at least a trouble to Burke, Boothe, and Venig. And those lockpicks? Seemed likely her uncle was a damned yeggman. Or maybe a locksmith just barely on the right side of the law. If it suited him. And what did that make Wilkie?

Just as well he'd made plans. A mile from the ranch, Hix heard a motorcar coming up behind him and quickly reined the mule off the road into a gully deep enough to hide him when he dismounted. Sure any local would recognize Jackson's big critter and accuse him of theft, he hid amongst some trees until the automobile swept past. The car had *Sheriff* painted on the side. That kind of surprised him. Who'd have thought in a little burg like Deer Lodge there'd be a motorcar at the law's disposal? Credit the prison, he supposed. He ended up pasturing the mule where Jackson would be sure to find it and walked on lugging his jar of gas until he reached the Triumph. He found it still tucked into the patch of bushes where he'd left it and undisturbed.

It took only moments to fill the gas tank. He cleaned the spark plug, but even then, it took ten minutes or more of jumping on the kickstarter to get the damn thing to run. Flooded, though he wasn't quite sure what that meant. By the time the machine coughed, and the engine turned over, he was so short of breath, he could hardly think. Worse, he hadn't eaten all day and was hungry enough to carve a steak off Jackson's mule and eat it raw.

That might've been why, when at last, secure in thinking the twilight covered him on his way back to town, Hix chugged past Jackson's side road without a glance. Stood to reason the sheriff had collected Eldon by now. No doubt both his cousin and the posse were sitting in the jailhouse as snug and well-fed as a litter of nursing kittens. Hix figured he'd scoot on into town free as a bird.

Turned out he was wrong.

***

As soon as Hix and the mule disappeared from sight, Wilkie sat down and purposely made her mind go blank.

Tried to make her mind go blank, that is, on the premise a few moments of respite from this pounding worry might let her think what to do.

But despite her best efforts, some things were simply stuck in her head, going round and round on a never-ending loop. The memory of her uncle Jameson lying in that damn hotel bed, diminished by death, for instance. Even now, knowing the dangers of the day, she hardly believed she'd let herself be chased out of Butte, leaving his body unclaimed in some undertaker's cold room. Hix said he'd made arrangements—decent arrangements—to get Jameson home, but could she trust him, a stranger?

She thought so. Her heart said so. But really? Doubts rose up like a cloud of flies.

Jameson had talked to her about what steps she should take if something happened to him while they were on a job. He'd mentioned possibilities such as arrest, incarceration, hanging, even shot to death. But she'd never believed any of those things would ever happen. And it had never crossed either of their minds that he might die of a heart attack or a stroke or whatever it was that had taken him. Not Jameson.

Regarding the possibility of being killed while on the job, his advice had been to abandon his worn-out old body and leave town fast. Hide her tracks always, so no one knew where she came from or where she went. Go home, taking the long way around.

"The adventure," he'd said, "ends when I do — or when the job does."

Ends when I do. She could almost hear him saying it.

Without warning, tears began cascading down Wilkie's cheeks. She sobbed unrestrainedly until the noise of her grief seemed to fill every corner of the empty room. After a time, although the pain in her heart lingered, she stopped.

He'd been her mentor, her teacher, her protector. Acting, almost, as a father from the time he came to live in her mother's boarding house when she was only eight. What was she supposed to do without him?

The question rang in her mind until she had an answer.

Finish the job.

Weariness dragged at her as the dusk gathered outside, darkening the room where she sat. She knew she'd better make herself as comfortable as possible before it became too dark to see. So, while some light still penetrated windows dirty with soot and grit from the trains, she searched around inside the station. Amenities included an indoor toilet and a washstand with icy cold running water in a little cubby just off the waiting room. She felt like jumping for joy.

Hardly limping at all, Wilkie hastened to make use of the facility. The washstand also meant she had water to drink and to wash in. A quick search behind the ticket counter turned up a single apple, and though her stomach craved more, she made do. As a child, her mother often sent her to bed without any supper for one infraction or another. She was no stranger to being hungry.

Tossing the apple core to the birds outside, she stretched out on one of the benches and, though she hadn't meant to, slept until the familiar sound of a motorcycle engine awakened her.

"Hix." He'd come back for her.

Wilkie jumped to her feet, ignoring the twinge in her ankle. She felt a surprising sense of relief sweep over her. Not only, she assured herself, because Hix had said he'd be back, but because he'd kept his word. She started toward the door intending to unlock it, a question of what had taken him so long on her lips when she stopped with her hand on the knob.

One of Jameson's first lessons had been to teach her to always check the way was clear before stepping outside. Even at home, but especially in a strange place. On the brink of ignoring his teachings, Wilkie steadied herself.

"Steady, girl," she whispered.

Certain she couldn't be seen within the station's dark interior, she peered through the window just as two men on horseback rode out of the trees. Behind them, another man appeared, wobbling side to side on the motorcycle. The rider seemed to be having difficulty keeping his balance on the rutted road.

The man on the motorcycle wasn't Hix. She

knew that much. Instead of a flat cap, this man wore a regular hat, one with a crown and a brim. Although he slouched over the handlebars, she saw he was taller and broader than Hix. Anyway, if she needed more proof, he really didn't know how to ride. Every once in a while, he'd jerk the throttle, the engine would roar, and the bike would jump ahead. But even seen in the weak light, she knew the machine matched the one she'd been riding for most of the day.

Frowning, she squinted out at the men on horseback. The reason for the men's backdoor entry into town seemed clear and made her shelter in the station precarious. Were they headed here? Had Hix told them where to find her?

Nervous now, Wilkie reached into her boot and, with a jerky motion, withdrew her pistol.

She settled back to wait.

The file of men, horses, and machine headed toward the station, hooves, and tires crunching in the gravel along the railroad tracks. At a mere twenty feet from where Wilkie watched beside the window, she identified the men. One was Eldon, looking worn out with the white handkerchief still wrapped around his hand. He also appeared no less angry and, unless the haggard expression on his face lied, scared along with his pique.

The one on the bike frightened her most. Laced Boots.

But it was the other horseback rider who caused her heart to gallop.

Hix.

He sagged in the saddle, close enough as they pulled up outside for her to see blood had streaked down his face and dried there, leaving a dark crust. His arms were tied behind him, his feet bound to the stirrups. Wilkie knew he was awake, although he never once glanced toward the building.

They stopped in front of the station. She froze. Any movement might be seen. Seen or sensed.

"What's that sign on the door say?" Laced Boots rasped; his accent thick.

"Can't see it," Eldon said.

"So get down and look."

She and Hix had been calling this man Burke's henchman, but apparently, he rated a step above Eldon in the criminal hierarchy. Eldon seemed to be the real lackey. Wilkie had heard of gangs where new members had to prove themselves somehow, usually by murdering someone. Burke, Boothe, and Venig. Were they *that* sort of gang? Did they plan on Hix being Eldon's first victim?

Or me? Me if they can catch me?

Her mind raced. How had Eldon gotten away

from Jackson? While she and Hix had been wasting their time staying out of what they feared was Laced Boots' vicinity, apparently, he'd been breaking Eldon loose. The sheriff had missed the window of opportunity. Was Mr. Jackson safe? Had they killed the old man and managed to blame Hix?

Eldon, thumping across the porch, regained her attention.

"The notice says the station is closed and will open at eight in the morning. First train is at 8:17. What are we going to do with him until then?"

Laced Boots cursed, though not in English. "I know a place. We can lock him up there overnight. The three of us will board the train in the morning. Then I know just the right spot for him to make a break."

"Make a break?" Eldon appeared doubtful.

"Yes." Laughing with a strange, evil-sound rasp, Laced Boots pumped the motorcycle's gas feed, making the engine's volume rise. "But not until he tells us what we want to know. It'll be too bad when his escape attempt fails, he falls from the train and is run over. Splash. Guts and blood everywhere." He laughed again, loud in the night.

Wilkie gripped her little pocket pistol with stiff, tight fingers, tempted to hammer out the window glass and take a shot. But her .32 held only five bullets. Worse, the light was uncertain where the outlaw stood with Hix's motorcycle propped at his side. What if she missed?

"Come here, Venig," Laced Boots said. "If you can't ride, it's your turn to push this machine. I'll ride the horse."

"We only just switched before we got here," Eldon protested.

She noticed he cradled the hand still wrapped in his handkerchief as if it hurt. Worse than her arm? She doubted it. What a pansy man.

"No arguing. It's time we go. Now." The threat in Laced Boots' voice had Eldon vacating the porch in a hurry, even as panic serrated the edges of Wilkie's composure.

They planned on murdering Hix. Perhaps not so surprising considering the breadth of their embezzlement enterprise. And the fact they'd evidently murdered Eldon's father, a partner in the firm. The good Lord only knows how many more. Didn't Eldon care? Maybe, but she felt certain he was too frightened to go against them. With good reason, she supposed. She had no doubt but that he'd be even easier to drop beneath a train's wheels than Hix.

Not that she intended on allowing any such thing.

The moment they passed beyond the station

windows, Wilkie flew about, gathering her valise, making sure it was latched and that she'd leave nothing behind.

Dread filled her as she slipped out the door, relocked it, and followed the sound of the Triumph's idling engine.

Chapter Eleven

When Eldon walked out into the road in front of him, Hix applied the brakes hard enough to almost flip the motorcycle end-over-end. Not that he'd had much choice in the matter as his cousin stood there with a gun clasped in both hands and pointed straight at him. Meanwhile, his own weapon was stowed in the side-holster under his jacket. Unreachable at the moment. Even then he didn't worry too much. Not until the lawyers' enforcer, the foreign man Wilkie insisted on calling "Laced Boots" joined them. About then he wished them both, and Eldon in particular, to perdition.

Backed by Laced Boots, Eldon opened the conversation. "Where," he demanded, "is Wilhelmina Van Slyke? I need to talk to her."

"Who?" Hix said.

"Don't act stupid, Hix. You know who."

"Huh. Guess I didn't catch her name." Shrugging, Hix steadied the bike. "I don't know where she is. I dropped her off at the train station a while ago to catch the 3:45 to Missoula. She's probably halfway there by now."

"Lies," Laced Boots said. "I was there. The train didn't stop at the station."

"Didn't it? Well, I don't know then. I didn't wait to see. Had my own fish to fry. Been trying to get rid of her all day. Ever since you handed her over to me, to tell the truth."

Laced Boots and Eldon exchanged a glance, whereupon Eldon shook his head. "You two seemed pretty cozy to me, back there at that cabin where you tied me up."

"What did you expect? You were holding a gun on me. Then you shot *her*." Hix wondered if he had time to pop the clutch, hit the throttle, and get past the pair before Eldon shot him, too.

"I didn't shoot her." Eldon acted outraged. "If you remember, she shot me!"

Hix refused to argue about it. "Anyhow, I guess I know how you got loose. What did you two do to the old man?"

Eldon's chin wobbled. "Nothing much. Balakov knocked him around a little is all, then we locked him in the bedroom with his wife. His dead wife."

Balakov. Hix filed the name away as the man chuckled at humor that escaped him.

Always able to tell when Eldon was being untruthful, Hix knew his cousin was lying. He figured the pair of them had killed the old man.

"How'd you get past the sheriff?" he asked, mostly just to give him time to think of what to do.

"Beat them out of the house by the skin of our teeth." Eldon laughed. "They came in the front as we went out the back. We laid up in the woods behind the barn until they left. Those cracker asses couldn't figure out what's what if their lives depended on it."

Balakov scoffed a little and made a quick motion.

"Which it did," Eldon continued.

"Sitting geese," Balakov said.

"Du..." Eldon started, then stopped.

Hix judged Balakov to be a man who most likely didn't appreciate being corrected. Then again, his cousin was not only a liar but had always been a bit of a coward. Too bad Wilkie hadn't shot him a little more thoroughly while she was at it. He decided to stir the pot.

"Eldon's trying to tell you that's sitting ducks, not geese," he told Balakov helpfully.

Glaring, Eldon waved the pistol at him. "Shut up and get off that motorcycle. But don't kill the engine," he added quickly. "Hand it over. I'm going to take it for a ride."

"You are?" Hix, figuring he'd rather trust the

bike to little Miss Wilkie than to his cousin, didn't see he had any choice but to do as Eldon said. At any other time, he might even have been amused as the second he dismounted, Eldon, still hanging on to his pistol, grabbed the throttle and swung his leg over the bike. But then, being unprepared to balance the machine and staggering under its weight, the clutch slipped out of his grasp. The machine jerked, the engine died, and the pistol spun on Eldon's forefinger.

Anything funny about the situation faded when Balakov took over pointing a gun. His expression said he'd take great pleasure in putting an extra hole somewhere in Hix's body.

Yelling something rude, Eldon leaped free as the bike fell over. He glared at Hix as if the crash were his fault. "Get this thing started. We need to go."

"Why don't you start it?"

"Because I told *you* to."

Hix, reminded forcibly of their schoolboy days, wanted to tell him to go to hell. He quelled the urge when Balakov stuck the pistol barrel in his back and shoved like he was trying to bore a hole there. No sense taking the pair of them on now, Hix told himself. For some reason, they'd neglected to search him, and he didn't want to give them cause. His chance would come.

Making a show of it, he reefed the motorcycle into an upright position, made some adjustments to the choke and the gas, and gave a mighty jump on the kickstarter. The engine sighed but didn't start. He made the jump again... and again, and again.

Not much to his surprise, it took quite some time to get the bike running. He didn't know if all motorcycle engines flooded when they fell over, but the Triumph's had a real bad habit. While he enjoyed the speed of travel when all went well-meaning roads, gas, tires, breakdowns — he missed the reliability of Tap, his chestnut gelding. Step aboard, lean forward in the saddle an inch, and off they'd go. That's all there was to it.

"Hurry up." Eldon, never noted for his patience, returned to pointing his pistol at Hix's mid-section. "We've got to keep a close watch on him," he told Balakov when the man appeared leading two horses from the woods behind them. "He's a tricky bastard."

Speaking of tricky, Hix hadn't even noticed Balakov was gone, if only for a few minutes. Resuming his efforts to restart the bike, sweat dripped from his nose when he finally succeeded.

But then, Eldon being Eldon, he killed the engine again during the transfer from Hix and denied blame.

Even Balakov saw through his weak excuses. "Enough," he said. "We need to go now, get off this road. This one..." he pointed at Hix... "will push the motorcycle. It's best not to leave it here. You..." he pointed at Eldon "... ride the horse. We'll look for the girl in town. He..." he pointed back at Hix "... knows where she is. He'll tell us where. Sooner or later."

Hix, remaining expressionless, didn't say a word. No "aye, sir," no "no, sir." He figured they were keeping him alive for just this reason. Why would they even bother with him, otherwise? He figured the best bet was to keep his mouth shut and wait for the opportunity to make a break for it.

Balakov, however, proved plenty tricky himself. "Venig, you lead the way to town. Then you..." he was back to pointing at Hix "... are next with the motorcycle. I will ride last and keep watch."

Which meant, Hix was certain, he'd have no chance to pull his gun. The four miles into town seemed an awful long way to push a motorcycle, but maybe not long enough to figure out what he should say about Wilkie. Stick with the original story or make up something else?

They started off at a far brisker pace than Hix liked. When he'd more or less caught his breath, he called ahead, speaking to Eldon's back. "Why do you even want her, that girl? I doubt she knows anything that'll help you."

"What did she tell you?"

"Nothing. All I know is we were a little busy getting away from people who scared her almost senseless. Then her uncle turned up dead, and she didn't know what to do. Said she wanted to go home."

"Yeah?" Eldon turned in his saddle to look back at Hix who was puffing away, legs pumping, trying to keep from being trampled by Balakov's horse. "She didn't seem all that scared to me."

Balakov spoke. "Where is her home?"

"Damned if I know. I didn't ask, and she didn't say. She just wanted out of Butte. Out of Montana, period." *Almost as bad as me,* he added silently.

The Slav's eyes narrowed to slits. "Liar."

"No lies," Hix said. "Truth."

He never saw the blow coming as Balakov forced his horse close to the side of the bike. Just as Hix looked over at him, the Slav reached across and backhanded him with the full weight of the pistol. The barrel struck his cheekbone a wrenching blow. At the same time, something, probably the pistol's sight, gouged a track under his eyebrow, just missing the eyelid. Blood poured from the cut, blinding him. Hix dropped.

Dropped the bike, too, the metal clattering.

"Son of a bitch," he said.

Balakov fought to rein in the horse, which had taken to jumping wildly as it protested the metal critter landing under its feet. "Where is she?" His tone menaced.

"I don't know. She said she'd find her own way. I just took her to the station." Fighting mind-numbing pain, Hix let the blood run.

"Get up." Fixing him with a threatening stare, Balakov backed the horse far enough for Hix to rise. He gestured at the fallen motorcycle. "Move."

Hix moved all right. He lowered his head and rammed it into the horse. At the same time, he grabbed for Balakov's gun, caught hold of something, and yanked. It seemed like a golden opportunity to unhorse the man and get him onto the ground where he stood a fighting chance. He hadn't counted on being blinded by his own blood.

Instead of grabbing any part of Balakov's anatomy, Hix got hold of a portion of his shirt. Losing leverage as Balakov jerked away, what he received for his pains was a boot. Balakov slammed the flat of his foot into Hix's chest and shoved. Hix went down again. He thought maybe his heart stopped for a few seconds. He knew his lungs ceased to work.

"Fool," Balakov growled. "Try again, and I'll kill you."

Hix believed him.

"Now pick up the motorcycle and go."

With no other choice, Hix did as the thug told him, following Eldon along the narrow path while holding the Triumph upright.

After a while, Balakov called a halt and told Eldon it was his turn to push the motorcycle, and Hix's to ride the horse. It gave Hix's legs a rest and a chance to wipe some of the blood from his eye. Couldn't stopper his ears from hearing his weak-kneed cousin complain, though. And worse, to his disgust, Balakov took up a position riding too near for him to chance drawing his weapon or forcing the horse to bolt. The horse was a slug, anyway. A critter rented from a livery stable, no doubt. Or maybe a youngster's horse stolen from a rancher's corral.

Eldon, with Balakov's approval, traded places again with Hix long before Hix was ready. His eye had swollen shut, and blood crusted his face. They stopped just outside of town.

"Venig," the Slav told Eldon, "Start the bike. I'm going to ride it."

"You are?" Eldon sounded surprised. Or maybe worried as he slid from his horse and went to take the Triumph from Hix. Never known to be successful at so much as filling his pen with ink, Eldon's half-hearted kicks amounted to nothing more than playacting.

Finally, his lip curling, Balakov said, "Enough. You—" he pointed at Hix, "you do it."

Not seeing any other choice, Hix took a turn. To his surprise, one strong anger-fueled kick sent the engine roaring. Didn't earn him any points, though, as Eldon tied a rope around Hix's arms and wound it under the horse's belly before attaching it to his feet. The two weren't taking any chances.

Balakov managed a wobbly ride, although frequently putting his feet down in order to remain upright.

Hix had an idea Balakov would abandon both Eldon and him if he found the law waiting when they reached Deer Lodge. But they bypassed the silent town, circling around to reach the western edge. He estimated it was nearing midnight when he saw starlight shining on the parallel steel rails of the train track. They led right up to the station.

Balakov called a halt in front of the dark building.

Once Hix thought he saw a shadow of movement through the window. Silently, but as though she should be able to hear him, he commanded Wilkie to use common sense. *Don't open the door.*

Stay still. Stay quiet. He hadn't come to save her. Hearing Balakov's plans, it was clear he needed saving himself.

Wilkie must've figured all this out for herself as the door remained locked when Eldon tried it. If he hadn't known differently, Hix would've thought the room empty.

"Get a move on," Balakov told Eldon, shrugging. They reentered the woods along the railroad track and headed out of town. Hix had no idea where they were going or what he'd do when they got there. Most probably die.

His only hope remained the pistol concealed under his coat.

***

Several hours rest had helped Wilkie's ankle, although exhaustion still dragged at her. Her stomach rumbled as she started off on foot following the men. Her valise, in lugging it along, felt as though it had gained a good ten pounds. Every few minutes, she changed the weight from one hand to the other, trying to convince herself the discomfort didn't matter.

Hix was her only concern. Somehow, she had to free him from the clutches of Laced Boots and Eldon Venig.

One girl against a hardened criminal and a self-important embezzler? The odds were against her. Against Hix.

She groaned as she stepped around a pile of fresh horse apples and staggered into a rut. Pain shot through her ankle, but she gritted her teeth and limped on.

How had those two gotten hold of Hix, anyway?

Her head whirled, recalling the man's words. Did he mean what he said? Did he truly intend to dump Hix from the train to be mashed beneath its wheels? Who did things like that? Who even thought of them? Uncle Jameson used to talk about outlaws and evil-doers, but she'd never heard him speak of anyone as cold and wicked as this man.

She touched her little pistol, kept handy now in the pocket of her split skirt. A talisman against the night.

Yeah. A talisman with only four bullets, she thought, remembering the one spent in shooting Eldon in the hand.

An owl hooted from high overhead. Startled, her heart pounding, Wilkie gave a leap to the side as the bird spread its wings and shot into the sky. A sudden swoop, like a ghost descending from heaven, took it down to the ground. When it rose, something small squealed, wriggling in its talons.

Wilkie swallowed hard. She'd rather not have seen that.

The men were easy to follow, thanks to the idling motorcycle acting as a guide along the dark, circuitous route. Except she almost went the wrong way once when the trail split in two. But then a wet spot in the trail where a horse had voided showed her the way; it's strong odor leading her toward the right.

God bless horses! She hurried then to catch up, afraid of the sounds they made, even the *phut phut* of the motorcycle, fading out of her hearing.

It seemed to her as though they traveled for hours.

Then the motor died, and the woods went silent. Even the susurrant whisper of the trees stopped. Wilkie froze, listening with all her might.

What did it mean? What had happened to the Triumph? Where had they gone?

The answer came when, off to her left, voices rose out of the darkness. Shouts, cursing, meaty thumps, yells of triumph, one of pain. At least one of pain. It went on and on, until a man, Eldon, she thought, protested. Silence followed the last groan. A few moments later, a door slammed.

Peering ahead, she inched closer, until she spotted a rundown, obviously abandoned shack.

"Are you crazy?" Eldon said as Laced Boots fiddled with the shack's door. "Why'd you have to do that? He has to look good enough to get on the train in the morning."

"I felt like it is why. Besides, you'll think of something. An excuse. A good lie." Laced Boots chortled. "That's what you lawyers do, yes?"

Apparently a quick thinker, Eldon soon came up with a plan. "We tie him up, gag him. Say we're lawmen taking a prisoner to Missoula."

"Why a gag?"

Eldon hardly paused. "We'll say he bites. We'll say he's a madman who resisted arrest, and that it took six of us to subdue him. That'll account for the blood and his ragged condition. Right out in the open, brazen as can be."

"Brazen?"

"Bold."

The men were coming toward her, each leading a horse. She stepped — or threw — herself off the path right into some prickly bush that threatened to make her sneeze. Pinching her nose hard to quell the outbreak, she dropped to the ground and flattened full length. A flash caught her attention. *Stupid blouse. They'll see me, for sure.*

But they didn't. They passed within a couple

yards of her as they stopped some distance from the shack.

"We camp here." Laced Boots sounded as if Eldon should be content with sleeping on bare ground. He strung a picket line between a couple of pine trees. Unsaddling, they tethered the horses and dropped their gear beside a circle of stones.

"Here?" Eldon, looking around with his hands on his hips, seemed less than impressed. "You call this a camp? A bedroll and a fire pit? Why don't we go into town and get a hotel room? I don't care to sleep on the ground. Come on, Balakov. Hix isn't going anywhere. Beat up, tied up, and locked in that shed? He's not some mythical hero, after all, regardless of what he sometimes thinks."

The last part struck Wilkie as a bit jealous sounding.

Laced Boots — or, she had a name for him now, Balakov — ignored all this. "We are close enough to watch the shed, but far enough not to hear him cry." He laughed. "And by morning, he will cry. We'll take turns. I will watch for three hours, then it will be your turn. By then, it will be dawn, and we'll go back to Deer Lodge. Be ready for the 8:17."

Cry? Hix? What did he mean?

Dawn. Wilkie had to free Hix before then. She

hoped they were heavy sleepers.

Meanwhile, she lay at the edge of their camp, afraid to move for fear she'd end up in that shed right alongside Hix.

Chapter Twelve

Wilkie loathed Laced Boots or, as she'd learned his name by now, Balakov, with every fiber of her being. Although the day had been warm, the ground had lost its heat and gotten damp. Worse, Wilkie was aware of every stone beneath her. Each seemed to grow larger, harder, and pointier the longer it prodded her flesh.

Meanwhile, apparently wide awake, Balakov sat by the fire he'd built, at intervals tossing a broken limb from a small pile he'd gathered earlier into the embers. Every sleepy murmur of a bird or twitch of a horse's tail caused him to turn his head toward the sound and peer into the dark.

Which meant she lay frozen in place — almost literally frozen — aching to shoot him where he sat. After an hour or so, avoiding the path they'd brought the horses up, he walked across the acre-sized meadow to the shack and checked on Hix.

While he was gone, Wilkie had a chance to move. Eldon, busy stirring something in a skillet, kept his back turned toward her. She slipped behind the biggest tree around but dared not go any farther for fear of meeting Balakov on the way back.

Better to wait, she thought. As she knew from experience, Eldon was the weak link in their chain. She'd make her move when it was his turn at watch.

Wilkie, stomach growling so loud she feared Balakov would hear, settled in while the two men ate whatever Eldon had been stirring. Silently ate, Balakov evidently no dinner conversationalist. Soon after, Eldon plopped down on his blanket. Crossly, like a petulant boy.

Speaking of Eldon, well, Jameson had been quite the snorer, but not in Eldon's class.

Wilkie catnapped a couple times, although she hadn't meant to. She came wide awake when Balakov called out to Eldon, proclaiming the designated three hours of his watch up. Receiving no response, he prodded Eldon in the back with the toe of his laced boot. The prod didn't appear particularly gentle since Eldon, yowling like a stomped on cat, shot upright. Wilkie winced along with him.

"Get up." Balakov yawned. "Your turn. Go check the lock. I don't trust Forry. His reputation speaks of a slippery character."

"He is." Eldon, dodging another toe kick,

threw his blanket aside and rubbed the spot on his back. "All right, all right, I'm awake. Watch yourself, Balakov. Remember who's paying your wages."

"I remember. And it ain't your name on the pay stub. You don't like it, talk to Burke."

Hix a slippery character? The exchange gave Wilkie something new to think about as, with a murderous glare, Eldon rose stiffly, belted on a holstered pistol and trod off across the meadow to the shack.

"To your right," Balakov called after him. He fed the fire again before settling into his bedroll. Wilkie didn't think he slept, though. Not right away. Not until after Eldon returned, sat down with a grunt and wrapped himself in his blanket.

"Well?" Balakov unduly concerned from all appearances, had his eyes shut.

"Hunky dory. What else would he be? He's trussed up like a Christmas goose, for God's sake."

Balakov slept then, and later, just as she'd expected, so did Eldon. Treading carefully, as she didn't want the noise of a cracking branch or surprised animal to disturb the men's rest, Wilkie retreated, taking a circuitous route through the trees to approach the shack from the rear.

The night felt deeper to her than normal, quieter, more secretive, even though her eyes had long ago adjusted to the dark. Shadows bounced out at her. Once a stick poked in her side and she imagined, just for an instant, and before her common sense took over, it was a gun barrel. The trek around the meadow did nothing to calm her nerves. Finally reaching the shack, she stumbled over the Triumph laying on its side where one of the men had dropped it. Hix, she knew, would hate that.

Using her uncle Jameson's picks, the padlock on the door took only moments to open. Removing the lock from the hasp, she pulled on the rickety door, drawing it ajar. If Hix hadn't been beaten and tied, she figured he could've kicked his way through the half-rotten boards. She figured *she* could kick a way through it. But not now, with Eldon and Balakov so close. Another deterrent. Sound carried farther at night.

"Hix," she whispered. "Hix, where are you? Are you awake?"

She couldn't see a thing.

"It's Wilkie, Hix. I'm here to free you."

A muffled groan answered.

The relief made her dizzy. She'd been afraid she'd find yet another corpse. Her breath went out on a shaky sigh.

"Where are you? I can't see."

Another groan, or more precisely, a half groan-half grunt, drew her attention to the far corner of the shack where a dark bulk huddled against the wall. The bulk moved a little. Enough to indicate a living person and his location.

Though reluctant to enter the interior, she didn't have a choice, especially since Hix was trying to sit up and failing, all the while sounding as if he weren't getting enough air.

She hurried to him. Starting at the top of his head, she patted her way down his face. Felt a lump and blood, sticky on her hands. He'd been slugged hard at some point. Lower, she found the gag tied so tightly his mouth gaped wide. Wrenching open her jackknife, a tool of her trade and kept sharp, she slipped the blade under the handkerchief and sliced through the cloth. It fell away and hurrying now as he seemed to be suffocating, Wilkie reached two fingers into his mouth and pulled out a wad of cloth.

He took a deep shuddering breath, then another and another. He didn't — couldn't most likely —speak.

The ropes binding him came next. She followed the ropes by feel. A complicated wrap held his bound wrists to his feet. If he'd struggled, he would've been bent severely backward.

And he'd struggled. He groaned again at their

release.

She cut him once, on the back of his hand, only aware because of the way he jerked. "I'm sorry," she said, blinking tears. *Torture. This had nothing less than torture.*

Once freed, he didn't move. He didn't try to say anything, either, but some minutes later, rolled himself upright until he sat braced against the wall. Wilkie wished she'd thought to bring some water. He must be thirsty to death by now. The gag — she hated to think of the gag.

After a while, Wilkie didn't know how long, she said, "It will be dawn soon. We have to go before one of them comes to get you. Do you think you can walk?"

"Take... horses?"

"They picketed them right next to their camp and hobbled them besides. I can't get to them without making noise and being in plain sight."

"Huh."

He must've known his motorcycle wasn't a viable solution. Awkwardly, using the wall as a prop, he rose to his feet. With Wilkie's shoulder under him, they had no more than hunched along toward the door and escape — Wilkie wondering how on earth they were ever going to make it back to town — when she heard the sharp pop of a snapped tree branch and a distant curse.

"Oh, no!" She stopped in the middle of the room. "Someone is coming. Eldon, I expect. That other one is too canny to give any warning."

"Hide." Hix managed real words, his tongue too thick for perfect clarity. "Lock me in. I can take Eldon."

"Nonsense. You can't even hold yourself up right now." But Wilkie didn't disagree with the plan of action. As far as it went. "You distract him. I'll get the drop on him. Again."

"You hide."

What they shouldn't do, she realized, was waste time arguing. "All right," she said. "*You* be careful."

She slipped outside, got the door shut and the padlock closed, before whipping around the side of the building an instant before Eldon, apparently in no hurry, reached the shack. Her heart thumped. Had he seen her? She didn't think so. His head was down, watching where he stepped. Pressing against the worn boards, she waited, hoping he'd just check the padlock and leave when he found it secure.

The fingers on her left hand crossed, even as she took a grip on her .32. If worst came to worst, she had to get rid of Eldon without firing the pistol, as that would bring Balakov down on them. And, though she hated like the dickens to admit it, Balakov scared her spitless.

Around the corner, as though simply to thwart her, Eldon's key turned in the lock. The hasp scraped, and the door swung back. Eldon stood in the opening; hands braced against the jambs.

"You still kicking, cousin?" He sounded cheerful. "Oh, sorry. Kind of doubtful about the kicking, isn't it?"

Wilkie didn't think he was the least bit sorry.

"I suppose you're a little cramped." Eldon went on with his one-sided conversation. "Consider it payback for you and that girl messing up our plans yesterday. Are you enjoying yourself now?"

Hix made a noise and Eldon chuckled. "When will you ever learn? Hix, you've got to choose better friends and allies. That's the trick to getting ahead. And let them think it's their idea to do your work for you."

He took another step inside. "Well, I guess it's a lesson come too late for you, but it is..." A match scritched, a small flare of light indicated a closer look. "What the hell? How did you..."

Hix tackled him, grabbing him around the knees and shoving backward. The flame went out, extinguished beneath their bodies as Eldon went down under the attack.

Wilkie figured Hix's advantage was due more to surprise and superior weight than to fighting strength. She heard a resounding thud of fist to flesh though, and it was Eldon who cried out. To her, entering silently behind him, it seemed clear there was a race in progress. One to see if Hix could deliver a knockout blow before he fainted.

The faint appeared most likely. Time for her to take a hand.

Wielding the pistol like a club, she bent down and thunked the barrel against Eldon's skull. The blow didn't knock him out as she hoped it would, perhaps due to her lack of experience in such things. Or maybe she'd hit him in the wrong spot.

She swung the pistol a second time. Harder, with a broader swing, but turned out it still wasn't enough. Wondering if his head was made of concrete, she tried yet again.

This time, on only a sigh, he collapsed. On top of Hix, as it happened. Dark streaks of blood flowed from a gash where the revolver's front sight had cut through hair and skin. It soaked slowly into his collar.

"Ugh." Hix's muffled voice came from somewhere around Eldon's shoulder. "Get him off."

Using her foot, Wilkie moved Eldon's inert body a few inches to the side, leaving Hix to manage the rest. Once free, he sat up and tried to spit. "Got a mouthful of hair. Eh. Bear grease."

Wilkie gave a shiver. "Is he dead?"

"Nah. But I expect he'll have a headache when he wakes up." Panting, Hix struggled to stand. "I hope it's a bad one and lasts for days. If Balakov doesn't kill him when he finds out what happened."

"We should go."

"Yeah. I know." Though not showing much anger on the surface, it became clear when Hix found the wad of cloth and the handkerchief the two had used to gag and torment him. He even smiled a little as he crammed the wad into Eldon's mouth.

At Wilkie's indrawn breath, he looked up. "Eldon likes soft beds and fresh linens, clean clothes, and gourmet food. He's gonna hate this."

"Serves him right." Still, she was relieved when Hix refrained from tying the gag until Eldon's mouth gaped open. Nor did the rope around his wrists connect backward to his feet.

They left the shack, padlock intact on the door, the key tossed into the bushes. In a matter of seconds, Wilkie retrieved her valise from where she'd stowed it when she approached Hix's prison.

"You know where to go?" He gawked around in a bewildered sort of way.

His question made her wonder if he'd lost his

wits. "Yes." Wilkie handed him a stout, fairly straight branch to use as a walking stick. She imagined he needed all the help he could get. "But we need to bypass Balakov's camp. Let's just hope he's still asleep."

***

Hix, casting a rueful glance at his fallen Triumph as they walked past, nodded as if agreeing with Wilkie's wish, but he wasn't so sure he felt the same way. In fact, he didn't. During his time with Eldon and Balakov, through the intimidation and that last beating, it hadn't occurred to either of them to search him. He still had his gun, even if he hadn't been able to use it. A blessing. God only knows how Balakov had missed striking it with his fist. Maybe he hadn't and was using it to tease Hix.

But now he felt free to fire on them. Or, one of his better ideas, set the scene up just right and he could shoot Balakov and pin it on Eldon. It'd be easy.

One problem and she had a name.

Wilkie.

Chapter Thirteen

At daylight, Wilkie and Hix paused along a small creek running through what he figured was somebody's cow pasture. A few cottonwoods lined the bank, their rustling leaves adding a fresh aroma to the air. Sure beat the acrid odor coming from a thick array of cow patties in a low section. At least none of the patties were fresh.

Upstream a way, Hix dropped the walking stick, knelt down, and shoved his whole head under water. Blood, sweat, and a whole lot of grime washed into the current. The water, icy cold, cleared some of the fog from his brain. When he'd cupped his hands and, lapping like a dog, drank his fill, he felt almost smart Smart enough, anyway, to be glad he hadn't stuck around and killed either Eldon or Balakov back at the shack. What the Bulgarian might do to his cousin when he discovered Hix gone and Eldon tied up in his place, he didn't know. Didn't much care, when you got right down to it.

He glanced over at his traveling companion

and grinned. She'd taken a page from his book and, like him, was drinking from her hands. Daintily, as if trying not to slop water down the front of her blouse. Not that it would've made much difference. She'd started out fresh as a flower when he'd picked her up at the store in Butte yesterday morning but resembled more of a dried up weed now. Grass stains and soil sullied both skirt and top, not to mention wrinkles and a tear in the split riding skirt at about the knee. The least of it, when you considered her blouse had only one sleeve. He was thankful to see the wound in her arm, true to Jackson's opinion, apparently didn't bother her much.

Earlier, he'd taken the lead when they got back to the railroad tracks with little Miss Wilkie blindly following as if she were exhausted. She probably was, lugging that valise — he could vouch for the weight of it—all this way. He wondered how her ankle was holding up. Most of the women he knew would've been crying their eyes out, but not her.

Before he could ask, she winced, sat back on her heels, and wiped her chin. "Where are we?"

He chuffed. "Middle of nowhere'd be my guess."

"You don't know?"

"Not right on the dime. Somewhere west of

Butte and Deer Lodge. That's what you want, isn't it? To head west?"

"Yes. But I'm hoping not to walk all the way to Spokane."

Her tart answer made him smile, a stretch of his lips that made the upper one bleed. He dashed cold water on it.

"How many miles to the next town?" she asked.

"Dunno. I'm not going to worry about it. I don't think we have any choice, do you?"

She caught her breath, and he figured she planned on chewing on him about that, but he overrode whatever she meant to say.

"There's a freight train water stop some way up ahead. Not too far. Probably not more than a couple miles. You can make it that far, can't you?"

"Yes, but—"

"These tracks along here are a freight line. The next stop is where they fill the boiler before heading into Missoula and from there, over the mountains into Idaho. We can hop the train at the water tower."

"Hop the train?" She didn't sound real happy about the idea. "What about the railroad police? Won't they be watching?"

Wondering what a girl like Wilkie knew about railroad police, he said, "We'll avoid them. Don't worry. The thing is, freight haulers usually come through between passenger runs on the main-line. We may have to wait for a train."

"Is there food at these water stops? I'm awfully hungry."

Hix wished she hadn't mentioned food. He hadn't gone this long without eating since he'd been seventeen and in the Philippines during the late Spanish/American war where his unit had been fighting a whole crowd of natives. Supplies had been unable to get through the jungle. Peering at Wilkie through the water dripping from his head, he had the impression she looked a little gaunt, too.

"Afraid not," he said. "Just an unattended tower."

Sighing, she unbuttoned her blouse's right cuff and rolled the sleeve as far as it would go. At that moment, the sun hit the creek, creating a dark pool in the shadows. Wilkie eased her hand, then slowly, the rest of her arm into that section of water.

"What are you doing?" Hix frowned. "We should be on our way."

Wilkie shook her head. Hix leaned over the creek bank and saw her fingers moving in the clear water, slow and wavy following the current. But that's not all. Even as he watched, a big bull trout swam up to nibble at those enticing white digits. It looked as though she were petting the fish. He figured maybe the fish thought so, right up until a quick flip and the creature landed on the bank, almost between his feet.

His mouth dropped open. "I'll be jiggered," he said.

"Don't let it flop back in the water." Wilkie inserted her arm into the stream again.

A few minutes later, a second fish joined the first, and Wilkie, shaking water from her arm and complaining of the icy water, turned to scouting the riverbank. She came back holding a fistful of wild green onions. "Got a match?"

Recognizing a hint when he heard one, Hix gathered the makings and started a small fire while Wilkie cleaned the fish using her jackknife.

"Where'd you learn to do that?" Hix's mouth watered as he waited for the trout to cook. Wilkie had impaled the fish, onions stuffed inside, on green sticks and propped them over the fire. To take his mind off the scent, he periodically splashed cold water on the knot over his eye. As the swelling went down, he was relieved to see again.

Wilkie turned her fish. "At home, my mother hires an Indian girl to help in the kitchen and clean rooms. Millie and I are friends. She taught me. And Uncle Jameson thought tickling the fish was good practice, teaching me to be quick and accurate with my hands. Even if they're numb with cold," she added thoughtfully.

"I'd say he was right." The aroma of broiled fish soon became overpowering. Hix tore into his trout; aware Wilkie had given him the biggest one. Some potatoes fried in bacon fat would've been good with it. And biscuits with jam or honey, but he wasn't about to complain.

***

A hard-won couple hours later, they reached the shingle-sided water tower with its cone-shaped top rising above the trees. Sunlight beating down on the shiny metal rails in front of them brought tears to their eyes when it hit at just the right angle. Hix had long ago removed his jacket, carrying it in one hand while leaning on the walking stick. His shoulder holster fully revealed; he was surprised when Wilkie asked no questions. Like why hadn't he shot his way clear of Balakov and Eldon?

The fragrance of fresh-cut wood emanated from several cords lined up alongside the track as they approached the water tower, but the area appeared deserted. Pleasant. Peaceful. He relaxed.

"We made it." He turned to find Wilkie lagging behind, her limp grown more noticeable as the day wore on.

"Yes," she agreed, then said, "Who is that?"

"What? Who?" He spun around, looking for whatever, or whoever, she'd spotted while his back was turned. "I don't see anybody. Are you—" His intended question got interrupted when a man holding an old pepperpot pistol stepped out from behind the stack of wood cut to lengths to fit in the train's boiler.

The man fired a shot that hit just in front of Hix's boots, then pinged off somewhere to the side. Hix let go the walking stick.

Birds startled by the shot swooped from their perches in the trees. Insects went silent. And Hix broke out in a sweat, thinking of the direction the ball could've taken. "What the hell are you doing?" he yelled. "Put that thing away."

The man didn't. Without taking time to aim, he emptied another barrel at Hix who, thinking he heard something buzz over his head, ducked and leaped to the side, pulling Wilkie along with him. Too busy reaching for his own gun to think how many shots the fellow had left, he about had a fit when Wilkie walked in front of him. She held her valise up like a shield.

"Sir," she said, just as if the blackguard hadn't taken two shots at Hix and, holding the pistol in both hands now, seemed fixed to fire another.

Maybe at her, this time. "Sir, can you help me? I think I'm going to faint."

Faint? Wilkie? Hix didn't believe it.

Swanning forward, she kept going toward the man who gaped at her, his mouth hanging slack. And truthfully, she *did* look small, frail, and weak as she walked right up to the four-barreled pepperpot, shoved it aside with her valise, and straightening, rammed her .32 into the man's ribs.

Not weak at all.

Hix didn't know what the fellow saw in Wilkie's expression, but he dropped the antiquated old pistol on the ground and raised his hands. Fast. "Don't shoot. I give up," he said, as cowardly as a lone coyote with a wolf on his tail.

"Give me one good reason why I shouldn't shoot you where you stand." Wilkie's voice had risen an octave. She gave him another good jab. "You're just a cold-blooded murderer, trying to shoot down two innocent people minding their own business. Nobody'd blame me if you turned up dead. It's called self-defense, Buster."

The man backed away from Wilkie as if thinking of escape. She kept right on pushing and poking. Hix just stood there with his pistol half-in, half-out of his shoulder holster.

"W... well. I... uh..." Buster stuttered like a two-year-old baby. "D... on't shoot."

Hix felt a touch of unease himself. Wilkie wasn't really gonna shoot the guy. Was she? At least not until they found out his intentions. But then, who'd have guessed she could be so fierce?

"Who put you up to this?" Wilkie demanded.

Good question. Hix liked the way she thought.

"Mister, I'd speak up if I was you. Tell her the truth, and maybe she won't shoot you," he said, reseating his pistol in the holster.

Wilkie shot him a look. "It had better be the truth. I hate liars."

"Yes, ma'am." He kicked the fellow's pepperpot into some weeds. "Well? And stick to the truth."

Buster's hands fluttered in the air. "Sure. Sure, the truth. Hell, yeah. Nothin' but, I promise."

He appeared to believe this meant he could put his hands down. For a moment at least, until Wilkie made a motion with her .32, her stern expression indicating something different. Hix almost laughed when she said, "So?"

"So? Yeah. Sure. Well." Buster's idea of speaking seemed a little more as if giving instructions to a mule, gee, and haw making more sense.

Wilkie's next poke in the ribs finally got him started.

"I live over thataway." A jerk of his head—an unkempt head in sad need of a haircut and a face in need of both a wash and a shave—indicated a northernly direction. "Got a small ranch, a few cows, a few horses, some good timber. I cut this here wood for the railroad." He meant the wood stacked beside the tracks.

Hix nodded.

"So, I was felling a dead tree this morning when a man rode up. I axed him if he was lost and he says 'no.' He says he's looking for two outlaws, a man and a woman. Says maybe they're on foot. So, I axes him if there's a reward. He says, 'maybe,' and axes if I've seen'em. I says 'no' but people what are lost turn up at my homestead ever now and then. So, he says he'll give me a hunnert dollars if I bring'em over to Deer Lodge, dead or alive but best if they're dead. Say's they're dangerous—" he stared at Wilkie's unwavering gun "—and I should oughta shoot at first sight if I see'em. Says the man kilt an old rancher and his wife what lived outside of Deer Lodge yesterday."

Hix drew a deep breath, aware of Wilkie's dark eyes turning toward him. Only for an instant, before her attention turned back to Buster.

"Was this man a foreigner of some sort who speaks with an accent?" she asked.

In Hix's opinion, Buster had enough of a twang in his speech to qualify as a foreign accent.

"Yeah. How'd you know? He talked like one of

them high-class lawyer boys. That's what he said he is. A lawyer in Butte. Said the girl is a thief." Buster avoided looking at Wilkie.

Probably just as well since Hix thought maybe there'd be steam issuing from her ears at the "thief" moniker. He had no doubt the lawyer boy had been Eldon inquiring after Wilkie.

"Huh. Apparently, Balakov didn't kill Eldon after all," he said.

"Too bad," she said coolly, and then to Buster, "What are you doing here? I don't see a fresh load of wood."

"Oh, no. No. Quick as the lawyer boy took off, I headed right over to the water tower. This is where they all end up, ya know."

"They?"

"Them who gets lost. If they don't wind up at my place, it means they've followed the tracks, and I'll find them here. Why this ain't the first time I've shot down a criminal." Buster stopped then, maybe thinking over what he'd said.

Too late. Wilkie had caught the implication. Her eyes narrowed. "Are you saying you've shot people here? Killed them? Without even troubling to find out who they are first?"

"Maybe," Buster said, all cagey-like.

"Murdered them?"

Buster gawked between Hix and Wilkie. "I

wouldn't say *murder*. Anyways, they was all bad men. All wanted by the law, else they wouldn't have been stumblin' around out here. Bums tryin' to steal a ride on the train."

"I don't think that's a killing offense," Hix said.

"Stealin' is stealin'."

"And murder is murder." Wilkie looked helplessly at Hix. "What are we going to do with this yahoo?"

"I know what I'd like to do with him," Hix gritted.

Wilkie smiled, Hix's implied threat diverting her attention. Her guard dropped, and she discovered, for all of Buster's bumbling ways and words, he could move real fast when he wanted.

A short-bladed knife dropped from his sleeve into his left hand even as he swatted her .32 to the side with the right. He reached for her, his hand dirty and missing a finger.

He almost caught her, too, snatching at the single remaining sleeve on her blouse. Plenty fast herself, she twisted to the side, but regrettably, not quite out of his reach. His fingers touched her wrist and grabbed on with fingernails like filthy claws. The knife blade swung at her, slicing through the loose fabric of her shirtwaist where it covered her ribs as she twisted again. She cried out. Not loud, but gasping.

The interaction gave Hix the time he needed.

His gun was in his hand, snapping off a shot as Buster swung the knife for another try at Wilkie. The woodcutter smiled down at her, eyes glazed as if he didn't even see Hix. At least until the bullet slammed into him. A surprised look crossed his face as he stared down at the blood pumping from the hole in his chest, even as he kept his hold on Wilkie.

Hix shot him again. And again, until Wilkie finally pushed him, dead on his feet, and Buster toppled to the ground.

Wilkie, Hix saw, was bleeding too. But not toppling. Nor even fainting.

"When I get home," she said, a determined note in her firm voice, "I am never coming back to Montana."

Hix laughed, a forced laugh, as he shoved his revolver into the holster. He strode to her, his relief making him almost giddy. Or as if he'd been shot or knifed, right alongside Buster and Wilkie. "Me either. I'm gonna find somewhere else to call home."

Alarmed at the amount of blood running down her side, he bent to examine the wound. "We've got to get the bleeding stopped."

She acted as though she didn't hear. And then, just like he'd known she would, she posed the big question. He would've asked her the same, if he'd been sitting in her chair, except when you got right down to it, what she said wasn't a real question.

"You didn't do it, Hix." Her hand pressed against her side, blood welling between her fingers. "I know you didn't kill Mr. Jackson. And nobody killed Mrs. Jackson. She just died."

That's what she said, and he didn't pretend to misunderstand. Had no idea what to say, though. Either yes or no sounded right, neither providing an answer to both her statements.

He'd kept the handkerchief she'd given him last night in a pocket. Folding it into a pad, he pulled her hand away and put the pad there before pressing her fingers back over it. "Press this tight, even if it hurts." It'd hurt all right, but he didn't know what else to do.

"When I first walked up to the house," he finally said," I found the poor old feller with his wife and dog out by a pond. His missus lay there dead. Jackson told me it was her favorite place, and she'd walked out there by herself. I carried his lady back to the house and put her on the bed. That's when Eldon showed up and pulled a gun on us. Next thing, you came along and rescued us both. That's the last I saw of Jackson when you and I left together on his mule."

Wilkie nodded.

"I turned Jackson's mule into the pasture on the way to pick up the Triumph. Didn't even go to the house as I figured folks would be there soon, if they weren't already, to help with Mrs. Jackson's funeral. When I was coming back on the motorcycle is when Eldon and Balakov got the drop on me. Guess you pretty much know what happened next."

He snorted a bitter sound. "I don't know about you, but I've about had enough of folks jumping out and holding me up. And trying to pin their crimes on me."

"Yes." She nodded. "And it's past time we did something about it."

Yeah. And like he'd noticed before. While she might've *looked* dainty, Miss Wilhelmina Van Slyke was tough as any man and not the fainting kind.

The problem with this diagnosis is that she had begun to tremble as she stood. Her creamy skin had turned an ashy gray, and the bleeding showed no sign of slowing.

"Here, darlin'. Let's get you off your feet." He knew a little about treating a wound, due to his service in the Philippines. Not as much as he wanted to know, right about now.

Wilkie didn't argue. He would've felt better if she had.

Chapter Fourteen

Wilkie's wound bled freely and hurt like hell. Which was a fortunate thing, according to Hix. The bleeding that is, not the hurt. Wilkie begged to differ. At this rate, she wouldn't have any blood left in her body.

Shot and knifed both within a twenty-four hour period. What next?

Hix picked her up and carried her over to a stump where he bade her sit. Going by the ring of cigarette stubs and hard-packed earth around it, the stump had often made a convenient resting spot. She nearly had a fit, thinking that, if Buster told the truth, he might've been the one doing the smoking and tamping the ground.

"Here, let me take a look." Ignoring her protest, Hix moved her fingers and the sopping pad aside. Plus, causing her to look away in confusion over his boldness, he pulled up the tail of her shirtwaist and spread the slit in her corset far enough to study the wound. "It's deep. But be glad it's a gash and not a stab," he told her. "A stab likely would've reached your kidneys, and you would've bled out by now."

"Oh, good." She sniffed. "So instead of dying fast, I'll die slow, probably from blood poisoning due to that man's filthy knife."

Wilkie thought she saw concern in his hazel eyes when he glanced up at her.

"Which is why I say it's a good thing to let the blood clean out the wound. I'm not going to lie to you, Wilkie. It's serious. You need a doctor. The bleeding may help prevent infection, but that cut needs a more thorough cleaning and then stitched. Take care of it, and you'll be fine. But it needs done as soon as possible." He shrugged. "Wish I had some whiskey."

"Whiskey?"

"Disinfectant. Not the best, but better than nothing. And a shot or two on the inside wouldn't hurt, either."

She huffed. "Inside me or inside you?"

"Both."

Although she wouldn't admit it for the world, Wilkie felt quite woozy at the moment, with or without whiskey. Kind of like some of the men who lodged in her mother's rooming house appeared after a night on the town. Or Jameson, when he went on a spree and suffered the next day, sick to his stomach and disoriented. Her heart stuttered, thinking of Jameson. It didn't help that when she raised her eyes, Buster's body lay where it had fallen, flies already gathering to feast on the spilled blood. She could hear their buzz from her seat on the stump.

Hix had evidently been thinking and planning while she sat with her thoughts simply swirling and getting nowhere. "Do you still have that cloth you used to wrap your ankle?" he asked.

"What? Yes. Why?"

"Need it to bandage your wound. Hide it from the flies."

"Oh." She bent over to take her boot off but cried out instead. "Son of a..." she started.

Hix chuckled. "I'll do it."

"... shenanigan," she finished.

He made a good job of it, opening the laces wide, so all she had to do was slip her foot out of the boot. Her ankle, still swollen and sore, was turning purple. All their walking hadn't done it any favors.

Slicing off a length of the cloth, he made a pad. "Hold this over the cut," he said, which she did. He got up and went over to Buster. Reaching down, he dabbed parts of the cloth in Buster's blood, the puddle already thickening. Holding the cloth at arm's length, he brought it back.

To her horror, he made motions like he was

going to wrap the disgusting thing around her. "Stop that." She slapped him away.

"Listen to me." He glared, though he wasn't mad at her. "I know you're put off by this, darlin', but what do you think is going to happen when the train comes through?"

"I haven't thought anything about the train. Why should I?" Truthfully, just about everything had slipped her mind since they'd met Buster. For instance, right now, every single thought, every object she looked at, and even her words had a black edge to them. She sighed. "I don't know, but I suppose you're going to tell me. What about the train?"

"Not the train, exactly, but the men who work on it. They're going to take one look at Buster's dead body and drag us off to the sheriff in Missoula. That's if they don't just leave us stranded here."

Thinking it over, Wilkie figured he might be right. "So hide the body. Stack this woodpile over the top of him."

"And then what? Do you think you can run fast enough to jump on board the train when it starts up again? Because we can't get on while it's stopped. The crew always check the cars at water stops. They're not gentle when they find a non-paying passenger, either."

He seemed to speak from experience.

"I can pay our fare."

"These freighters don't allow passengers. They don't have a place for them."

"Oh."

"And then," he added, "if we did manage to sneak on board, we'd have to get off again before it quits moving at the next stop."

The way Hix described it, Wilkie wasn't so sure either the on or the off were anything she could manage. Ever, let alone with a bleeding wound and a sore ankle to boot.

"Oh," she said again, her voice small.

"So all this calls for a change in plan. The way I see it, we've got a couple choices."

At first, Wilkie thought the buzzing in her ears was the result of blood loss and the strain of recent events. And maybe the lack of food, too, as one trout flavored with wild onion hadn't assuaged her hunger for long. Anyway, eating had been hours ago. She listened harder. As the buzzing progressed, it steadied out to a familiar rhythm.

"You'd better figure it out," she said, "because the train is coming. Can you hear it?"

He frowned. "You sure?"

"Yes."

"Well, then, whatever we decide, you'd better

let me take care of this first." He shook the cloth in front of her, a real attention getter.

Gritting her teeth, Wilkie nodded. "I don't understand, but... what are the choices? Why *are* you smearing more blood on me? Isn't there enough of my own?"

"No. You want this to look bad."

"It *is* bad."

He didn't disagree.

Fingers spread across her middle, Hix held the cloth steady and made the first wrap, centering the part wet with Buster's blood over the pad already in place. At least it didn't touch her skin or the edges of the cut.

Wilkie winced. Yes, it hurt, but the thought of the subterfuge affected her more. *Buster's blood.* Two words she had a hard time getting out of her mind.

Hix didn't say anything more until he'd tied off the bandage and wiped his hands in some grass. Sweat beaded his forehead when he finished, and truth to tell, he looked a little green around the gills.

This hadn't, Wilkie thought, been so easy on him either. After all, it was Hix who'd killed the man. Hix who had, or so it appeared, barely taken time to aim before shooting right past her as she struggled with Buster. Not once, but three times.

And the grouping of bullet holes in Buster's chest took up an area no larger than a quarter dollar. She didn't think that had been luck.

Cocking his head, Hix had apparently caught the sound of the train clacking its way down the track toward them. He knelt in front of her. "Here's one way to do it," he said in a rush. "We tell them we were out for a ride when a man and a woman stepped out of the bushes, held us up at gunpoint and took our horses. We followed the tracks here to the water tower, and he —" he jerked a thumb at the body "—showed up and started shooting at us. He said *we* were the outlaws and he was gonna hold us for the reward. We disarmed him, but all the sudden he got out a hidden knife and slashed you with it. So I pulled my gun and shot him. But you're badly hurt, and we need a ride into the city where there's a hospital." He clasped her hands. "The more blood, the better. They're bound to take every care of a pretty young girl cut up by some deranged maniac. Hopefully, they'll ignore me and tend to you."

She nodded. After all, it was almost the truth. "I hope the girl doesn't have to be too pretty."

He gave her fingers a squeeze. "Or, easiest for you—easiest for everybody—you tell them you were riding, got bucked off, and when you limped in here, this feller attacked you with a knife. You managed to fight him off and shoot him. They'll believe it if you cry a little. But just a little. Men don't like too many tears. Tell the story back to me, and I'll believe you."

He grinned, but Wilkie didn't feel like smiling back. "In that case, what about you?"

"I'll fade off into the woods. Maybe backtrack this one." He meant Buster, of course, though to tell the truth, his wasn't making much sense. "See where he came from. Railroad men, they're not trackers. And they won't have any reason to *not* believe you."

It seemed there was a reason to dispute his last comment, but she had a higher concern. "But then you'll be stranded."

"I'll catch the next train." He paused. "Give me your pistol."

"What?"

"Your pistol. You can't have shot this lout and still have a clean gun. Hurry now."

No more argument. She handed the .32 to him. Hix dashed off behind the woodpile and fired three shots into the ground before handing the gun back. She figured it for a right smart ruse.

Down track, a couple puffs of smoke became visible in the high blue sky; the clacking of train wheels grew louder. Hix, without further discussion, faded into the scraggle of trees and brush surrounding the water tower and disappeared before Wilkie had a chance to say, "thank you" or "goodbye," let alone "Will I see you again?" He'd made his own decision on what course to follow.

Had he meant to cut their parting so close? Wilkie felt hurt at the thought. She'd grown used to him.

Casting a last look around to see if the evidence would support the fibs, she planned to tell—and deciding it came fairly close—she waited for the freight to come to a stop. When it did, men seemed to boil off the train, leaping down and running toward her. She allowed her shoulders to slump; her body to sag. She had no doubt her face was several shades paler than usual. To tell the truth, aside from the pain, she did feel drained and listless. No acting necessary.

One long, lanky man with a sooty face reached her first. "Ma'am, ma'am..." He took a second look. "Miss, what's happened here. Are you all right? Who is that? Who are you? You just hang on. We'll help you."

He was shouting to be heard over the locomotive, his voice vibrating in her head and even into her heart. Wilkie didn't speak, merely pressed a hand against the cloth wet with her own and Buster's mingled blood as if afraid she'd split in two if she didn't hang on.

Another man had broken off to take a look at the body with its gathering of flies. "It's Wilmer Spreck, by Gawd. Somebody finally done him in, the dirty bas..."

A more stately older man, one wearing a striped cap with a bill askew on his shiny scalp, made a cutting gesture, stopping the speaker in mid-sentence. This was the engineer, she thought. The man she had to impress.

A fourth man came running from the end of the train, which had only ten cars plus the locomotive. Some of the car doors were open, some closed. Five stock haulers filled with bawling cattle made up the middle. A couple flatbeds with huge bins strapped to them brought up the rear.

"What's happening?" The brakeman called out. Taking in the scene, his mouth dropped open. "Well, I'll be damned. Somebody killed Spreck."

He didn't, Wilkie noticed, appear too concerned or sorry. None of them did.

The engineer knelt beside her. "How did this happen, miss? Can you tell me?" His voice was loud too, though not so earsplitting as the first man's.

"I... I... he attacked me," she said as if still surprised by the fact. No mistaking what she meant. "I was out riding this morning, and something spooked my horse. I don't even know what, but he took me by surprise and bucked me off. My ankle..." she stopped at that since she didn't want anyone looking too closely at it. Most anyone could tell the injury hadn't happened this morning, but they could see the swelling beneath her stocking without looking further. "I walked until I found the railroad tracks and followed them here, hoping I could get help back to town."

"We're headed for Missoula," the engineer said. "And it looks like you need a hospital. We can get you there. But him." He pointed at Buster. Or Spreck, apparently his name. "What happened to him?"

"I don't know why he did it." She decided a little excitement was called for. These men probably wondered why she wasn't hysterical, sitting here beside a dead man and bleeding profusely, so maybe she'd better see if she could meet their expectations. Her voice went up an octave. "He came at me with a funny pistol—I think it's called a pepper shaker."

Hah. The misspeak seemed a mistake a silly female might make. The trainmen nodded at each other as if in agreement.

Satisfied at seeing this, Wilkie went on with her story. "But my daddy always says when I go riding, I should carry a gun in case—just in case. Which is very good advice as you'll see. That man dropped his gun when he kept missing. But before I could run away, he grabbed me and started stabbing at me with his knife instead. I managed to escape long enough to pull my boot pistol. And I shot him." She pointed a bloody finger in demonstration. "Just closed my eyes and shot as he came at me again. Bam, bam, bam."

Willkie opened one eye a slit to see the engineer and the other men staring at her.

"You shot him with your eyes closed?" the lanky fellow said.

"Yes. I guess so." Wilkie sagged again. "I didn't even know at first he'd done this." She removed her blood smeared hand from the wound and fluttered her fingers. "But, but then... oooooh..." She allowed her voice to trail away as though completely spent by the effort to talk. Not so far from the truth. In fact, much too close.

The man who'd first recognized Spreck joined the others crowding in on Wilkie in time to hear her story. "Don't hurt my feelings any. Lord knows we've hauled a few of his victims off to Missoula to be buried. He said he caught 'em stealing from the railroad, but I always figured he murdered them just for the fun of it."

"I heard Joe and the boys transported a sorry-looking sonofa... gun in just last week," the engineer said, nodding. "It don't surprise me

Spreck'd molest a lone woman if he thought he could get away with it. Odd he'd start shooting first, though."

"You'd think he'd want her alive," the lanky one said.

"For a while at least," the brakeman muttered.

It struck Wilkie they were not posing questions precisely, but simply filling in all the blanks for themselves. And she was thankful. But they were also taking all the air, and she couldn't get enough to breathe. "Please," she said. "Please."

The trainmen, belatedly aware of her pain and distress, swung into well-practiced motion. The lanky one threw chunks of wood into the car behind the engine's cab. Another guided the water spout over the boiler and released the valve for water to gush in. The engineer and the brakeman, between the two of them, hoisted Spreck's body. They argued over who got the shoulders and who was left with the feet, before tossing him into one of the cars that had doors.

Then they turned their attention back to Wilkie. The engineer plucked her off the stump with barely a grunt.

"My bag," she said. No matter what, she couldn't leave the valise behind. Not when it contained over three hundred dollars in gold, her uncle Jameson's stash, and those all important papers pointing towards a sad case of malfeasance by the Burke, Boothe, and Venig law firm. An outfit more than willing to kill in order to bury the evidence. An unfortunate word—*bury*.

"Bring it," the engineer told the brakeman, who jumped to the task. The engineer was frowning, though, like maybe he wondered why she was carrying around a bag when she'd gotten bucked off a horse in the middle of the wilderness.

Through shattering waves of pain, it occurred to Wilkie that she'd better polish her story before she arrived in Missoula.

Chapter Fifteen

Hix stuck around, silent and out of sight, until he saw Wilkie safely aboard the train and on her way to Missoula. He'd barely smothered a gut-splitting laugh when he'd heard her say she closed her eyes and shot Buster. Maybe they even believed her, given her own wound and innocently trembling lips. Yeah. Not to mention those beguiling dark eyes of hers.

Giving himself a shake, Hix took stock of the situation. It galled him no end to think of his cousin's plan to defraud their Aunt Magdalena. Not only her but those other widow ladies Wilkie had mentioned, as well. That the defrauders were the very people the women trusted to oversee the safety of their investments struck him as particularly low. And to heap on more burning coals, by doing a simple favor for the girl on his aunt's say-so, he'd somehow gotten suckered into the deal.

He figured Eldon would try—and probably manage, given his connections—to shift the blame for the whole shebang onto him. It wouldn't be the first such incidence, after all. This time, in all good conscience, Hix wasn't going to let the situation pass without doing something about it.

His cousin had made a mistake when he persuaded Hix to give the girl a ride to her hotel. Or, Magdalena had done the asking really, he supposed, even though Eldon had been the messenger. But he'd made an even bigger error when he and his lawyer partners tried to pull a fast one on Wilkie and her uncle. Oh, yeah. Wilkie had told him all about it.

But by God, when they forced him to leave his Triumph motorcycle dumped in an out-of-the-way clearing to rust, it was the last straw. One he refused to tolerate.

The way he saw it, he had a couple options in front of him. Number one, he'd find his way back to the clearing in hopes of finding his motorcycle, if not rideable, at least repairable. Balakov and Eldon were sure to be long gone, presumably without taking the bike since neither was able to start the engine, let alone ride it. Whereupon, best case, he'd beat it out the country on the Triumph.

Of course, they, meaning Eldon mostly, might've destroyed the machine out of pure cussedness.

His number two option meant he'd return to

Butte on the sly and contact his aunt. She was a wise old gal. Hix figured by now questions about Eldon's part in this had raised themselves in her mind. Together with the other women, she had enough clout to get higher authorities than the county sheriff involved. Maybe even the governor. They'd put facts together and bring the embezzlers to justice. The problem with this being she needed to know all the facts. Facts he needed to tell her.

Maybe a telegram would work, sent from somewhere out of state.

Hix knew his wisest move was to stay the hell out of Butte or Missoula either one. Out of Montana for good, and never come back. He was still wanted for rustling John Robertson's cattle when it turned out one of Eldon's get rich overnight schemes originated on the wrong side of the law. Funny how Hix had been caught and Eldon got away clear. Hix had his suspicions on how it all came about.

But Miss Wilhelmina Van Slyke stood squarely in the way of following any of these various options. Wounded and alone and being chased by some very bad men trying to get those damn incriminating papers back.

He scratched his head, wondering. How had she become his problem?

She isn't. Or so he told himself.

When the rear of the train disappeared around a curve, Hix stepped from cover alongside the water tower. He wasn't looking forward to hoofing it back to Deer Lodge, let alone Butte. And damn, but he was hungry.

Buster, or, as he'd heard the trainmen call him, Spreck, had to have come from somewhere nearby. If he cut wood for the railroad, he probably lived within a mile or two. Hix had a notion to see if he could find where Spreck holed up. He probably had food laying around. And maybe even a horse he could borrow.

Or steal. It didn't much matter which. Spreck wasn't going to complain.

***

As it happened, the horse spotted Hix first.

It wasn't much of a horse. In Hix's estimation, only about what you'd expect from a man like Spreck. He didn't even see it right off. Then, as he started backtracking the dead man, the horse, who'd been standing immobile, moved. Gave Hix, who'd been blundering along like a greenhorn, a start. Leaves rustled as the critter shifted its feet and nickered as if asking a question.

The thin, Roman-nosed plug didn't appear to

have seen a curry comb or brush in its entire life, so its mottled brown color blended well into the background of sapling trees and undergrowth. It bore a tattered saddle, cinch pulled tight, and the bridle reins knotted over a tree limb that held its head too high for comfort.

Hix got the silly idea it recognized him for a stranger and was asking for help.

"Whoa, boy," he murmured, approaching with all due caution. A mistreated horse might not be friendly, and he'd as soon not get kicked in the face. If the poor creature could summon the energy to kick.

But the horse stood calm and resigned, ears pricking forward when he released the reins so it could lower its head. He thought he heard it sigh with relief when he removed the saddle, not surprised to find raw spots on the horse's hide. Rid of the burden, the horse shivered.

Hix patted a spot on its rump that seemed unharmed. "You don't need to worry anymore, feller. He's dead." He figured he'd done the world a favor in killing Spreck. He'd wager the horse thought so, too.

Afraid he had no chance of riding such a poor creature the five miles back to his motorcycle, Hix spotted a saddlebag lying in the shade, away from any danger of the horse trampling it. Not that it had been able to move so far.

"What do we have here? Lunch?" he asked the horse. An ax, propped against a tree trunk, appeared the only item, excepting the razor sharp knife he'd used on Wilkie, where Spreck utilized care. The ax head gleamed, honed to perfection. Spreck must've arrived here with the intention of chopping more wood for the railroad and found what he thought was easier prey in Wilkie and Hix.

Since the horse didn't answer his question, Hix opened the saddlebag to see for himself. As he'd hoped, he found food. A couple apples a little on the underripe side rolled out, along with slabs of bread and some cold fried ham, all wrapped in second-hand butcher paper.

His stomach grumbled. Hoping it wouldn't make him sick, he slapped the ham on the bread and took a bite, chewing the tough, dry ham slowly. His mouth still hurt from the gag and being busted in the chops.

Slipping the bridle bit, he fed the horse one of the apples although it seemed a little uneasy about taking the slices from a stranger's palm. In the horse's place, Hix would've too. He was already unsettled. Although he felt justified in doing whatever he wanted, he still hadn't made a decision on his next move. Go after the girl? Get out of Montana? Find Eldon and pound some sense into his head?

He talked the situation over with the horse.

"Way I see it, Brownie, if you take me back to where my Triumph is, I'll do you the favor of turning you loose. Hell, if that rat bastard hadn't killed old man Jackson, you'd've had a good home there with a couple mules for company. As it is..." Hix didn't like thinking about Jackson or the mule or even this brown horse.

The horse, looking for more apple slices, nuzzled his shoulder and blew a little sound.

***

The view out the train window made Wilkie dizzy. What seemed an endless bunchgrass prairie kept moving up and down in a disconcerting fashion. Black dots filled her vision, remaining there even when she closed her eyes. And really, she hated to complain, but the joggling motion as the engine swayed over the tracks not only made her queasy but caused the slash in her side to hurt something fierce. A slow seep of blood kept the pad Hix had placed there wet.

"Sir," she said after an interminable amount of time. "How much farther to Missoula?"

But no one heard her over the noise. She realized now why the men spoke in such loud voices.

After a while, the engineer turned to her and yelled, "We're almost to Clinton. It won't be long now. We're ahead of schedule. I've been pushing the old girl hard." It took a moment for Wilkie to realize he was referring to the locomotive when he said, 'old girl'. Still, to Wilkie, the trip seemed to take an eternity. The only respite she found was when they stopped once to take on water and fuel. Oh, and the time they pulled onto the siding near a small town and picked up another full cattle car bound for the stockyards in Spokane.

But finally, as it was getting dark, they rolled into Missoula.

"Here we are," the engineer said as the train shuddered to a stop. His name, she'd discovered, was Bill. He looked at the fireman and jerked his head. "Better fetch a deputy, Farley. Try to find Summers, if you can. I'm hoping it's Bodeen's day off. And a doctor. Tell 'em we got a lady needs to get to the hospital right away."

Kneeling beside Wilkie, he touched her hand, causing her to startle. "Sorry," he said. She hadn't realized her eyes had drifted shut again. "I've sent Farley for the deputy and a doctor. You hang tough just a bit longer, missy."

She managed a nod. "I will, sir," she whispered. A loud whisper, to be sure he heard her. "Thank you for your help. Thank you all. I would've died if you hadn't come along."

He blushed, no doubt pleased at being taken for a hero, a role she was happy to assign him. Him and the whole crew.

***

Hours later, Wilkie awakened, sick, scared and in pain, not knowing where she was. No longer on the train, that much was certain.

At first, due to a darkness broken only by windows set high in the wall, she thought she might be in jail. She lay on a hard, narrow, dreadfully uncomfortable mattress, with blankets tucked so tightly around her she believed they, whoever they might be, had tied her down with straps.

Trapped.

Panic, followed by a terrible lassitude, wrapped her in what felt like black fog. Her heart fluttered.

Sickness rose in her throat. She fought the blankets free and scooted upright. The pain in her side flared as if being ripped open by an eagle's talon. Turning her head, she caught sight of a lamp burning at the far end of the room. Five more beds lay between her own and the lamp, two of which were occupied.

Where was she? Was this a hospital or a jail?

She never been in either one, not even as a visitor. But here she was now.

A sudden churn of nausea forced her to lean over the bed and spew onto the floor. Just as well, she thought, guilty at the mess, her diet the last couple of days had been almost non-existent. Involuntarily, she cried out, a weak mewling sound.

In response, a door opened. A woman dressed in flowing white garb and a high white hat with a short veil hurried into the room. She had what Wilkie thought of as a stern face, although that may have been from the shadows formed by the lamp she carried.

Wilkie froze. Almost literally, as she realized she was icy cold. "I'm sorry," she whispered, shivering. "I'm so sorry. I didn't mean to. It just happened."

The woman put her finger to her lips and, setting the lamp on a bedside stand, stepped back out, returning in moments lugging a bucket, some newspaper, and a mop.

"To be expected," the woman said, her voice, in contrast to her stern visage, soft. "Do not worry. Ether makes one sick. That's just the way it is. I should have been here to help. You awakened sooner than expected." She spoke with an accent of some kind. "Lie back and cover up. The shock has given you chills."

"Ether? Am I in a hospital?"

"*Oui*. St. Patrick Hospital. I am Sister Marie Therese." She plied the newspaper and the mop. Quickly finished with the chore, she gathered her cleaning implements, then paused. "Are you quite through with this?"

"I think so. I hope so."

The nun chuckled. "Good. Hold on. I will be back in a moment."

When she returned, the nun—a nursing nun— Wilkie realized, plumped a pillow beneath Wilkie's head and fetched another blanket, spreading it all the way to her chin. The comfort lasted only moments until another thought struck her, and she struggled up again.

"My valise. Where is my valise? And my clothes?" At the harsh panic in her voice, the woman in the farthest bed moved a little, moaning and asking for water. The nun held up one finger in a 'wait a minute' sort of motion and hurried off to check on the other woman.

Wilkie fought back weak tears and oddly enough, for all her anxiety, blanked for a few moments before awakening again, her cheeks still wet.

This time, the nun, finished tending the other patient, appeared at Wilkie's bedside carrying the now scuffed valise under one arm. A clipboard with some blank paperwork and a glass of tepid water occupied her other.

"*Voilà!*" Sister Marie Therese smiled. "Your clothes are being cleaned. I hope you have a clean blouse in this valise of yours because the one you wore is destroyed. No amount of mending can fix it."

Wilkie, trembling with relief, took a deep shuddering breath and tried to ignore the pain that shot through her side. "I have a sweater," she conceded. "And the pistol in my boot?"

"Will remain in your boot. You have a cupboard here, beside your bed. Your things will be safe in it, I promise." The sister made a show of stowing the valise in the compartment.

"Thank you."

Sister Marie Therese allowed Wilkie to sip sparingly of the water. "If it stays down, I will bring you a cup of plain tea," she said, taking up the clipboard. "Now, you may not remember how you got here. Do you?"

The best thing seemed to be for Wilkie to shake her head no.

"Well, do not worry. The memory lapse is to be expected."

She did remember though, part of it, at least. Even after the deputy had appeared at the locomotive's door and she conveniently went faint again. At which point, the engineer and the stoker got to tell her story. They did it so much better and graphically than she could have herself.

One would've said, she thought, listening to them, they were eyewitnesses. And perhaps because the deputy, Deputy Summers, as Bill had hoped, found it expedient to write the incident up the way they told it, she hadn't had to speak at all.

Clearly, Spreck had not been popular.

But what had been overlooked in the rush of getting Wilkie to the hospital and prepping her for surgery, the sister said, was any sort of paperwork. And by the time the omission struck home, the trainmen had gone on to Spokane and wouldn't be back for a couple days, so they had no one to ask.

Wilkie hid a smile at that. She'd never told Bill or Farley her name anyway. Everything was working out for the best. Especially since another patient called out for help just then and the sister dashed off to help the woman to the facility.

The break gave her time to think. Jameson had told her certain circumstances called for the utter truth when it came to names and addresses and such. Other times, obfuscating the facts seemed wiser. This, she thought, was one of those latter times.

Lying back, Wilkie closed her eyes. What name should she choose? Something close to the truth so she'd be unlikely to forget it in case someone woke her out of a sound sleep and took her by surprise.

Let's see... I'll be... Millie. Yes, Millie, her friend at home working in Esther Van Slyke's boarding house. And for a last name, why not take Jameson? It worked for a last name as well as it ever did as a first.

"Millie Jameson," she told the nun when she returned to Wilkie's bedside with her pen and chart at the ready. "I'm Millie Jameson from over in Idaho."

The water, as it happened, stayed down. So did the tea.

Chapter Sixteen

Sometime after dark, Hix arrived back at the clearing where he and Wilkie had left the motorcycle the night before. Unaccustomed to riding bareback, his groan when he slid from Spreck's brown horse told a story.

Except for nocturnal insects singing their songs, the place was deserted. Even so, he scouted the area and approached the shed with caution. The padlock was still attached to the shed door hasp, while the door itself hung askew. Apparently, Balakov hadn't bothered looking for the key. He'd simply kicked it in to release Eldon.

A pained grin flitted across Hix's face. The two were probably still trying to figure out how it had come to be open in the first place, never thinking a girl capable of picking locks. As far as he knew, they still thought it had been Wilkie's uncle who'd been in the bank and taken the papers. He doubted Eldon was being entirely forthcoming with Balakov on that score. Men like his cousin didn't care to admit being beaten by a girl. Or anyone else, for that matter.

He found the Triumph looking like a pile of abandoned trash as it lay on its side where Balakov had dropped it. It didn't appear damaged, although he'd have to wait for daylight to be sure. Fumbling in the dark, he found his small supply of tools still stored under the bike seat. At least he'd be able to make repairs if he found them necessary. But for now, he needed sleep. And food.

So did Brownie. Thinking back, he remembered Wilkie had said Balakov made camp some distance north of the shed. A quick look around showed him where. It appeared obvious Eldon and Balakov had left the area quickly when they found him gone.

The rope the two had used as a picket line hung from a tree. Concocting some hobbles out of it, he turned Brownie loose to graze in the little clearing. He'd have to find something to do with the old horse in the morning. Provided the motorcycle would run. If not, he and Brownie were apt to be partners a while longer.

Trying hard to ignore his growling stomach, he leaned his back against a tree and closed his eyes. Thirty seconds later, he was asleep.

***

A shaft of brilliant sunlight shining onto his closed eyelids jerked Hix awake. When he blinked his eyes open, he found Brownie standing nearby where he'd been grazing quietly. Wisps of grass hung from the horse's lips as he stared at two little boys who sat side-by-side on a log. They were looking back at him.

One kid noticed Hix's eyes were open.

"Hey, mister," this one said. "I like your horse. What's his name?"

Hix had to think a moment. *Name?* "Brownie," he said. With a careful turning of his neck, he gazed around the clearing. The children seemed to be alone.

"Brownie. That's a good name. It suits him."

Surprised into a laugh, Hix nodded.

"I wish we had a horse," the talkative one said. "So we could ride him to school. The school's a long way from our house."

Yawning, Hix checked the position of the sun, figuring it for about seven o'clock. Exhaustion had kept him sleeping longer than he'd planned. "Shouldn't you be on your way to school right now?" And he should be seeing to the Triumph.

"Nah. School's out until fall."

"Oh, right." Stiff not only from sitting on the ground but also aching from the battering he'd taken from Balakov and Eldon, Hix got to his feet. Muscles and cartilage popping, he stretched. An idea occurred. "You can pet ole Brownie if you want. He seems to like it." A minor miracle, now he thought about it, considering the mistreatment the animal had endured.

The kid who had yet to speak smiled widely, showing a gap where two front teeth were missing. He—no, make that 'she' regardless of the bib overalls—jumped from the log and without hesitation, approached the horse. Hix held his breath, but Brownie just whuffled the little girl's hair. She giggled.

Hix felt a little like giggling himself. Could it be that one problem had just slipped from his shoulders? He went over and removed the hobbles as the children watched his every move. He bridled the horse with a headstall that he'd amended to actually fit the old gelding, and directed the boy, the older of the two, to take the reins.

"Come with me and bring him," he said.

"I get to lead him?" The boy's sparkling eyes betrayed his excitement.

"Yep." Hix nodded, although when he turned once to see how they were doing, he found both children had their hands on the reins.

Back at the shed, he went to work on the Triumph, which, to his surprise, both young ones eyed with distrust. "It kind of stinks," the girl said, her snub nose wrinkling at the odor of gas and automotive grease.

Before going to sleep the previous night, he'd leaned the bike upright against the side of the shed. Now, when he went through the procedure of starting the engine—meticulously cleaning the spark plug and checking the oil beforehand—it let out a roar at first kick, then died.

Brownie, startled by the racket, jumped away, but when Hix looked, the little girl still held the reins and was cooing at him. The horse stood still, allowing himself to be soothed.

"Hold him," Hix said and gave the starter another kick. The engine caught this time, soon smoothing out and running like his mother's treadle sewing machine. Another of those weights drop from his shoulders. He'd paid more than he should've for the motorcycle even at a bargain price and sure didn't want to see the hard-earned money squandered on a worthless piece of metal.

All being well, this was decision time. One way or another. Back to Butte or on to Missoula? Which direction should he go?

***

The kids jumped up and down with excitement when Hix told them the horse now belonged to them.

"You've got to take good care of him, though." His stern expression went a long way in convincing them he meant what he said. "He's a fine fellow and looks to you to make sure he has feed and water and a clean place to sleep."

The two looked at each other. "We'll take care of him. We got a good barn, mister," the boy said.

The little girl's eyebrows drew together and crinkled as she stared at her brother. "What if Mama says we can't keep him, Harry?"

Harry shook his head. "But she wanted to get us a horse. You heard her. Now we got one."

"Yes. But what if she thinks we stole him? She'll make us bring him back."

Hix, having thought his problem solved, put a damper on this argument fast. "If you bring him back, I won't be here. And if you turn him loose, he might get lost." Or lead somebody to connect him with Spreck's death. "Tell you what I'll do," he said. "I'll write your mother a note. A bill of sale. Think that'll do?"

The girl nodded eagerly. "Mama writes notes to Teacher sometimes, if we're going to be late to school. And Teacher writes notes to Mama." Then her brows crinkled again. "But we don't have any money."

"That's all right." Hix dug in his back pocket

until he found a slip of paper, a receipt for the gas he'd bought in town. "This will do. *Sold to Harry and...*" he looked to the girl who grinned and told him her name "... *Annabelle Biggers, one brown gelding by the name of Brownie, for the sum of zero dollars and the promise to take good care of him.*"

He defied anybody to decipher the signature.

A satisfactory transaction all around, including to Brownie who plodded away with the two children astride his bareback. Hix was still smiling over their bliss-filled expressions when he rode the Triumph into Missoula a few hours later.

Stopping at the first decent looking café he came to, he propped the Triumph against the side of the building and strode inside. Sheer hunger made him weak. He didn't even mind that café's interior was dark as a tomb, the only windows a couple small ones facing the street. Three high wooden booths per side formed a center aisle, with an estimated twelve foot counter at the far end of the room forming a barrier to the kitchen. Small lanterns hung from supports extruding from the wall. A set-up sort of like most barns to Hix's mind.

Sure enough, didn't smell like a barn though. He caught the scents of pot roast and fried chicken and ham, along with cinnamon and... was that maybe cherry pie? Overcome with anticipation, at first, he didn't see the badge pinned to the vest of a tall, mustachioed man just rising from a stool at the counter. Settling his hat on his head, the man, a badge pinned to his shirt, headed his way.

Hix slid into the first empty booth he came to and, reaching for a menu, held it in front of his face. Words printed on the food-stained menu blurred out of his sight. The deputy's swaggering presence reminded him all too rigorously of Eldon and his cattle rustling scheme a few years back. Yes, and the fact that *he* was still a wanted man. Smart thing would be to lay low.

Then, just as the footsteps passed him, and he figured it safe to lower the menu, the sheriff— closer examination proclaimed deputy sheriff— stopped and turned around.

Although he didn't look up, Hix knew the man was studying him.

"Newcomer to town?" the deputy asked.

It seemed unwise to ignore the question, no matter how much he wanted to. "Stopped for a meal, is all." Unease moved through him. "On my way to St. Regis. I figure to find work in the woods." Like hell. He was no lumberjack.

The deputy, resting his hand on the butt of his pistol, nodded. "Saw you ride up on that fancy machine. Think it'll make it through those woods?"

"Guess I'll find out."

"If you make it that far."

Blinking at the cryptic utterance, Hix remained silent as the deputy stared a moment longer before going on his way.

The waitress, an overworked, overweight gal of middle-age, soon arrived at his table. "I see Deputy Bodeen stopped to talk to you. Is everything all right?"

Apparently, everybody in this town stuck his, or her, nose into a stranger's business. "Sure. Fine. Just passing the time of day."

At least he hoped so. As long as Eldon hadn't arrived and stirred folks up. Nevertheless, the idea disturbed him so much he absently ordered the special, a surprise when a big plate of liver, bacon, and onions was deposited in front of him. Ordinarily, it wouldn't have been his first choice. This time c he ate every bite. Hell, he figured he would've eaten cardboard if it'd been sautéed in bacon fat.

The waitress moved around the room, bringing coffee refills along with the bill. Smiling as she lay the chit upside down on the table, she poured coffee with the other hand without spilling a drop.

Hix patted his lean belly and spun a silver half-dollar onto the table. "Ma'am, can you tell me whereabouts I might find the hospital?"

She laughed a jolly sound. "I hope it wasn't the food here that makes you ask."

"Oh, no." His laughter joined hers. "My compliments to the cook. But a young lady came in on a freight train last night. She'd been wounded by a madman on a rampage. I just wanted to find out how she's doing."

The waitress, shaking her head over the sad state of affairs when a girl could be attacked by rough, bad men, willingly gave directions to St. Patrick Hospital.

Replete, his belly full at last, Hix finished his coffee before ambling out the door. For his next step, he intended to check on Wilkie Van Slyke's welfare. Then, in all good conscience, he could leave the state far behind.

All those plans went crosswise when he found Deputy Bodeen and two younger deputies standing by the Triumph waiting for him. The young deputies jumped him before he had a chance to reach for his gun, even if he'd been so inclined. Which he wasn't. Hix figured if he had drawn, he would've been dead before it was even halfway out of the holster seeing that Bodeen had a .45 pointed at him the whole time. He stood no chance against three of them.

"What's this?" he protested as one man jerked

his hands behind his back and snapped on thick metal cuffs. It took all he had to stand calm and let the deputy pushed him around. It seemed almost as if they were daring him to fight. And they, unlike Balakov and Eldon, didn't neglect to search him.

"You're under arrest," Bodeen said. "But I'm fairly sure you knew that already."

"Under arrest? What for? I haven't done anything."

One of the deputies spit on the ground. "That ain't what we hear."

"What?" Hell, he thought, Wilkie must've had to speak up about that damn Spreck.

"That's right, mister. You're wanted for murder. Twice over." Bodeen grinned.

Twice? "Murder? That's not right. I haven't murdered anybody."

Bodeen never lost his grin. "Yeah, that's what all killers say."

"No, wait." Hix couldn't stop his muscles from flexing, involuntarily striving to break out of the cuffs. Didn't work. Just encouraged the deputy with one crossed eye to buffet him on the shoulder. Hurt, too, since Balakov had kicked him in the same spot the other night. "Who am I supposed to have killed?"

"You killed so many you can't keep track? But

just to make it all clear, you're under arrest for the murders of Trench Jackson and Eldon Venig."

He'd half expected old man Jackson, but *Eldon?* Sheer shock kept Hix silent.

***

By evening, Wilkie felt some better. Oh, her side still hurt what with the stitches pulling every time she moved. But at least the ether sickness had passed. She'd even managed to keep down some clear broth at lunchtime, and a scrambled egg with toast for supper.

Her legs shook like a week-old kitten's when she tried to stand up. The nurse told her it was due to blood loss and the shock to her system, insisting she have someone with her if she got out of bed. That's why, when a girl about Wilkie's own age came to pick up her plate, refill her water glass, and turn on the single electric light bulb over by the door, Wilkie begged assistance to the water closet.

With the other two room occupants still completely bedridden—Wilkie didn't know why and hesitated to ask—the aide, who seemed the garrulous type, wanted to chat.

"My name is Janet Clement," the girl said, sticking out an elbow for Wilkie to grasp. "And I guess you're Millie Jameson. I saw your name listed on the chart outside the room. Last night you were still unknown."

"Yes. I'm Millie." Wilkie had almost forgotten she'd given that name.

"I know you were stabbed. A victim of a crime." Excitement colored Janet's voice. "I saw something interesting today that I bet will make you glad."

"Glad? About what?" Wilkie's interest mostly lay in getting safely to the water closet.

"One of our deputies caught a murderer this afternoon," the girl said. "Down at the Main Street Café. I live right across the alley, and I saw part of the arrest. Why, the man didn't even try to escape or to shoot his way out of town. It would've been ever so exciting if he had. Just like in the old days. Maybe if Deputy Bodeen had wounded him, they'd have brought him here in the hospital. Maybe Sister Marie Therese would've assigned me to take care of him. I'm not afraid."

"My word," Wilkie said. For some reason, one of those ghastly *feelings* she sometimes got raised goosebumps on her skin. A *murderer*? A compulsion nagged at her, making words come out of her mouth she'd rather not have said. "What did this murderer look like? Scary?"

She hoped so. As frightening as Spreck had been.

The girl put a forefinger over her lips and thought. "Not very. Actually..." she bent closer to Wilkie and whispered. "... he's nice looking; I'd even say handsome. And young. Don't tell anybody I said so, but he doesn't look like he'd murder anybody. Why, I'd let him take me dancing any day—or night. Or I would if I didn't know he was a murderer."

Wilkie wondered what standards the girl judged by.

"Who did he murder?" Her voice trembled, and she sought to steady it. "Is supposed to have murdered, I mean. I guess we don't know if he did or if he didn't. That's something the law has to prove."

Janet, who stood by while Wilkie attended to business, emitted a breathy harrumph. "I heard he killed some old man over by Deer Lodge. And a lawyer, too. My dad said the lawyer probably deserved it."

"Oh. What is... was... the lawyer's name?" Feeling decidedly weak, Wilkie made her way back to bed. *It couldn't be. Mustn't be.*

"Why? Do you know a great many lawyers?" Ignoring Wilkie's protest, Janet tucked her in. "This lawyer came from Butte. He has a funny name that starts with a V. I'm not sure of the pronunciation."

Wilkie's breath stopped. "Venig?"

"Why, yes. How could you know?" Janet

stopped what she was doing and stared at Wilkie, who shrugged.

The aide had one more item to impart. "Just before I left for work, a deputy came and dragged away a motorcycle they say belonged to him." Dishes clattered as she carelessly gathered them onto a tray. "To the murderer, I mean. Isn't that funny? A murderer on a motorcycle?"

"Hilarious," Wilkie muttered, although it wasn't the least bit funny. Her scattered thoughts kept screaming, *'No. Oh, no, no, no.'* Why had Hix come to Missoula, anyhow? Why hadn't he escaped Montana when he had the chance?

Guilt rushed in. *My fault.*

She fought her way out the smothering cocoon of blankets the second the girl left with her tray of dirty dishes. Anger provided impetus, allowing her to ignore the tug at her wound.

If she knew anything at all, it was that Hix hadn't murdered anyone.

Had he?

The answer came to her. No. She didn't count Spreck. After all, he'd been trying to kill her at the time. That had been no murder, just pure defense.

And now Hix was locked up on her account.

Chapter Seventeen

The stone jail, erected handily right next door to the courthouse a few years previously, proved as grim inside as it appeared from the exterior. Stunk, too, of fear, days-old sweat, of piss and vomit and maybe other body fluids, as well. Something about the building struck Hix as cold, regardless of the lingering heat of the day. The thin blanket issued to him did little to alleviate the chill. The bunk in his cell, when he lay down on the stained mattress, was every bit as hard and lumpy as the bare ground he'd been sleeping on the last couple nights.

Hix, disgusted with himself for acting the fool, expected Little Miss Wilkie could take care of herself. In fact, he was sure of it. There'd been no need for him to rush after her. What had he been thinking, that he was a knight in shining armor?

He snorted. Apparently, he could use one of them for himself.

Eldon dead. He still couldn't believe it. Why? A falling out among thieves? Had Eldon drawn the line when he knew what Balakov planned for Hix? If Hix hadn't escaped, that is. Or had it finally gotten through to Eldon that Balakov planned to eliminate Wilkie as well, first chance? Or maybe even Aunt Magdalena. Or both? And who else?

Or, considering Eldon's full-on participation in threatening old Mr. Jackson and beating on Hix, maybe it was because Balakov had simply gotten rid of an incompetent partner.

At eleven o'clock, the night jailer, a stooped older man long past his prime, came through checking all the locks, his keys rattling on his belt. "Not asleep, young feller?" He peered through the bars at Hix.

"No, sir. It's hard to relax, boxed up in here." Hix didn't suppose he was the only prisoner to feel that way. He had no idea how many were incarcerated at present, but he heard their noises, their cries, and shouts, once even someone weeping. All disturbing to one used to being alone—or maybe just born of a tougher breed.

The jailer laughed. "Better get used to it. This ain't nothing compared to over at Deer Lodge."

Too damned cheery by far, in Hix's opinion. "I won't be here long. I haven't killed anybody," he said, trying to sound confident.

"No?" The man chuckled again. "That's what

all killers say, even as they're being dragged to the gallows." He moved on, clanging the door between the cells and the office shut as he left.

Beginning to think he'd have been better off to put up a fight back there at the café—or in no worse case, anyway—Hix heartily wished it possible to take back the last few days. The last five days, to be precise, all the way to when he'd been doing fine working for Jarvis Pettit and his rumrunning operation outside of Idaho Falls. Right back to when his friend Ben Wakefield, who knew Hix had coveted a motorcycle since the day he'd seen a new red Indian with a camel-back gas tank, told him about the feller in Dillon, Montana with a Triumph to sell.

Long story short, Hix got excited and informed Jarvis he was taking a few days off. Though having frequently said he intended to stay out of Montana for good after that little mix-up with Eldon's cattle rustling deal, Hix succumbed to the lure of acquiring a new motorcycle for the amount stated. Off to Dillon, he went. And from there, since a new owner had to try out his purchase, and because he hadn't seen his friends or his aunt in Butte for some time and it was only a hop and a skip, he went ahead and did that too.

More fool him.

Stuck in the cold Missoula jail cell, Hix

groaned, joining the other, unseen prisoners in their misery.

As long as he was wishing, he wished he had a set of those lock picking tools Wilkie claimed were her inheritance from her uncle. Not that he knew how to open a lock with them, but she'd told him how they worked and, as she called them, the principals of unlocking a locked mechanism. He'd soon figure the process out for himself.

If he didn't hang first.

***

At one o'clock in the morning, Wilkie flung back her blanket and crawled out of bed. Barefoot, and as silent as though creeping down a bank corridor while the clerk's back was turned, she slipped past her roommates' beds and peeked into the hall. Except for one weak light above a desk situated near the stair landing, the hall outside was dark. She spotted a nurse's station at the far end, although at present it was unattended. Head cocked, she became aware of the murmur of voices issuing from a room just down the way. The gleam of a lamp reflected off the white walls, while a woman sobbed within.

A choice time for an escape. Wilkie hobbled down the hall, past the desk, and into the stairwell. Lucky timing, since the night nurse emerged from the room, said a soft goodnight, and headed back to the station where she sat back in her chair with a sigh, her voluminous attire settling around her.

Wilkie froze. Her bare feet already cold, she was beginning to think she'd have to confess to sleepwalking if she wanted to go back to bed. Which she did. Even this little excursion made her weak. But then, since she had come this far, she decided she should extend her knowledge and discover all the options. The plan forming in her head made her more than a little nervous.

Blame Hix, anyhow. He should've immediately fled to wherever in Idaho he'd started from. Forgotten the motorcycle and left it lay. Written it off as a failed experiment. Silly man. He didn't have the sense God gave a chipmunk.

Creeping down the stairs where lights were turned low enough one could barely see the bottom step, it occurred to Wilkie why he hadn't done the wise thing. And the guilt lay right at her door.

Upon reaching the floor below, she entered a hall. Lights shone at the end of it. Hugging the wall, she came to a jog. One way had a little sign that said, "Admitting." The other way said, "Waiting room." She took the latter route and soon entered a large, dark room, empty now, but scattered with a couple groupings of chairs and a desk barring the way to the rear. Across the empty space, the hospital entrance beckoned. The few lights still on downtown sent a glow through the front windows. Missoula was not a large town, by any means, she saw now. Small enough for a stranger to be remarkable.

She blew softly, relieved to have discovered the escape route—or maybe by rights she should just call it the way out—so easily. Truly, she could leave anytime she wanted. But not tonight. Plans needed made first. Plans no subject to failure. Turning, she retraced her steps. At the top of the stairs, she found the nurse, a gentle-faced sister with a wilted cap, snoring in her chair, her face turned into her shoulder.

Tiptoeing around her, Wilkie sympathized. The poor woman was certain to have a stiff neck when she awoke.

Once safely back in her room, Wilkie, chilled to the core, climbed into bed and burrowed under the blanket. If this small walk had exhausted her, the mind boggled at going all the way into town. *Tomorrow,* she promised herself. She'd be better tomorrow.

And she was, though disgruntled at being awakened by the chime of bells at six o'clock in

the morning. Time for prayers, one of her roommates informed her in a weak voice. Wilkie drew
the blanket over her head, not that it did much
toward shutting out the noise of a hospital preparing for a busy day.

At eight o'clock, a different girl from the one
last night brought her breakfast. Oatmeal and
toast with a smear of plum jam and coffee. Not
what Wilkie would've ordered if she'd had a
choice. She ate every bite anyway, determined
to regain her strength by evening. An hour later,
a nursing sister came around and checked her
wound.

The nun's smile at Wilkie was one of satisfaction. "You're doing well, healing fast." Giving a
little sigh, her smile faded as she nodded toward
the woman who'd told Wilkie about the bells.
"Unlike poor Mrs. Twist. Be happy you're young
and healthy."

Wilkie caught her breath. "I am. Happy and
grateful. Is she..." She nodded toward the woman,
in the throes of a coughing fit. "Will she recover?"

Jameson's death kept the question near the
forefront of her mind.

"We certainly hope so." The sister's lip quiv-
ered. "She has a large family of young children.
They will need their mother."

That wasn't how the scene worked out. Unfortunate for the woman, but good, as it happened, for Wilkie's rather nebulous, free-flowing plan.

Soon after breakfast, the third woman in the room went home. By noon, the mother's temperature spiked. Her breathing became labored. The nurses put a cloth tent over the upper part of her body and forced steam into it, but after one fierce coughing spell, she made no sound at all. Her family filed into the room soon after. Five stair-step children, a husband who openly wept, people Wilkie imagined were the woman's own mother and father. A doctor hovered, a nurse at his side.

Other nurses came to take Wilkie, trembling, and on the verge of tears, into a different room. They brought her a magazine and the morning newspaper, no doubt hoping she would entertain herself while they attended the dying woman.

Everyone, from their subdued demeanor, knew it was only a matter of time.

Hix's arrest took up a three-inch column on the front page. It didn't really tell Wilkie anything more than the aide had told her last night. Even so, put in print, the information seemed damning, even though she knew it wasn't true. The time was coming that she'd have to step forth and do her best to clear Hix's name. If the authorities even believed her. Backed by an outfit like Burke and Boothe—no Venig in the name now—it seemed possible her word would do no good, especially when it came out about Jameson and her own part in the story. She had information to back up her claims, however, if she lived long enough to get it to the right people. And for that, well, she could use Hix's help. His and his aunt's.

***

One o'clock in the morning seemed a slow time in the hospital. At least it had worked well last night. Wilkie, dressed in her sweater and cleaned skirt with the .32 in her pocket, patted the last of the bed's blankets into shape, left the lamp left burning on a low flame, and cracked open her room door.

Mrs. Twist clung to life. Lights shone in her room. Children slept on the floor, the grandparents nodded in chairs, and the husband, still awake, sat by the bed holding his wife's hand. A nun sat nearby, holding vigil with the family.

Wilkie stepped back as a nurse carrying a basin passed her room and entered Mrs. Twist's. This nun and the nursing sister conferred, leaning over the bed before one closed the door.

Perfect.

Wearing moccasins grubbed from her valise to ensure silent footsteps, Wilkie closed the room door behind her. She darted down the hall and past the deserted nurse's station. In a matter of minutes, she stood at the exit, waiting for the pain to ebb. A sense of dread hung over her. What would the sheriff do if he caught her? Would he lock her up in a cell next to Hix?

She couldn't let that happen.

While she did feel much better, the journey along dark, unfamiliar streets to the courthouse, and by association, the jail, exhausted Wilkie. Outside the lowering stone building, she took a few moments to catch her breath and again allow the pain from pulled stitches to recede.

Once recovered, she tightened her muscles and firmed her spine, then trod up the stone steps where she tugged on a heavy door. Halfway to her surprise, it opened. Slipping inside, she entered a large room with a high counter set along the back wall, behind which a deputy normally stood to take care of inquiries. And perhaps safeguard the jailers. Right now, the room was empty, and praise God for that. Plain wooden benches lined the walls, but certainly nothing that appeared comfortable. Not a place to take up housekeeping, Wilkie thought sourly, looking around. Behind the counter, a couple hallways with sets of stairs at the ends beckoned.

Now what? she wondered. Right or left, up or down?

With no one there to stop her, she felt brave enough to go on.

Once behind the counter, she explored the halls. Offices, some with doors open, some closed, had name plaques on them. She shrugged, except at the one marked Bodeen. The man, according to the newspaper, who'd arrested Hix. She stuck out her tongue, like a child.

Mounting the stairs, Wilkie reached the second story and spotted her objective ahead. Just as she stepped onto the landing, she heard a sound behind her. A toilet flushing, then footsteps before the creak of a heavily weighted chair. A close call.

There'd be no going back now. Not until—

Lock picks already in hand, Wilkie started forward only to stop as though she'd run into a wall. Propped against the wall on the two rear legs of a wooden chair, an elderly man sat with a cup in his hand. He sat so still that at first, it seemed certain he was awake and staring right at her. But then, as a minute, or maybe an eternity, passed and he didn't stir, she realized it wasn't so. In fact, he was so still, he seemed not to be breathing. She stepped forward to check, relieved when she saw his chest move.

Now to find Hix.

There was nothing for it but to look in every cell until she found him. Most of the cells, to her relief, were empty, the barred doors open. Beginning at the far end on the left, as if reading a book, Wilkie scanned each cell. Some contained two men, some just one. She hoped to find Hix by himself.

Wilkie's luck held, although the night guard erupted with a loud snore once that frightened her so badly, she nearly wet herself. Even so, his breathing immediately smoothed out, and he slept on undisturbed. The cup remained gripped in his hand. Wilkie's own hands were shaking.

She found Hix in the fifth cell from the end. He lay in the bottom bunk of the two-tiered set-up, on a mattress that appeared to have been in use since the first Missoula jail was built nearly forty years earlier. Although the dim lighting kept her from seeing his features, she recognized the flat cap and belted jacket hanging from the corner of a bedpost. She knew his scuffed boots, too, side by side below the cap and jacket.

After a look behind her at the guard, she pressed her face against the bars. "Hix?" she said on a breath, so low she knew he'd never hear. Rightfully. He didn't.

Setting to work, she inserted the tension wrench from Jameson's set of tools into the lock. Wishing for a squirt of lubricant, a bit of maintenance that evidently hadn't been provided for some time, she determined which way the key, if she'd had one, would turn. From there, she began ever so gently working the key wrench, her sensitivity telling her when to apply torque to the plug. A disquieting amount of time passed as she set the pins, but at last, the lock disengaged. Something scraped as she withdrew the pick and the wrench. A job, made more difficult than necessary by her nerves, finally accomplished.

Behind her, the guard snorted again, and she jumped, her galloping heartbeat loud in her ears.

Pulling the cell door open, Wilkie stepped inside.

Chapter Eighteen

Hix, who Wilkie was relieved to see had the cell to himself, lay on the lowest bunk with his face toward the wall. Something about his pose struck her as defensive. As though as long as the bars weren't within his line of sight, he could pretend he wasn't locked in. Well, he didn't have to pretend anymore. If all went well, he'd soon be free.

For now, a voice in her head whispered. *Then what?*

She crept forward and lay her forefinger across his mouth. "Hix?" she murmured into his ear. "Wake up."

He gave a monstrous jerk. His arm, which had been thrown across his forehead and over his eyes, shot out and grabbed her. Somehow, and even later she couldn't quite figure how the sequence came about, she ended up with his arm in a choke hold around her neck as she lay sprawled across him.

At least she had sense enough not to struggle. After a few seconds, he realized that and pushed her off. But then, as if not sure of what his eyes told him, he yanked her closer again.

He appeared to be trying to make words.

Shaking her head, Wilkie put her finger across his lips again and said, "Shh," so quietly she figured she deserved a medal. What she really wanted to do was scream as the wound in her side, unappreciative of the jolts and jars of his manhandling, blazed as though a fire had been lit in her innards.

Although she'd as soon stayed where she was until the pain faded, she couldn't afford the time. Sliding off him, she stood. "Come on," she mouthed and with a 'come along' gesture, moved toward the cell door.

Hix's mouth dropped open. Realization struck, and he shot up off the bunk. Who knew a man could shove feet into boots so quickly? Or don a coat and hat.

Wilkie realized he still didn't trust his eyes or senses, though, as he reached out and touched her arm before actually taking a step toward freedom. His knuckles, scabbed over from when he'd tried to fight Balakov and Eldon, hadn't healed much in the last couple days.

She grinned at him.

Letting him go first, she shut the cell door behind them as they left, soundlessly, so it didn't clang, on the premise that if an escape wasn't immediately obvious, they'd have more time to get away. On tiptoe, they passed the jailer, who, still sound asleep, snorted once just as Hix went past him. Wilkie thought for sure she heard Hix's heart pounding double time. Except she decided it couldn't possibly be his heart, but her own.

Hix led the way down the stairs, stopping at the office with Deputy Bodeen's name on a little plaque. He put hand to knob and twisted.

Wilkie glared, shaking her head. "What?" she mouthed at him, certain he could read the question on her lips. She'd begun to feel the walls closing in. They needed to get out of here. Right now. And run—as if she could.

But Hix ignored her warning and pushed on the door. Regretfully, in Wilkie's view, it opened. They went inside.

The room smelled bad, although she couldn't have described exactly what it smelled of. And even with the door ajar it was almost as dark as the proverbial dungeon, so she had no idea what they were doing there. But Hix did. He lost no time moving toward a desk situated under a high window and pulling open the middle drawer in a bank of three running down the right side.

He pulled a bundle from the drawer. His holster and pistol and a knife. A few other things, perhaps. She couldn't really see. But she could hear. For instance, the sound Hix made as he slid the drawer shut, a thud carrying well in the overall silence of the building.

"Well, hell," he said at the noise. Too loud, by far.

Wilkie felt like clouting him one. Next thing she knew they'd both be right back upstairs in his cell, her right along with him.

"Who's there?" Putting an exclamation point on her anxiety, a man's deep voice sounded from the front of the building. "Bletcher, is that you? What're you doing prowling around the offices?"

She didn't know which of them stood most solidly frozen. But she realized she had a death grip around his arm, and he, after the few seconds it took for him to thaw, was trying to shake her off. Stung, she let go.

"Get behind the door." He tugged her over to stand against the wall. "When it's clear, get on outside. I'll take care of this and be there in a minute."

With that, he stepped into the hall and walked away.

Fuming, some of those muleskinner words she knew rose up in Wilkie's mind. He'd closed her in here. How was she supposed to know when it was clear? Would she hear gunfire? Screams?

Bellowing? Sirens?

But when she put her mind to it, as she listened closely, she heard the clomping of a heavy-footed man walking down the hall. At every door, he paused long enough to thrust it open and peer inside. The search, she thought, didn't seem especially thorough.

Sure enough, the door opened on her, pressing her tight against the wall. She held her breath as the man looked around. He was a heavy man, corpulent, judging by the sound of his breathing and his shadow on the floor.

Just then, from the furthest end of the hall, she heard a rattle of metal, and what struck her as an animal's squeak. The fellow withdrew into the hall.

"Now what the dickens is that?" he said, just above a whisper.

Thankfully, or maybe not, depending on what Hix had in mind, the fellow set off to find out.

Wilkie, thankful she'd been slim enough to fit in the area behind the door without revealing herself, wondered too. Stepping from her confinement, she poked her head out far enough to see the man waddling off behind the staircase as he followed the direction of the sound.

This being her chance, she walked as Jameson had taught her—no running, being fully aware the faster pace added a noise level not found with walking — toward the jail's entrance. Once there, she simply opened the door, went out and trod down the steps to the road below the walkway. There was a bench in front of the courthouse next to the jail. Trembling, she sat on it.

How long would she have to wait?

What if the fat man caught Hix? Lord only knows poor Hix would be crushed if the guard sat on him. Or what if the jailer woke up and joined the hunt? Two against one and she'd seen Hix still moved as if his beatings had not yet healed. What if he had to shoot his way out?

Wilkie, well on her way into a nervous dither, jumped to her feet—nearly tearing out her stitches yet again—as Hix burst from the jail and, taking the steps two at a time, headed toward her. He barely paused as he came even, caught her by the hand and, though she gasped and resisted, pulled her along with him.

They didn't stop until they reached the drive leading to St. Patrick Hospital. A leafy tree stood on the grounds, and here Hix finally paused to whirl her into its shelter. Next thing she knew, his lips were on hers, and he was kissing the daylights out of her.

The kiss ended, to her regret, although he kept hold of her hand.

"I thought I was imagining you," he said. "I thought it was someone come to torment me. Or a dream. Maybe it's still a dream."

Wincing as he squeezed her fingers, Wilkie's voice came out shaky and breathless. "Oh, I'm real, all right. Then and now. Do you always try to choke your dreams?"

His teeth flashed white as he smiled crookedly. "Not generally. Do you always shout in a sleeping man's ear?" He stopped. "Sorry. I didn't mean..."

She knew what he meant.

"I didn't shout," she said. "I whispered, trying to warn you to keep quiet. You almost spoiled everything."

He opened his mouth and closed it again. "But you got me out. Cracked open that jail cell like it was a boiled egg."

"It was easy." A boiled egg, she reflected, didn't quite seem the right simile.

After that, there was nothing else to say, except for Hix's heartfelt "thank you."

He should've gone then, Wilkie thought, waiting for an alarm to go up about his escape. Apparently, the fellows guarding the jail hadn't discovered he was missing yet. But they would. Soon.

"What are you going to do now?" she asked when he lingered.

"Run for the border. Catch the first train out of here that's headed west." He shook his head in what might have disgust, but that Wilkie interpreted as sorrow. "Leave my motorcycle. They've got it locked up somewhere."

"I brought some money. I promised I'd pay you for the arrangement about my uncle, and for getting me out of Butte."

She knew he flushed.

"They confiscated my money," he said, "so I'll take it with thanks. Although you don't owe me anything. You got me out of jail. I reckon that's enough."

"Where you wouldn't have been in the first place if it weren't for me. Anyway, I do owe you. You saved me from that awful man at the water tower." Wilkie dug in her pocket and found the twenty-dollar gold piece she'd stowed there. Handing it over, she turned away.

"What are you going to do?" Looking down at it, Hix clutched the heavy coin.

Wilkie grinned over her shoulder. "I'm going back to the hospital, find my room, and go to bed. With any luck, they won't know I've been gone."

Huffing out a laugh, Hix shook his head. "You are some piece of work, Miss Wilkie Van Slyke. And that's a fact."

The hollow feeling in Wilkie's chest grew bigger as she made her way up the hospital steps. At one point on their way here, she'd mentioned to him she'd signed into the hospital under the name Millie Jameson. Not that he'd asked. But what if he'd forgotten? If he came for her—although why he should, she couldn't imagine—he'd be turned away. But then, that's what she'd wanted, isn't it? To hide her identity? And his?

I'll never see him again. The words echoed mournfully in her head. And it was true. When she got inside and looked back, she caught a last glimpse. Then he was gone, jogging down the street where the dark swallowed him.

It occurred to her he hadn't told her how he'd gotten past the jail guards. Or what kind of noise had lured the fat man away. Now she'd never know. It was like not getting to read the last chapter of a book.

No, not in *a* book. In their book.

***

Wilkie having disappeared within the hospital, Hix knew it was time to get out of Missoula. Past time. But how? The temptation to try regaining his motorcycle, riding him hard, he made a foray back toward the jail. Could be he'd find it stored behind the building, in a courtyard where he'd overheard the jailer mention he parked his bicycle. That idea ended when, still a couple blocks distant, he found the whole jail lit up and uniformed men guarding the premises.

Seemed obvious his escape had been discovered. It hadn't taken long for the guard to wrestle himself out of the supply closet where Hix had stored him. Not long enough, by far. Probably hadn't been too difficult for a man as weighty as him.

That wasn't all. Deputies were out in force patrolling the nearby streets. One, as luck—bad luck—would have it, spotted him right off.

"You," the deputy called. "Hey, you. Stop where you are."

"What's going on?" Hix called back.

"Prisoner escape." The deputy headed toward him with a self-important swagger to his step, his hand resting on the gun at his hip.

"Prisoner escape, you say?"

"Yeah." The deputy eyed him. "What are you doing out at this time of night?"

"On my way to work. Thought I'd come see why all the lights are on."

If it sounded like a pretty poor excuse to Hix, he could only imagine what the deputy must think, but to his complete surprise, the man, so caught up in excitement himself, bought Hix's story.

"Yeah, well, a murderer got loose. They're not saying how it came to happen, just that he's armed and dangerous."

Hix swallowed. Armed and dangerous. Holy smoke! He was having a hard time stopping himself from reaching for his gun.

"When did all this happen?" he asked, seeming casual.

The deputy shrugged. "Half-hour, maybe forty-five minutes. Or so they told those of us on night duty."

"Half-hour?" Hix made a point of staring around. "Then why are you all stomping around here? Don't you figure he's out of town by now?" As he would be if he had a choice.

The pointed question effectively caused the deputy to lose interest in Hix. "I just follow orders," he said. "Move along now. There's nothing here for you to look at."

Hix, the hard knot in his gut relaxing, was plenty happy to follow orders, too. He moved along.

Abandoning the idea of riding away on his Triumph, he jogged across the patch of lawn in front of the courthouse and hit the road leading to the rail yard. If he caught a ride on a freight as far as Frenchtown, the next small town west of Missoula, he'd drop off there and, as long as word of his escape hadn't reached them when the morning NP went through, he'd buy a ticket to Wallace, or maybe Enaville. From there—well, he guessed he didn't know yet.

Head to Spokane, maybe, then backtrack to Idaho Falls and take up transporting booze over the border again. Funny though. The exhilaration he'd always felt at tricking the authorities didn't seem to be there anymore. But, he consoled himself, at least the money was good. He'd soon make back what he'd lost on his abandoned Triumph.

The freight yard lights were glowing even though it was the shank of the night. Or, he supposed, depending on your inclination, early in the morning. Either way, the illumination made finding a hiding spot easier. On the other hand, it also opened him up to getting caught. Sometimes the railroad security detail had a dog sniffing out freeloaders, and Missoula was a big enough hub to qualify. He kept a watchful eye out, just in case.

As he slipped between tracks, he saw the locomotive on which Wilkie had ridden into Missoula idling while it built up a head of steam for the return trip to Butte. The burly feller was there, too, and the engineer with his striped cap.

And someone else.

Balakov.

Hix watched, a streak of fear running through

an anger-filled core, as the engineer and Balakov shook hands. Even at this distance, he could see Balakov looked happy as a hound with a cat up a tree. Which might mean he'd given up on pursuing Hix and gone directly after Wilkie. Right now, if found, she made an easier target. Hix had no doubt the engineer had revealed Wilkie's whereabouts to the man, although how the Bulgarian had come to look for these particular railroaders and pose the question in the first place was a mystery.

It didn't matter anyway. He knew the end result. Wilkie was in deep trouble.

Chapter Nineteen

Wilkie found the route to her assigned ward blocked at the top of the stairs by a group of nuns wearing frighteningly solemn expressions while speaking in low, serious tones. Barely managing to catch herself before walking right into their midst, she spun around before they spotted her. A quick retreat to the ground floor soon brought her to a kitchen where a couple women were already busy lighting stoves and putting pots of water on to boil. Slipping past them while their backs were turned, she discovered a rear access. It was a dark, narrow, and *steep* stairway that left her grateful to be a safecracker. She wouldn't be one of the workers in this building for anything.

Who, she wondered, breathing heavily and holding her burning side as she reached the top if in their right mind, would choose to be a maid or nurse traversing these steps Lord only knows how many times a day?

Reaching her room undiscovered with only the one close call, she closed her door with a soft click and flicked on the overhead light. Her room appeared just as she'd left it. The rolled blanket in the bed still looked like a person snoozing the night away. A quick check indicated belongings stowed in the cabinet were undisturbed. The newspaper where she'd read about Hix remained folded on the table by the bed. A half-glass of water sat there too.

Swiftly, or at least as quickly as possible, Wilkie skimmed out of her clothing, stuffed it in the cabinet, and donned the hospital gown.

By then, fatigue strong enough to draw the very marrow from her bones, she collapsed onto the bed, not even minding the light. Sleep claimed her between one blink of the eye and the next.

It was still dark outside when she awakened. Not a peaceful awakening, either, but a startling jump that burned her stitches. The sound of sobbing, and oddly, a man's angry voice rising all the way to a shout disturbed the hospital's usual quiet. Certain that no more than an hour had passed since bedding down, she tried to make sense of the commotion. The wound in her side protesting, she got out of bed and poked her head into the hall to see what had caused the uproar.

Three nursing sisters stood just outside the room Wilkie had previously occupied. Janet, the girl who'd told her about Hix and brought the newspaper, leaned against the wall, appearing to need its support as she wept. She looked a mess, cap knocked askew, a lock of hair hanging over one shoulder. While the nuns, although their faces were pale and drawn, spoke quietly and calmly, Janet made no effort to control her tears. The man doing the shouting stood with his chest thrust out, arms akimbo. He wore a policeman's uniform.

Wilkie had no choice but to overhear.

"How could all of you be on duty during the night, yet never see a thing?" he thundered. "What kind of a place is this, anyhow? People may come here to die, but they don't plan on being murdered. Now," he turned to Sister Marie Therese, "when did you discover the body?"

Murder? Wilkie's mouth turned dry as a salted cracker. What could he be talking about?

If the policeman's intention was to intimidate the sister, his plan failed.

"Please lower your voice," she said. "You are disturbing our patients."

Wilkie noticed then that other rooms had people garbed in hospital gowns standing in open doorways. All women, she noticed, before remembering she'd heard hospitals had wards separating men from women and children.

One woman, evidently a patient privileged

beyond the norm, had donned a silken kimono robe over what must've been her own nightdress as it reached all the way to her ankles. Unlike Wilkie's, which ended mid-calf.

The woman spoke in a firm, authoritative voice. "What's the meaning of this disturbance, Sergeant Moore?"

"Mrs. Townsend, ma'am." The police officer made a sort of bow, by which Wilkie assumed the woman was well-known and of some importance in this town. Or the wife of someone important.

"Nothing for you to worry about," Sergeant Moore said, although it seemed clear he was in a rage. His voice rose again. "Everyone go back inside your rooms. I'll be along to talk to each of you soon." At this, Wilkie felt a distinct chill, a precursor of one of those crazy insights she got. She hadn't been raised by Jameson Van Slyke for nothing. Or joined in his business of opening locks for people who most often were not the people who'd set the lock in place. Sometimes, as Jameson had been known to admit, his clients were of the sideways sort. People like Boothe, Burke & Venig. The fact never appeared to bother her uncle unduly. But it bothered her now. A connection between this and that. She just *knew*.

The policeman nodded at Mrs. Townsend. "I'll meet with you first, ma'am, if it suits."

She nodded back. "As soon as possible. I'll be waiting." Directing her attention to one of the nurses, she called out, "I need your attention, sister, if you please." She seemed to wilt as she tottered into her room again, as though her effort had exhausted her.

The sister, not one Wilkie recognized, hurried to do the woman's bidding. No surprise.

Other patients took direction from the commanding pair. Wilkie wanted to know just who Mrs. Townsend was and what position she held. She admired the woman's naturally assumed authority, a trait she decided would come in handy when dealing with clients—until she remembered she had no clients. Not with Jameson dead. But still—

Taking a deep breath, she called, "Janet, please, can you help me?"

Janet, her sobs thankfully diminished, glanced at the policeman, who nodded permission. Now the others had quieted, and the sergeant ceased yelling, Wilkie heard men's voices coming from inside the room she'd previously occupied.

"She's been cut to pieces!" one exclaimed.

"Lot of blood," said another.

The sound of retching carried clearly to Wilkie. Janet, too, who turned from pale to an odd greenish gray color. Maybe Wilkie did as well, as what the men said sank in.

"Oh, my God," Janet kept repeating as she entered Wilkie's room. "Oh, my God. Oh, my God."

It was as though the needle had stuck in the groove on one of Mr. Edison's gramophone cylinders.

"Close the door," Wilkie said.

Janet did, effectively shutting out the men's voices. "Oh, Miss Jameson, it's terrible. You're so fortunate they moved you last night, or you might have been murdered, too."

A heartbeat or two passed before Wilkie remembered she'd told them her name was Millie Jameson.

"Who was murdered?" she asked Janet. "I thought,—" she paused to swallow. "I thought that lady, Mrs. Twist, was dying anyway. Who would do such an awful thing?"

"No. It wasn't Mrs. Twist. Didn't you hear? She passed at exactly 3:23 a.m. Right before they took her away, they moved a girl into the room from... well... a girl from the wrong side of town whose... um... well, she'd gotten beaten rather badly. It must've been her... um..."

"Her pimp?" Wilkie was perfectly able to supply the word. Better to get on with the story than look for euphemisms.

"Yes." Janet's eyes, red from crying, narrowed.

"Oddly enough, she looks... looked... a lot like you. Dark hair and eyes. And her... pimp... had cut her with a knife, too. It says so right on her chart."

Wilkie's sense of wrongness, the premonition, settled in with a thud. Though Janet didn't lift a hand to help her, she sank down on her bed, her strength gone. "Did you see her... after? Who found her?"

Janet shuddered. "I did see her. Sort of. From the room door. But Sister Marie Therese found her when she was doing a follow-up check. It happened while the other sisters were seeing the Twist family out. That fast!" She shook her head, causing more blonde hair to straggle from under her cap.

"What was her name?" Wilkie forced the words from a dry throat. And though she asked, she didn't look forward to the answer.

"Nobody seems to know. I wish we did. It's just wrong for her not to have a name." Janet's tears spurted again. "But she was unconscious when they brought her in, and we couldn't ask, so we just marked the room as for Jane Doe."

"Jane Doe?"

"Yes. That's what we, and the police too, of course, call anyone whose name is unknown. Jane Doe for women, John Doe for men."

That could be me. And she had the thought it should have been, that it was supposed to be. "I hope you learn her real name," she said after a moment.

Someone else knocked on the door and called for Janet's services then, leaving Wilkie alone to stew. Although still exhausted by her efforts of the night, sleep eluded her. She lay in bed covered up to her chin, shivering and staring wide-eyed at the ceiling. Was it possible her medical journey here also began as Jane Doe? Most probably. Had calling herself Millie Jameson saved her life while causing another girl's death?

Janet had left the room door ajar as she departed, which meant Wilkie heard the police sergeant's rapid progress through the women's ward. Sister Marie Therese accompanied him, introducing each woman by name, injury or illness, and general state of being. He only had a few questions for the patients. Each easy to answer, especially when one had time to think those answers through. Since he'd started in a clockwise direction from the dead girl's room, Wilkie, although only a couple doors away, was the last.

A heavy-knuckled rap on the outer wall announced the policeman's arrival. Wilkie sat up, drawing the blanket with her. "Come in," she said, her stomach roiling.

Sister Marie Therese, reading from the chart, announced her name, injury, and present state.

Sergeant Moore read over the nun's shoulder. He straightened up, stared hard at Wilkie, then said, "Thanks for your help, Sister. This one is the last. I'll take it from here."

The sister started to protest, mentioning something about impropriety, but seeing Wilkie's nod, she gave in and excused herself, leaving the room with a swish of her voluminous skirts.

The policeman waited until sure she was gone before stepping over and closing the door. He pulled up a chair and sat, legs crossed.

Wilkie's stomach growled a warning.

"I seen on the chart that your name is Millie Johnson. That right?" he said.

"Jameson," Wilkie said, surprised by how quiet her voice had become. "My last name is Jameson."

"But I also seen that when you were admitted, you were a Jane Doe. Just like the little gal that got killed here last night."

Thinking she heard an accusation in those two statements, Wilkie nodded but said nothing. The resulting silence seemed to go on forever. After a while, he started in again.

"Chart says you have a stab wound, too," he said. "Just like the dead girl. Anything you want to tell me about that?"

Wilkie cleared her throat. "If you know what ails me, you probably know a train crew brought me into town when they found me wounded at one of the water towers." She put shock and fear into her voice, most of it real. "They brought the man who'd done it on the train, too. Dead. To save my life, I shot him." Her eyes met his. Bland. Innocent.

Sergeant Moore's eyebrows went up. "You don't seem unduly disturbed, considering you killed a man."

"Disturbed? He was trying to kill me at the time. I didn't have time to be disturbed. Ask the trainmen. They'll tell you."

His head nodded, not as if he was agreeing, but as if he were listening to distant music—or maybe stray thoughts passing through his mind. "I read the report they made to Deputy Summers. Looks as if you're in the clear about that. Spreck was a known violent criminal. We know he'd killed several men. Maybe women, too."

Wilkie replied before she could stop herself. "Perhaps you should've done something about him before he got to me, then."

As though surprised by her bitter tone, Sergeant Moore drew a small pad of paper from his uniform pocket, along with a chewed pencil stub.

"Yeah, well. Now, about last night. What do you know?"

"Me? I don't know anything about last night."

"Nothing? Yet here you are right next door. You must've heard something. The gal threshing around before she died, for instance. Maybe she cried out."

Wilkie knew her eyes went wide and staring as she imagined the scene. Her mouth trembled. "No," she said. "I didn't hear a thing." Guilt felt ready to consume her. Maybe she would've heard something if she hadn't fallen into bed worn to a nub from breaking Hix out of the county lockup. Maybe the girl would still be alive. *Or maybe I'd be dead. Maybe it's me who should be dead.*

"No footsteps in the hall? Doors opening or closing? People talking?"

"If I did, I'd not pay attention. People are walking in the halls all the time. Going in and out of rooms and speaking. Bells ring when someone needs assistance. It's a hospital!" *Easy.* Wilkie took firm hold of her emotions. That had sounded a little desperate.

More calmly, she asked a question of her own. "What about whoever caused her the harm that brought her here? Don't you think he might've come to finish what he started?"

"I see her story has got around already." Moore

put his paper and pencil away. "Ordinarily, I'd say yes. It was probably him. But in this case, it isn't. He happened to be in the city jail at the time." He snorted a trumpet-like blast of air through his nose. "Just about the same time a man was escaping from the County Sheriff's hoosegow."

Wilkie thought she heard laughter in his voice. Or in the snort. But one thing she was relieved about, they couldn't blame this on Hix.

Or could they?

Chapter Twenty

Hix had watched Balakov walk away from the freight yard like a feller with a settled purpose in mind. His strides were long and fast. A man in a hurry.

Not an observation soothing to Hix's nerves. What had the railroaders told the man?

He knew the answer. They'd told him where to find Wilkie, sure as dogs chased squirrels.

Hix, himself, was of two minds. One part said he oughta follow his plan to hop aboard the nearest unguarded car—never mind where the train was headed—and get himself out of Missoula before Bodeen found him. Lord knows there were enough deputies on the streets searching for him to box him in good. Another part nagged at him, saying he owed Wilkie a debt and his duty was to make sure she escaped meeting up with Balakov.

He thought he saw a solution to the quandary. If he went on down to where the locomotive idled and struck up a conversation with the engineer, he figured to learn what Balakov had asked. And if he asked the right questions, he'd get the same answers. Then he'd know what to do.

The plan might've worked better if, three seconds after the plan formed, two deputies hadn't arrived. One walked with a lantern held at arm's length in front of him. Every once in a while, he'd swing the lantern from side-to-side, and while the other deputy pointed a shotgun in the general direction, they'd both take a gander into the shadows.

Hix froze where he stood at the edge of the stock pens. The area as a whole was rank with a sickening stench, but at least this pen stood empty.

Once the deputies stopped to question a black man, they caught crossing the yard. They held him hostage a good ten minutes while they examined some papers he handed over. Hix saw the man wore the dark britches and white jacket of a Pullman car orderly. Finally, they let him go and went on to the engineer who shook his head several times. After only a couple minutes the deputies went on their way.

So did Hix.

Ducking around a stock car where a couple drovers were chasing cattle up a ramp, he approached the engineer. Above him, he saw the fireman stoking the locomotive's boiler, preparing the train to pull out as soon as the cars were all coupled.

The engineer saw him coming and hesitated, giving him a narrow-eyed stare.

Hix, confidence waning, raised his hand in greeting, thinking he wasn't prepared for this. How much had the deputies told them? Was he walking straight into a trap?

Cursing himself for a fool, Hix said, "Howdy, friend."

The engineer held up a hand, his palm facing Hix. "Stop right there. Another deputy just talked to me. Said there's a murderer on the loose and wanted to know if I've seen him. I'll tell you what I told him. The only folks I've seen tonight are deputies and a man looking for a girl."

Under different circumstances, Hix might've whooped and hollered. Seemed the man had mistaken him for another deputy.

"Good to know," Hix said. "You sure don't want to meet up with a murderer. Say, you're the crew that brought that girl in from the water tower east of here a couple days ago, aren't you?"

The engineer dug a finger under the edge of his cap and scratched. "Huh. Seems to be real popular question tonight. What's it to you?"

"You saved a girl's life." Hix assumed his most sincere expression. "That makes you and your crew heroes in my book. In her's, too, I expect. And makes folks want to meet you. Including me."

"Yeah? Why is that?" the engineer said.

"Because I'm a friend of hers. She's doing better now, and when I saw her, she asked me to see if I could find you fellers and tell you thanks. She's pretty sure she would've died if it hadn't been for you fellas showing up when you did."

The fireman had paused his stoking and was unabashedly listening in. He gazed down at them from the cab, sweat dripping from under his cap. "Say, feller, you're the second man tonight come around talking about the girl. In fact, you just missed the other one by a half-hour or so. Although he's a hard-assed looking pilgrim, who talks funny."

Hix pasted a surprised expression on his face. "A man with an accent? I don't suppose he said who he is. I'm pretty sure she'll want to know."

The fireman, shaking his head, climbed down from the cab and looked to the engineer. "Don't think he mentioned his name, did he, Bill?"

"No," Bill said and laid his hard stare on Hix. "But I don't guess you've said who you are, either. Or for that matter, neither of you mentioned the girl by name. Which she didn't tell us either, seeing she was pretty well out of it that day."

Hix nodded. "Yes, that's what they said at the hospital. Her name is Millie Jameson. She wanted me to let you boys know." To tell the truth, he wasn't so sure of any such thing. "And my name is Ben Wakefield. I'm an old friend of hers and work for her family. Her pa sent me to look for her when her horse came back with no sign of Millie. She'd been out delivering some papers, see, and the folks have been fretting themselves sick. Me too." Smiling, he offered his hand around for both men to shake. "Pleased and proud to meet all of you."

Kind of tickled him to use Ben's name in introducing himself. Served his friend right since Hix wouldn't be here and in this predicament if not for Ben.

But then he allowed his expression to grow serious. "This other feller, the one I just missed meeting—you don't suppose he's related to this Spreck that got killed, do you? If he is, he might mean harm to Millie." An idea to put in their minds. Just in case.

"Nah," Farley, the fireman said. "I heard Spreck say once he didn't have any relatives, and that he was damned glad of it."

"Then I wonder who he is?"

"Well," Bill said, "I hope we didn't do wrong telling him where they took her. Anyways, all we could tell him is to ask at the hospital for a Jane Doe."

Farley sent a halfway worried look at the others. "I took him for another newspaper guy. You know, like the local feller with the daily newspaper, only maybe somebody out of Butte. Or even Spokane. What happened to a pretty girl like her is big news."

Big news? Hix knew for a fact Wilkie wouldn't like hearing she'd made the papers, not under the name Millie Jameson, nor even under Jane Doe. Hix'd noticed she didn't talk much—or at all—about her home. Only a little about her uncle. A girl with secrets.

Bill's solemn nod agreed.

A ding sounded from inside the train's cab, and Bill lifted his foot onto the first rung of the ladder to climb aboard. "You tell that girl to get well soon, you hear?" he said, and to his fireman, "Time's burning. We got a schedule to keep."

And that was that.

Hix didn't stop to ponder what his next step should be. Swearing, he headed for the hospital. Seemed he was doing nothing but running around in circles tonight. And laying himself open to recapture by the lawmen swarming about.

A few minutes later, he walked into a situation.

If he'd thought the rail yard a dangerous place, it was nothing compared the police presence around the hospital. Hix didn't think they were there by chance waiting for him, so why were they? Something besides his escape must've happened. Something real grim. All he could do is find a place to hole up and wait his chance to find out what.

*****

Wilkie's mind spun like a yo-yo at the end of its string. Even so, her body remained motionless after Sergeant Moore left the room. A paralytic trance held her still.

It's me who should be dead. The words pounded through her head, over and over.

A minute later, she heard Sergeant Moore's voice boom from down the hall. Truthfully, he was loud enough to be heard throughout the entire ward as he hollered for a stretcher to remove the body; at someone to not miss anything if he wanted to keep his job; that he'd done his part and was heading back to the station.

Then came silence. As if the lack of sound gave permission to move, Wilkie tossed the hospital gown aside and donned her clothing. Settling her revolver in her boot holster, she retrieved the valise and checked the contents. As Sister Marie Therese had assured her, the contents appeared safe. Her gold, Uncle Jameson's tools, and the papers she'd taken—or did she mean *stolen*—from the bank vault were all there and intact.

She placed a shiny double eagle on her pillow, right in the dent her head had made. Far be it from her to shaft the people who'd taken such good care of her. Even so, she couldn't help thinking that if she kept on handing out twenty-dollar gold pieces as though they were pennies, at this rate, she'd be lucky to make it home with a single one of those pennies to her name.

Not that she begrudged any of the money she'd spent. Not by a long shot.

A glance at the windows high up on the room's wall showed the night outside waning. It would be dawn soon. Time for her to be gone.

While the killer still thinks he's killed me.

The thought made her skin crawl. Laced Boots. Balakov. She knew it.

When she was ready, Wilkie flicked off the light switch before slipping into the corridor. A murmur of voices came from the room where the police were still working, altogether a great deal more quietly now Moore had gone. A splatter of blood drops showed where the woman's body had been transported to the morgue portion of the hospital. Wilkie had heard the cart's wheels squealing as they'd taken her away.

The hallway, empty, dark, with the only light spilling from the murder room, beckoned her forward. Every other door along the corridor was closed. Moore must've told the sisters and their helpers to stay out of the way for what remained of the night.

Wilkie sent him a silent "thank you" as she headed for the exit. Luck favored her. Even though she needed to pass the open door, the two men had their backs turned as they poked around the bloodstained bed.

Sickened at the proof of carnage, Wilkie slipped past, scurrying around the nurses' station and down the stairs with the valise weighing heavily on her arm. Downstairs, she found the sisters had gathered in one of the rooms, a sanctuary, she decided, noting the altar and benches. The women were on their knees, eyes shut, praying along with an older woman clad in black. Lucky again, none noticed as she crept by them.

Wilkie paused for a moment then, her heart racing, and let the women's soft voices wash over her while she regained her breath.

According to Jameson's oft-repeated counsel, if your intention was to remain unnoticed, you should never just barge through a door. One never knew who or what might be waiting on the other side. With his voice in her ear, Wilkie took time to examine her surrounding before exiting the hospital.

At the bottom of the steps a buggy, the horse hitched to a post at the entrance, bore police insignia. Transportation for the remaining men, most likely. At the end of the hospital driveway, a policeman leaned against a street marker as he smoked a cigarette, its glow brightening as he took a puff. Even at a distance, she saw his head rotating as repeatedly he looked this way and that. His counterpart stood farther down the block, almost obscured by shrubbery. The old adage about buying insurance after the house was destroyed occurred to her. Any self-respecting murderer would have escaped their net long ago.

Still, she supposed they were enough to scare off any interlopers. When the man nearest the hospital turned away, she hastened down the steps and, at the cost of a scratch across her cheek and a splinter, thrust a passage through some landscaping shrubbery where she hid in their shadows. The building took a jog, convenient for a girl to disappear and rest for a moment.

Her stitches pulling and burning in the aftermath of effort, Wilkie leaned against the rough brick outer wall. It took every bit of her remaining energy to force herself to stand upright and move. Keeping a watchful eye on the policeman, when the way cleared again, she worked around to an opening where she finally slipped beyond his line of sight. Just as the sun broke over the horizon, she left the hospital grounds and crossed the street.

Where now? That was the question. Missoula being unfamiliar territory, she didn't even know how to reach the train depot, having been unconscious when she arrived in town. And she had no desire to revisit the county jail, the only location she did know.

A half-roof over a section of sidewalk offered respite while she thought. A bench sat beneath a darkened window fronting the last building on the block. She thought perhaps if she sat there and rested for a moment, her mind, cloudy with distress and pain, might clear and she'd know what to do. It had been imperative that she leave the hospital in case Balakov discovered his mistake, but she hadn't planned beyond that one act. Now she must.

Besides, from here she could just whip around the corner and be out of sight if someone showed up and it became necessary.

A small whimper, quickly smothered, escaped as, limp and exhausted, she settled on the bench.

The activities of the night had been much too onerous for a woman who'd been stabbed only a couple days ago. Closing her eyes, she willed the pain away, not, perhaps, very successfully. Maybe if she let the dark take her? Only for a minute, she told herself. Or maybe two.

Or until the touch on her shoulder. And a voice saying in a gruff, raspy tone, "What the hell are you doing here?"

It felt as though every last hair on her head stood on end. Wilkie snapped erect much too quickly. "Ouch," she yelped. "Sacré bleu."

A disapproving click of the tongue responded. "Language."

Even then it took a moment for Wilkie's confused mind to recognize the owner of that voice. "Why aren't you gone?"

"Why aren't you in bed asleep?" Hix countered.

"Because a girl was murdered in the room I occupied until they moved me this... yesterday... afternoon. I think it was supposed to be me who died. I thought it better if I cleared off before he discovered his error and came back."

Hix, like a marionette with cut strings, dropped onto the bench beside her. "Before who came back?"

"Balakov. Who else?" No more Laced Boots. She knew him now for a cold-blooded murderer who warranted more serious treatment.

Hix's hazel eyes narrowed, his jaw flexed. His face told a story. Anger, fear, disgust, and... awareness?

"You knew he was here?" she asked.

"I knew he was around. I saw him. I'd gone down to the rail yard after you and I..." he hesitated. "After we split up, I meant to catch a freight out of town. Then I spotted him talking to the crew who brought you in from the water tower."

Wilkie gasped. "Oh, my Lord."

"Yeah. When he left, I went over and talked to the crew. Found out they'd told him where to find you. As soon as I had the chance, I headed this way. Got held up by patrolmen walking the streets is why I'm late. They're thicker than flies on..."

He stopped. Wilkie knew what he'd been going to say anyhow. It was an old reference she'd heard boys use quite often when they didn't know their mothers—or sisters—were listening.

"I don't understand how he knew to look for me." Wilkie wanted to cry, although no tears fell. "Or how to find the train crew."

"I think you can blame the newspaper. They ran a story about the train crew bringing you in, and they were calling you Jane Doe."

"Oh." She went silent. How had she missed seeing that? Why hadn't Janet, who seemed to know everything, pointed it out to her? "News about you was reported in *The Missoulian*, too. About your capture. That's how I knew you were in jail and that I had to get you out." Funny, she thought, that they hadn't gotten around to talking about it earlier. Probably because she hadn't wanted to bring up the charges against him. Charges she knew weren't true.

Hix forced out a laugh that sounded anything but amused. "Aren't we just a pair?"

"A pair of what?" she asked, grimacing.

Shaking his head, Hix stood and reached down to her. "The morning will be heating up soon. Time for us to go."

She put her hand in his but didn't rise. Shoulders sagging, she said, "Go where, Hix? And how are we going to get there?"

"Dunno, darlin', but we can't sit here and wait for somebody to rescue us. Not you and not me." He tugged, urging her to her feet. Taking the valise from the seat beside her, he put it under his arm. "Balakov..."

"Balakov!" Her harsh whisper carried over the top of his as, finally upright, she peered over his shoulder. "Don't turn around. Maybe he won't—" she didn't finish.

"He's here? Are you sure it's him?" Hix seemed

made of stone. "Why would he hang around if he thinks he killed you?"

"I don't know. Maybe too many police around for his taste. I not sure, but I think he sees us."

"I think we can't take the chance. C'mon."

A few steps took them around the corner, concealing them from Balakov. Or Balakov from them. For the moment. Even so, Wilkie had an answer to her question. The Bulgarian had seen them, all right. The heels of his laced boots pounding on the sidewalk grew louder as he raced toward them.

Hix reached under his coat for his pistol.

Chapter Twenty-one

"Can you keep up?" Hix, peering into Wilkie's big dark eyes, thought he'd never seen such misery as that reflected there. He figured whatever'd happened in the hospital before she decided to run must've been fearsome. She'd always been frightened of Balakov, but now she seemed terrified.

And she hadn't answered him.

"Wilkie, can you run?" he asked again, realized he was pulling her along as if she could match his longer strides, and slowed.

"I don't think so," she said, her words coming on top of gasps. She pressed a hand against her wounded side.

No. He didn't think so either.

They rushed past a door, the room inside dark, the shades drawn. Hix glanced behind them. Nope. Balakov hadn't reached the corner as yet. Maybe there was time to... before the thought was complete, he stopped and went back. Reversing his pistol, he used the butt to smash through the window in the door. Reaching in, he opened the door from the inside and pushed it open.

That was it, though. When Wilkie started through, he pulled her back. "No. We're not going in." Half-carrying her, he hustled her on, guiding them into the alley with only a second to spare before he heard Balakov, boots sliding on some gravel, turn the corner. The Bulgarian had gained on them. No surprise.

Wilkie gave a breathless little laugh into his ear. "A ruse. Hope it works."

Yeah. So did he. Force Balakov to stop and reconnoiter. Slow the murdering bastard down long enough for them to give him the slip. He'd almost be glad to see a bluecoat looming up in front of them. Almost. God only knows the law had been thick as ticks on a sheep the last hour as he made his way here. Looked as if most everyone, sheriff's office and police constables alike, must be gathered in this area.

Which is how his grand idea came to him. Except for Wilkie. He didn't think she'd be able to keep up.

"Hix," she said, interrupting his thoughts as though attuned to them. "Hix, there's something the matter with me. Everything seems a little... d... dar..."

Spinning, he managed to catch her before she

hit the ground.

Not that she didn't make a nice armful, but Hix found juggling his pistol, the valise, and Wilkie all at the same time somewhat taxing. *What now?* Lugging an unconscious girl around town didn't seem like much of an option. He thrust his pistol back into the holster.

He'd begun stumbling over his own feet when a towering tan-colored brick building caught his eye. Not just any building. A church. A Catholic church, St. Francis Xavier, according to the sign out front, and if his memory held true, the priests usually kept the doors unlocked day and night.

Sanctuary. That's what they called it.

And if anybody ever needed sanctuary, he guessed Wilkie did. Him, too, most likely.

Still carrying Wilkie like a baby doll, he crossed the street to the church. Putting his shoulder to the heavy door, he forced it open and staggered inside with his burden. Rows of pews lined the route to an altar. Although the huge room was dim except for a few candles burning at the front, he made out a ceiling painted with biblical scenes, and Jesus on a cross on the wall behind the altar. All quite beautiful, really, as well as peaceful and quiet. Burning candles or not, the place was empty.

Perfect. And not a place Hix hoped Balakov

would dare to enter for fear of being struck down by God.

At the fifth row pew, Hix stopped and lay Wilkie on the bench. Kneeling beside her, he patted her face. "Wake up. Wilkie, darlin', wake up."

Maybe the pats were a little harder than he intended although he didn't truly think so. At any rate, she responded by slapping at him. Eyes opening, she stared up at him before her focus changed. She blinked her eyes down hard, then opened them wide.

"I'm dead," she whispered. "Am I in heaven?"

She'd lost her mind. But then he remembered and looking skyward, huffed out a chuckle. "It's a ceiling, darlin'. A ceiling in a church. Pretty, isn't it?"

Her gaze shifted back to him. "Hix? Oh, my. Did I faint?"

"Afraid so."

"How embarrassing." She paused, her forehead knotting. "Did you call me darling? Twice?"

The question made him grin. She was recovering fast. "I might've. You got something against being a darlin'?"

This time, her hesitation went on for quite some time before she said, breathlessly and very small, "No."

***

Hix's plan to retrieve his motorcycle may not have met with Wilkie's approval, but even she didn't see any other choice.

Because, as she confessed to him, this crazy chase had only one ending if she—they—didn't agree on an achievable outcome.

"What do you mean?" he asked. "An achievable outcome."

"I mean one that is attainable," she said. "One that is permanent. Final. All the loose ends tied up. Burke, Boothe, and Venig out of business. Best case, the ladies they embezzled receive their money back, you're cleared of all charges and I..." She stopped, then started again. "I mean an outcome where we don't die."

The last part sounded a little more doubtful than he liked.

She was sitting upright in the pew by this time, still looking pale and drained, but no longer, she'd assured him, feeling as if she'd pass out.

"There is that. A tall order," he said when she finished her list. "And I think you left one thing out."

"What?"

"Balakov. Dead. Without him, the rest sounds easy."

She didn't argue.

Hix pushed himself to his feet. "You got an idea of where we start?"

"Butte. We need to enlist your aunt's help. And get with the other ladies to prove our case. And... and... "

"Think those ladies will believe you? They've probably been dealing with Burke, Boothe & Venig for a long time. They probably trust them."

At this, a small smile breaking over her face, Wilkie patted the side of the valise. "I've got the proof right here that says they oughtn't."

"Yeah, I might've known you've been keeping that valise close for a reason." The girl was smart as a whip, for certain.

Admonishing her to keep her head down, her gun handy and to hide if anybody came into the church, after a slow and careful check outside, Hix slipped out the church's side door and wended his way through a small garden until he reached the street. Keeping an eye out for any sign of Balakov, who seemed to have lost their trail, he made his way in a roundabout fashion to the county jail.

He'd been right when he surmised the police were busy surrounding the hospital. Only once did he need to hide his face, when a lone bluecoat emerged from a bakery with a fistful of doughnuts, one of which he proceeded to stuff in his mouth.

Unable to resist the temptation, Hix, telling himself Wilkie must be as hungry as he, entered the shop. He left with half a dozen sugared doughnuts packed in a brown paper package and an extra one to eat on the way. The sleepy-eyed clerk didn't even look at him as he paid.

His sense of peace held all the way to the jail. Figuring the jailer and the desk sergeant were occupied feeding their prisoners breakfast about now, Hix walked openly around back. Sure enough, he found his red Triumph leaning against the jail's stone wall. Trying to appear as though he belonged there, he released the wire they'd twisted around the tire spokes, and wheeled it away, half expecting a bullet in the back at any moment.

A block's distance between him and the jail later, he stopped. Tying the doughnut packet to the back fender platform, he cleaned the spark plug, set the choke and gave a firm stomp on the kick starter. The engine caught. Leaping aboard as the bike rumbled noisily to life and spewed a black cloud of smoke out the exhaust, he opened the throttle and sped away.

Seemed as though his luck might be changing.

***

Not that she'd ever tell Hix, but Wilkie was relieved to have a few minutes to herself. A moment with no need to hide her pain. Most importantly, quiet in which to think, to plan.

Plan! As if I can.

She slumped against the pew's hard seat back and closed her eyes. "I'm fine," she'd told Hix before he left. It had been a lie. She felt like a wrung-out mop and figured her hair, loose and streaming down her back in tangles, looked the same.

The girl's death, back there in the hospital, had changed everything. Before, she'd thought that if she could just get away clean, it would be enough. Hadn't she done her duty, if duty it was, by telling Mrs. Badrac about the embezzlement? She could, anonymously by preference, mail the documents stored in her valise to the other fraud victims. Set things in motion and let them carry on the fight. Truly, it was no business of hers. It didn't seem sensible to put herself—or Hix, for that matter—in any more danger. They weren't the police.

As for Eldon's murder... well, what had she to do with a falling out among thieves?

Except, what about poor Mr. Jackson?

And the girl—Jane Doe—murdered in her stead?

And Hix, who somehow had gotten the blame for all this?

What would Jameson do? The question hammered at her. A tear leaked down her cheek, which, disgusted with herself, she impatiently brushed away. Tears were good for nothing but to wash dirt out of a girl's eyes. Hadn't her mother told her so often enough?

The church door creaked open, interrupting these heavy-hearted thoughts. A ray of bright white sunlight peeped in through the crack. Wilkie jerked upright, watching as the ray grew wider. Just wide enough for a man to pass through sideways, causing the sunlight to flicker. Not Hix. Too tall, Wilkie thought, shrinking down farther in her pew. Too soon for him to be back, anyway.

But not the priest, either, unless the good father had taken to wearing white shirts and carrying an unsheathed gun as he entered the church. Besides, no priest would move so furtively. All of which probably meant the man was not a member of the congregation.

And he wasn't a city policeman, either, or he'd be garbed in blue.

Which left one other possibility.

Balakov.

Although unable to see him clearly, she was sure of it. Somehow, he'd tracked her down.

Wilkie willed herself still, still and silent, when she wanted to run. Maybe to scream a little. Instead, she reached for the pistol in her boot. She didn't cock it, fearing the click of the cylinder spinning would let the man know the church wasn't empty. Cautiously, she slid down in the pew until her knees rested on the floor and peered through the slats in the pew's back. The first time she'd seen Balakov she'd crawled under a bench. If her side didn't hurt so badly, she'd do it again, but this time, folding herself in half was out of the question.

He must've been waiting for his eyes to attune to the dimmer light because several seconds passed before he started up the center aisle. The hard heels of his boots thudded against the floor with every step. He moved slowly, checking each pew as he went.

Wilkie's thumb caught on her pistol's hammer as she prepared to cock the weapon, noise or no noise.

A voice from the front halted the action, both hers and Balakov's.

"Welcome to our church, sir. I'm Father Alonso, pastor here." A man spoke in a rich baritone. "Can I help you?"

The newcomer didn't reply right away, but then he said, "Maybe. Have you seen a man and a woman? Young. The woman is good looking, with dark hair and eyes. She has been hurt and needs help to walk." He paused. "The man has a bruised face and wears a flat cap." He paused for the second time before adding, "She may be in danger."

Wilkie had been wise to hide. Balakov's voice and accent were unmistakable.

"I have seen no one," Father Alonso said. He had an accent of his own but still, something, an intonation, seeped through that hinted he might've been fibbing. She'd thought she heard something once when she and Hix had been talking earlier. Had the priest, in his turn, been listening to them?

"A parishioner told me a girl was murdered last night over at the hospital," Father Alonso continued, "Are you, sir, looking for whoever did it? I don't recognize you as a policeman."

Wilkie's stomach clenched. Father Alonso tread over dangerous ground with his questions. She had no doubt the Bulgarian felt few qualms at killing whoever got in his way. Priest or no priest.

But this time, he surprised her. "I am a friend from out of town, only looking for this woman. To help her."

"Ah. I am sorry, but I cannot assist you. I have

not seen a young, dark-haired woman today." The priest remained standing at the front. He didn't come forward, but he didn't leave, either.

Wilkie's stomach muscles eased, but only a little. She couldn't relax yet.

After a few ticks of the clock, Balakov seemed to realize they were at a standoff. "You are sure you haven't seen the woman?" he asked again.

"I am sure."

"Well..." Balakov nodded, casting one more suspicious look around the church. As though against his better judgment, he moved toward the door, boot heels thumping a threat.

"Peace be with you, my son," Father Alonso said as Balakov paused at the entrance. Only when, finally, the ray of sunshine disappeared, did the priest move from his position at the altar and come forward. He stopped at the end of the pew where Wilkie crouched.

"He's gone. You may come out now," he said softly, almost in a whisper.

"Wait," she answered just as softly.

Wise, as it turned out. A full minute, maybe more, passed before the door eased open again and Balakov peered in. The priest, who appeared to be praying, looked up.

"Yes?" he said, smiling. "You have a question?"

"No." The door slammed shut. This time it

remained closed.

Wilkie noticed the priest's smile had turned into a grimace. Sweat rose in small drops along his temples.

"I sense evil in that man," he said at last. "And yet, he says he wants to help you. It is you he's talking about, yes?"

Wilkie snorted. She pulled herself from the floor and regained her seat in the pew. "The only help he wants to give me is to see me dead."

"He means to kill you?"

"Yes. I have something he's been hired to take from me—no matter what he has to do. He murdered that girl at St. Patrick because he thought she was me."

Silence. Then Father Alonso said, "So that *was* blood I saw on his shirt. From a distance, I couldn't be sure. Even so, I knew that man has dead eyes."

Feeling more than a little sick, Wilkie stuffed her pistol back in her boot, trying to hide the motion from the priest. "I think you're lucky you didn't get too close to him."

"Yes. I, too, think I am lucky. And so are you."

"I am. If you hadn't spoken up when you did... well, a moment longer and he would've found me."

Staring at each other in the dim church, the

welcome and familiar sound of a motorcycle broke the silence.

Wilkie stood and grabbed her valise. "My real friend has come for me. I'll get out of here." She smiled. "Father, you told Balakov a fib. I hope you don't feel penance is necessary."

Chuckling, he bowed slightly. "No penance. I did not lie. Truly, I did not see you, even though I knew you were here."

"Thank you." Wilkie couldn't help thinking the clergy weren't above taking truth to the edge when they considered it necessary. And in this case, thank goodness!

Belying Balakov's claim she needed help to walk, she took herself down the aisle to the entrance. And even then, though she knew Hix waited for her outside, she took time to scan the area before stepping from the church.

Chapter Twenty-two

Hix felt an odd lurch inside as Wilkie rounded the corner and hurried toward where he stood beside the motorcycle. She leaned slightly to her left, favoring her wound, but at least she'd regained some color in her cheeks.

His eyes narrowed. Regained some color, yes. But he saw worry on her face, too, and if he didn't know better, fear. Fear in a girl who'd sneaked into a jail and picked the lock to his cell? Moreover, right under the nose of a jailer as he dozed on the job?

He kept the motorcycle running. "What's happened?" he asked when she reached his side.

"Balakov." Wilkie's dark eyes swept the area before coming around to meet his. "He showed up at the church. Even came inside."

"While you were there? He didn't see you?"

She shrugged, but her darting eyes and tight lips showed she wasn't as sanguine as she pretended. "Apparently not. The priest there, Father Alonso, convinced him the church was empty.

But I don't know. He asked only about me as if he knew we'd separated. Could just be Balakov backed off thinking we'd get together again. That I'd lead him to you. And keep an eye out. Maybe I did."

"How long ago?"

"A few minutes. We should go, Hix. Right now. I don't know where he's gotten to. He may be able to hear the motorcycle. That's how I found you. The Triumph guided me."

"Climb on, darlin'. You're right. Besides the fact, Balakov isn't the only one after me. It's only a matter of time before the police catch up."

Hix cut the string holding the packet of donuts onto the platform and handed it to her.

"You hungry?"

"Starved." She smiled. Her nose twitched as she took a hearty sniff. "Is this donuts I smell?"

"It is. Hop on. We'll find someplace out of town to eat."

An old hand at riding passenger by now, Wilkie settled onto the platform with her valise, and the donuts squeezed between them and grabbed Hix around the waist. Just for a second, he could've sworn she leaned her head into him, but then the pressure withdrew. He goosed the throttle, dirt spewing from under the rear tire as they shot away.

A frantic cry from Wilkie alerted him all was not well. "What?" he shouted over the engine's clatter. Except he had an idea.

"Balakov."

The warning heralded the loss of his cap, gone as a bullet snagged the cloth and sent it flying.

Wilkie's shriek rang like a clarion bell. "Hix?"

He felt no pain. "Hang tight," he said, taking up a zigzag course. They didn't topple over at the quick changes of direction, so he figured he must be riding fine.

The Triumph ran wide open as they made a skidding turn and shot down the first cross street they came to. Hix caught a glance of the Bulgarian, on foot, racing to keep within shooting distance. And doing a pretty good job of it, damn his soul.

A second shot plowed the dirt in front of them. A clear miss, but close enough to tell he had the range, if not the target.

Hix took a sharp left turn back onto Main Street, another shot following them, where they found more people forming an early morning crowd. Men on the way to work. Women going about errands. He swerved, avoiding a boy chasing a small black dog that darted between horses, and impeded a Hambly Brother's delivery truck.

The truck's air horn blared.

All to the good, except for the noise the Triumph made and the looks it drew as they raced through the mélange. But if residents didn't care for the way Hix rode the motorcycle, a rare item of interest of Missoula's streets, they cared even less for Balakov shooting in their midst.

As he swept past a store, Hix saw a woman pointing behind him and yelling. A glance to the side showed a couple men running toward the shooter. They paid bare notice to anyone else. A man on a horse racing faster even than the Triumph headed in that direction as well. The quick glimpse allowed Hix to recognize one of the men on foot. Deputy Bodeen.

The deputy halted, staring at the motorcycle, then plunged forward again.

"Hold on," Hix told Wilkie, but felt her slip and cry out as they sped around yet another corner. He reversed direction once, twice, until finally, a clear road lay ahead as they left the commotion behind. He heard a shot, then a second, neither aimed at him. Two different guns. One a rifle. The man on horseback had been carrying a rifle.

They went on for a few more miles before reaching a copse of cottonwoods that marked a small stream, and he pulled off the road.

Wilkie's valise dropped to the ground first, joined by the slightly smashed packet of donuts.

Then Wilkie herself, only she caught herself before she hit the dirt. She leaned against the same tree where Hix had parked the Triumph.

She reached for him, her hands shaking. "You're bleeding."

Yeah, he felt it now. A scrape deep enough to draw blood. The bullet that had stolen his cap took a little skin along with it. "It's nothing," he said. "You all right? You weren't hit?"

"No. I'm good. I almost fell off once, though." Fumbling in a pocket of her riding skirt, she procured a hanky, miraculously still snowy white, and attempted to dab his head with it.

He grabbed her hand and held it still. "Don't. It's all right, Wilkie. I'm fine. Here, I'll wash the blood off in the creek while you share out those donuts."

She studied him a moment before electing to take him at his word. "We need to decide what to do, Hix. Which way we should go."

"We will. Soon as I get back. I'll... you wait here." Stepping behind some bushes, he knelt by the creek, one that ran clear and cold over a jumble of rocks. Its frigid temperature felt both good and painful at the same time. He wasn't quite as fine as he'd let on to Wilkie. To tell the truth, his head plain hurt, and he came over as being a little top heavy. Not a weakness he wanted to show to her.

She'd found a sun-warmed rock to sit on, perching there with her hands clasped before her, when he emerged from the bushes. Opening her mouth, she started to say something, then stopped and waved at the two small stacks of donuts.

"Dig in," she said, watching with narrowed eyes as he joined her.

He sank down on a neighboring stump.

The donuts may not have tasted as good as the one he'd had at the bakery earlier, but he choked down his share anyway, hoping these stayed in his stomach where they belonged. From the look on her face, Wilkie wasn't having much better luck. Anticipation gone wrong. Same, Hix thought, as the simple act of doing his aunt and this girl a favor had done.

Wilkie flicked the last grain of sugar from her fingers onto the ground—"treats for the ants," she said—and went down to rinse her hands in the creek. When she returned, her lips were set.

"I imagine you'd like to leave me off right here and forget you ever saw me," she said, perched on the rock as primly as a girl with two buttons missing on her sweater can.

He half-smiled.

"Not that I'd blame you," she went on. "But I hope you won't. Leave me here, I mean."

Listening carefully, Hix wondered if that meant she also hoped he wouldn't forget her. Huh. Small chance of that. He'd been beat up, hunted like prey, jailed for murder and—was he forgetting something? Oh yeah. Shot at. Several times. He'd also been rescued from pending death and been broken out of jail. All since he'd met her. What was it? Three or four days ago?

A lifetime.

"Didn't figure on it," he said.

"Oh. Good."

From the look on her face, that wasn't the answer she expected. But by George, for all his faults, he'd never been the kind of man to run out on his promises, and he'd promised his aunt he'd get her home. Or at least, to where she wanted to go. He meant to see the job through.

His attention had wandered, but it came back when she sat up straight, wincing a little so he figured her stitches must've pulled. Her expression was real serious.

"I think," she said, "that we need to go back to Butte and, once and for all, untangle this predicament we're in."

"Predicament? Is that what you think this is?"

"What do you call it?"

"I call it..." he hesitated. "I call it one hell of a mess."

Huffing, she sent him a one-cornered smile. "Yes. That too. But I believe there's a way out."

"Yeah? What? How?"

Now she looked uncertain. "I don't know if you'll agree, but in my opinion, we ought to talk to Mrs. Badrac first thing. You see, I believe the fix depends on something I saw, something I'm certain your aunt can tell me if I'm reading right. If I am—"

But about then Hix lost track of what she was saying because the sound of several horses headed in their direction registered on his consciousness. He held up one finger in a shushing motion and listened harder.

Wilkie's eyes widened. "What is that?"

"Who, you mean. A posse."

"Posse? What makes you think so?"

"Only reason I can imagine for a bunch of riders to be racing their horses down this road is if they're chasing somebody. Namely me... or us."

"But... but haven't they gone after Balakov instead of you? Instead of us? Father Alonso knows about him. He'll tell them. Surely he *has* told them."

Hix appreciated the way she included herself. "Unless," he said, his bitterness plain, "he doubled back and murdered the priest, too."

He'd have given anything to take his words

back soon as they left his mouth. They didn't sit well given the look on her face and the way she turned three shades paler. Lord knows she could already have passed for a ghost.

"Or maybe," he hastened to add, "the good father just hasn't got a chance to talk to them yet. Either way, I don't want to be here when they arrive. You ready to go?"

She stood and gathered her valise. "When you are."

To Hix's relief, the bike's engine caught on only the third try. Wilkie hopped, a bit laboriously, onto the rear fender platform and gripped him around the waist. As soon as she settled, valise between them, they were off. Hix tried his best not to hear Wilkie's muffled grunt when every now and then they hit bottom on the rutted road. His admiration for her grew when she never once voiced a complaint.

Some hours later, having bypassed Deer Lodge by a slow, circuitous route, they reached the cut-off to the Jackson ranch, the faded sign still pointing the way. In the pasture closest to the road, the mule they'd ridden into town grazed side by side with a second long-eared beastie that looked to be an exact replica.

Hix stopped but kept the motor running.

"This is where Eldon and Balakov bushwhacked me. After they murdered Mr. Jackson." His voice thinned with the anger running through him. Anger at them and their evil deeds. Anger at himself for letting them take him unawares.

"It all looks the same." He sounded sad. "Wonder how Jackson's old dog is doing. Do you suppose anybody is feeding him? And taking care of the livestock?"

Wilkie's arms pressed harder around him. "The mules look all right."

His eyes rested on them. "Yeah. They do. Long as they've got grass and water, they'll be fine. But the dog—"

He felt Wilkie's shudder,

"Let's go," she said. "Maybe when we... when we get done, we can come back and make sure someone took him in. If not—" She took a breath. "If not, I'll take him myself."

A rash promise, in Hix's opinion, considering that she might be putting in time behind bars right alongside him. Or did the Deer Lodge prison have facilities for women? He didn't know. It had never mattered before.

They started off again. A couple miles farther down the road, very near where they ran out of gas the first time, they passed this way, a tire went flat.

"What else can go wrong?" Wilkie fumed as she dismounted.

Hix, undismayed since he'd been happy it hadn't happened sooner, got busy with patches and pump. "That's why I carry these. Wouldn't be any different with a motor car. Worse. They've got four tires to worry about."

Wilkie walked about, stretching her legs while Hix worked. Finally, tire patched and tools stowed, he called to her to mount up.

They pulled into Butte as night fell, the Triumph's headlamp lighting a course through the emptying streets. Slowing to avoid a rider-less horse that, due to its determined path through vehicles and pedestrians appeared to have a destination in mind, Hix turned his head only a little when Wilkie prodded his cheek.

"Look left," she said. "We're passing Burke, Boothe & Venig law offices. Second floor. The lights are still on."

The form of a man passed in front of the window as Hix craned his neck. Since he was trying to keep one eye on the horse, he almost missed seeing the man gesticulate with wildly swinging arms while holding a pistol in his hand. Hix, sure enough, felt Wilkie's arms tighten around him, however, and heard the catch of her breath.

"Is that Balakov?" Her voice shook.

He wasn't able to stop the involuntary clench of his fingers that cranked the motorcycle's engine and, in a sudden spurt, almost set them onto the back wheel. Wilkie let out a squeak and held on. The thing is, this time as he eyed the window, he saw they'd drawn the man's attention. He didn't figure it boded well, no matter the identity of the man standing there.

"Is it?" she asked again.

"Looks as if."

Once past the window, he didn't see any point in trying to hide his destination. Balakov and the lawyers knew he and Wilkie had arrived and where they were likely to go next. He took the most direct route to his aunt's house and drove around to the rear.

Even when they stopped, Wilkie clung to him. "How did he beat us here?" she demanded. "How did he get away from Missoula and not only the city police but the sheriff's men? Why didn't they catch him? Are they still after us?"

Hix held the motorcycle upright and balanced on unsteady legs as he waited for her to get off so he could, too. Most of all, he wished she didn't sound so hysterical. After all they'd been through together, he was a little afraid she might shatter like a dropped glass now they'd reached Butte.

"Wilkie, darlin', you know as much as I do.

What say we go in and talk to Magdalena. See if she's heard anything."

Wilkie seemed to deflate. "Sorry. Yes. All right."

So slowly that Hix knew it hurt her, she dismounted. He followed suit, propping the bike against the porch decking.

"Your aunt, she'll be surprised to see me again," Wilkie said, hesitating as Hix led her forward.

"Not at all," came Magdalena's disembodied voice from inside the dark house. "Come in. I've been expecting you."

Hix's laugh caught in his throat. "One step ahead of anybody else as usual, eh, Auntie?"

Her reply failed the lightheartedness of what he'd meant as a compliment. "Not this time, dear boy. This time, sadly enough, I am still catching up."

"But you are catching up?"

"Oh, yes. I just hope it's not too late. Come in. Hurry now." The door swung wider, allowing them passage. "Someone has been watching the house for most of the day, and I'm certain they still are. Are they looking for you?"

"Expect so. We... Wilkie and me... we're in a peck of trouble, aunt."

No lights shone inside. Hix, used to the house's vagaries, took the one step up into the kitchen.

Wilkie cried out as she stumbled over it, his warning coming too late.

"What is it?" Magdalena's question sharpened. "What has happened? Young lady, are you hurt?"

"She's been stabbed," Hix answered for Wilkie. "Spent a couple nights in the hospital. In Butte."

"Eldon?" Magdalena asked on a note of dread.

"No. Some crazy galoot we met along the way. Eldon saved his devilry for me."

"Most of it," Wilkie found the breath to mention. "The stab wound isn't the only blood I've shed."

"I remember," Hix said, although truthfully, he'd almost forgotten the incident at Jackson's place. He locked the door behind them. Not that the lock would do much good against determined invaders. A couple hard kicks would bring the whole door down, though it was a good sturdy piece of oak.

He smiled, remembering Wilkie and her lock picks. Good thing not many were as proficient as she was at silently overcoming such obstacles. Most would make more noise and give a little advance warning.

Inside the kitchen, warm and smelling of fried ham and Magdalena's famous peach pie, his aunt had left a small lamp burning. It stunk of kerosene while giving off enough light for them to see each other and not fall over the chairs. Or the cat stretched languidly on the linoleum floor. Not much beyond that. A piece of cardboard covered the window over the sink. Another blocked the window in the eating nook. His aunt had been busy.

He guessed she hadn't been joking about someone watching the place. While cardboard wouldn't do a thing to block a bullet, at least it might spoil any chance of a "stray" shot finding a target.

The way he relaxed of a sudden left him feeling limp as an empty oat sack.

Magdalena, insisting they sit and rest their bones, bustled around the kitchen fixing them a bite of supper. Hix wasn't about to say no to one of his aunt's meals, even if she did make excuses, insisting it poor stuff made up of things she had around. Like the ham, and the pie, and a pot of garden bean cooked with bacon and onion.

Stirring the fire and taking thin-sliced cabbage dressed with cream and vinegar from the icebox, she placed the food on the table. Plates, the nice ones with flowers around the rim followed. And the second best silverware. Hix smiled to himself, thinking he'd have to tell Wilkie she was privileged. That his aunt had made a special effort for her. Sure wasn't on his behalf.

The thought brought the tension of the day back. His smile faded. What was Magdalena going to think when he told her about Eldon? About the thefts and the conspiracies? And the murders?

Dread came over him so strong it almost killed his appetite. But not quite. His gaze fixed on Wilkie, matching him bite for bite. He couldn't remember his last real meal, and he bet she couldn't either. He wasn't counting the donuts from the start of this day. That had been a long time ago.

His aunt, quickly clearing the table but leaving the dishes in a pan of hot water, brought brandy instead of coffee when they finished the meal.

"Now," she said, filling her own crystal brandy snifter with a generous helping of fine old Laird's Applejack brandy and leaving the bottle open on the table. She twirled the glass. "We must speak. Wilhelmina, you first, I think. Start from the beginning. Tell us how you became involved."

"Do we have time for this?" Hix started to gulp his brandy, noticed his aunt's disapproving eye on him, and sipped instead.

Wilkie wet her tongue with the liquor, tasted, and followed up with a swallow. "Some of it, I think. Cards on the table, as Uncle Jameson would say." She tasted her drink again. Sighing

then, she cocked her head to the side as if thinking, and said, "My uncle is... was... renown for his
expertise in opening safes, vaults, or any other
locked item, large or small. He took great pride
in using finesse rather than brute force, by which
I mean dynamite or nitroglycerin. Those were
saved as a last resort or big jobs. And although he
has... had a set of English steel drill bits suitable
for boring through metal, he preferred to use his
talents. And, of course, he always kept his clients'
secrets."

Magdalena smiled kindly at her. "You told me
some of this already, I remember, but I was dis-
tracted at the time. Say again, how do you come
into the equation?"

If he'd been a dog, Hix's ears would've pricked.
He and Wilkie had been too busy to talk much
while they'd been together, or else she'd been
mad and not talking. Or one or the other of them
hurting too much to think about anything else.
Frankly, she'd been kind of leery of him, too. Or
no, she'd been *real* leery of him or of saying anything much about herself.

Right now she was gnawing on her lower lip
as if still undecided whether she could trust him.
Him or Magdalena.

"Damn it, girl." He slammed his glass onto the
table. "What have I ever done except try to help

you? What difference do you think it makes to me if you—"

"Hixson Forry!" Magdalena exclaimed. "You stop shouting at this girl right now. Can't you see you're frightening her?"

Hix set the brake on his temper outburst. No, as matter of fact he couldn't see that Wilkie had taken any fright. Hurt her feelings, maybe, as those big brown eyes welled with tears all the sudden. But scared?

Funny thing is, he got teary-eyed himself when she said, "I know, Hix. You've been nothing but kind and helpful. I don't know what I would've done without you. I just don't know where to start."

That wasn't the part that made him go all soppy, though. No siree. The soppy part came about because of what she so kindly didn't say. She knew he'd just as soon Magdalena never heard how the helping worked both ways.

A hard core relaxed inside, and, sitting forward, he winked at her. At last, he'd learn how their present predicament came about. He was tired of hearing a piece here and a piece there. Shrugging out of his jacket, he took another swallow of his aunt's good apple brandy.

"Start at the beginning," he said.

So she did.

Chapter Twenty-three

"Jameson Van Slyke, my uncle, is... was... well, I guess some people would call him a yeggman—or a safecracker. He preferred to be called a lock-smith. It probably depended on what side of the fence you're standing on. His business consists of opening any lock that seems impenetrable, where the key was lost or..." she hesitated "... or the opening of it needed to remain clandestine."

Magdalena made a small sound, which Hix echoed with a snort. Both of them knew this but repeating it helped Wilkie to think.

"There are legitimate reasons this can be the case," Wilkie glared at them, daring either to contradict her. "And when Burke, Boothe, & Venig, known to be a reputable firm of attorneys contacted him, my uncle thought the excuse they gave made sense."

Wilkie took another sip of her apple brandy. The liquor made her stomach feel better than at any time since she'd boarded the train east to Butte with Jameson. Even better than the food, if that were possible. Oddly enough, she felt as if she were blushing on the inside, turning her all warm and fuzzy. It was nice.

It also made Hix's simple act of shedding his jacket seem oddly intimate. He looked tough and capable, sitting there in his shirt sleeves with his underarm holster fully revealed at last. He made her feel safe.

But thinking of Hix as their savior was a dangerous precedent to let start, she thought, watching the way Magdalena's cat, a long-haired tortoise-shell beauty, woke up and pricked her ears toward the door. Safety was a total illusion. She and everyone else in this room had never been in greater danger. The sensation surrounded her like a cold fog.

"I'd best keep this story short," she said. "Mrs. Badrac, I'm afraid you have company gathering as we speak."

Magdalena's lips tightened. "I know. I warned my neighbors to stay inside tonight. In the morning, if it is to be, they will pick up the pieces."

"We'll be all right," Hix said, but going by the way he loosened the flap on his holster, Wilkie didn't think he believed it himself.

"What excuse?" Pouring herself a tad more brandy, Magdalena offered the bottle around to Hix and Wilkie. "I want to be very clear. Tell me again, what excuse did Mr. Boothe give your uncle?"

Wilkie declined the applejack with a wave of her hand. "In his letter, he said some papers dealing with their clients private business had inadvertently been placed in a local bank's vault. To retrieve them required both the attorney of note and the client, although the client by herself could demand them. The attorneys, afraid of being deemed incompetent, hoped to get the papers back without the client's knowledge." She snorted. "He said proper precautions had been put in place, so it never happened again."

Magdalena's eyes went narrow and beady. "And?" Her tone could've stripped the bark off a tree.

"And my uncle, although he figured it might not be strictly legal, thought maybe it wasn't strictly illegal, either. Nothing was being stolen, after all. Just some misplaced paperwork put back in its correct order. Mr. Boothe, the attorney he dealt with, seemed on the up and up, and has a high reputation in Butte. Jameson checked. Boothe also offered an excellent fee, so my uncle agreed."

"And?" The tone was only slightly less sharp. Hix sent his aunt a worried look.

"Jameson has... had been teaching me the business since my tenth birthday. He liked to bring me along on jobs that didn't seem dangerous. This is the first time he brought me along on a truly important job. He said if all seemed well, we'd go into the bank together. He said," she smiled at the memory, "I could watch the master, meaning himself, at work and if there were no alarms, he'd let me try my hand on the Spooner Bank's big Mosler safe. You see, while I opened a safe in a nearby town once, I had no real experience with anything like a Mosler."

Wilkie neglected to mention the part about the safe she'd opened previously being a much smaller one located under the bar in the most prosperous bordello in town. Or that Jameson had been kept busy while she managed the job on her own.

"Yes, yes," Magdalena said, her impatience growing. "Your uncle became sick, and you went alone. But there were alarms, yes?"

"Yes. I barely escaped without being caught. Balakov and the bank manager," she added for Hix's benefit, "who'd evidently been forewarned."

"By whom?" Magdalena asked.

"I don't know. Possibly the bank manager had detected some irregularities. Or..." A possibility occurred to her. "Or Balakov, who'd taken a job at the bank while working for the attorneys, had failed at retrieving the papers, which is why they hired Jameson."

Hix cocked an eyebrow. "Weren't you scared?"

Starting a denial, Wilkie changed her mind. She might as well tell the truth. "Terrified. But crazy happy when I completed the job and got away clean. I thought Jameson would be so proud of me."

"And was he?" Magdalena's eyebrows lifted over her sharp, dark eyes.

Wilkie's smile almost split her face. "Yes." Then her smile faded. "But he acted so strangely when I got back to the hotel, I knew something was wrong. At first, I thought he might be drunk, but he figured out about the embezzlement scam fast enough after I pointed it out. It turned out he was sick. And the next morning, even worse. He told me I had to go to the attorney's office and complete the deal. But, afraid they'd try to take advantage of me because I'm young, he told me to doctor up my face and dress like an older woman. I guess my efforts didn't fool anybody."

"Darlin'," Hix drawled, "that was the poorest excuse for a disguise I've ever seen."

Magdalena shot a glance at Hix and nodded agreement.

Lips compressed, even though wondering who else Hix knew who went in for disguises, Wilkie decided to ignore their jibes, and went on with her story. "Mr. Boothe tried to cheat me... us... out of the agreed-upon fee. And though I was already undecided on whether to deliver all the paperwork, his dishonesty decided me. I withheld the amended files, along with the copies Jameson had made of part of the original. It all worked out that Mr. Boothe's reluctance to cause a commotion in his law office where he had clients waiting gave me enough time to get out of there."

"Then you met Eldon. My nephew." A world of sadness mixed with anger colored Magdalena's staccato interjection.

"Yes." Wilkie paused. "You know what happened then. After Hix and I left here, it didn't take long to discover Eldon was part of the Burke, Boothe & Venig gang. All in, as gamblers like to say."

Hix shot her a funny look.

"And there's a man who works for them who follows Burke's orders explicitly. If he's told to dispose of someone, that someone is soon dead. Man, woman, or, I wouldn't be surprised, child. And that's who is out there right now with the intention of cleaning up the loose ends."

Magdalena frowned. "Loose ends?"

"Us," Hix said. "He killed Eldon, although I still don't know why. He also killed an innocent old man who'd helped Wilkie and me."

"And, mistaking her for me, he crept in and murdered a defenseless girl in the Missoula hospital," Wilkie added.

Drawing herself up, Magdalena's face paled although her voice remained steady. "I suspect then, that it was he who killed my husband. The sheriff said Bartholomew killed himself, but I know better. He would never have suicided. This man probably killed Eldon's father, too. I wonder if my nephew knew."

Hix stared into the distance. "I think so," he said. And a second later, as if it were an explanation, "They never got along."

At that point, the tortoise-shell cat got up and stalked away to crouch in the darkest corner of the kitchen, sheltering between the rungs of a stool.

Wilkie took the cat's action as a sign. She blew out the light.

"Oh, dear," Magdalena said with no trace of agitation. She sounded resigned.

Hix's chair legs scraped the floor as he pushed back and sprang to his feet.

***

The next instant, the threat announced itself

with little fanfare. A step onto the porch outside the kitchen, causing a board to squeak. The spin of the doorknob and a *snick* when, found locked, it came to a stop and was released. Then the window by the eating nook shattered as someone slammed a pistol barrel into it. The cardboard tore, and the pistol roared; the muzzle flashed bright in the dark kitchen. Wilkie had no idea where the bullet went.

Glass was still falling from the window frame when she grabbed onto Magdalena, pulled her from her chair, and dragged her beneath the heavy oak table. Wilkie tucked in alongside her. She didn't feel the pain radiating from her side until afterward; only gratitude the older woman was so tiny.

Hix, meanwhile, had responded faster than she thought possible, the glare from the exploded cartridge glowing on her retinas as he fired back, point-blank. A man cried out. An uneven thud of footsteps indicated retreat of a wounded man.

"Get down," Magdalena hissed at Hix. "That one is not alone."

Hix didn't answer. He sidled over the window where, moving the torn cardboard aside, he peered out. "There's three of them that I know of," he reported, "plus the one I nicked."

"The neighbors will have sent for the police,"

Magdalena said. "They'll be here soon. Please, Hix. Just stay down and wait. Let them handle these people. The doors are locked. We'll be safe."

Hix didn't say anything.

Wilkie thought it was up to her to explain. "We don't know if the police will be in time, Mrs. Badrac. These men, they won't wait for the police to organize. We have to be prepared to defend ourselves."

"Hix has already scared them off. That man ran. You heard him. The others will not be so eager to attack now they've seen we mean business." Magdalena poked her head out from under the table and grunting, started to rise.

A bullet thudded into the wall behind the table. Low, so that if they'd been only crouched, one of them would've been hit.

Magdalena squeaked as Wilkie pulled her back. "That depends on who the four are. I don't think they can afford to wait. Afford to let us live."

Hix, giving a short chuckle, moved over to see out the glassless window. "Plus, it's personal to Balakov. He doesn't like being bested."

"Balakov?" Magdalena seemed bewildered. "There's a Balakov who works at the bank. Is he involved?"

"He may work at the bank, but his loyalty

belongs to the lawyers." On the move again, Hix ducked below the window sill and hunched over to the sink window for a different view. "Two of them are milling around by the corner of the barn," he reported. "I figure they've got some kind of plan going."

"Surrounding us," Wilkie said. "Ma'am, are there any other ways into the house except for the front door?"

Magdalena thought a moment. "The cellar," she said on a gasp. "But they won't get into the house from there. I can see to that. It's the front door we must worry about." Magdalena pushed Wilkie gently aside, determinedly crawling from shelter.

Wilkie, remembering the first time she'd met the old lady she had been carrying a derringer, believed her.

She scooted out from under the table, too. "And I'll see to the front door." Ignoring Hix's, "Wilkie, no," and checking her .32 as she went, she felt her way down the dark hall to the foyer with its umbrella stand, the small table, and chairs.

A little turned around, she fell over the elephant's foot before, side aching fiercely, she sat on one of the chairs to keep guard, the pistol clasped in both hands.

Meanwhile, back in the kitchen, she heard

Magdalena ask Hix something, something that included her name, and Hix rumble a reply. What had Magdalena's question been? she wondered. And what had he answered?

Just then Hix banged off another shot. Magdalena yelped, and a loud crash indicated someone had fallen.

At that instant, almost as though an explosive charge propelled it, the front door slammed open, and a man plunged through.

Balakov! Even in the dim light, she recognized his shape and the way he moved.

Wilkie thought maybe her heart was going to fail her. Silly, come right down to it, but for some reason, she hadn't counted on having to deal with him. She'd believed Hix would engage him, leaving Magdalena and her to contend with lesser men, not an accomplished killer like the Bulgarian.

How was she to fight him? There seemed only one way.

He didn't see her at first, sitting on a chair in the unlit room as though expecting a guest. Then she moved, just a little, and he did. The knife in his hand turned toward her. And he smiled. A smile she couldn't see, but one she felt.

"Ah," he said. "Here you are. You tricked me once, but I have got you now."

A vision of the dead girl at the hospital rushed through her head. The blood. The gaping wounds.

Knives. She hated knives. Why did everyone have to come at her with sharp-edged weapons?

He made a twisting motion with the knife it's polished blade gleaming even in the darkened foyer. Not hurrying, he took a step toward as if anticipating what came next.

Aim for the target you can't miss, Wilkie, a voice said. *That's how you fight him. The chest. Go for the heart.*

Almost as though she heard Jameson's voice, or maybe Hix's, she couldn't be sure, Wilkie lifted the .32 from her lap.

"Now, Wilkie!" the voice shouted.

Obediently, as though pointing her finger, she aimed the pistol at Balakov and pulled the trigger. One time, two times.

Her ears rang from the noise in the enclosed room.

Balakov stood there, his mouth a black hole rounding into an O.

Oh Lord, she thought. I missed. How could I miss?

The knife dropped, turned a somersault, and landed point down, sticking straight into Magdalena's beautiful red fir floor.

She thought he tried to say something as he toppled forward, his hand coming to rest on top of the knife's hilt. A dark puddle seeped from under his body.

Ever so slowly, she got up and stood looking down at him.

Footsteps pounded toward her from the kitchen. Hix first, Magdalena right behind.

"Wilkie!" Hix gathered her into his arms. "Are you hurt, sweetheart? Bring a lamp, Magdalena. We need light."

He didn't seem to hear her when she said, "I'm all right, Hix. I'm not hurt."

"Light the lamp," he said again, and Magdalena said, "What if—"

"Don't worry," he told her. "They're done. Burke is lying on your porch, not dead, but out of the fight. One of the men has a gimpy leg, and this one—" he nudged Balakov's body with the toe of his boot "—isn't gonna be getting up again. Ever."

He turned so Wilkie's back was to the bloody corpse. Considerate of him but wasted. She doubted she'd ever get the vision out of her brain. What would happen to her now?

A couple more shots echoed from somewhere along the street. Men called out; lantern-light gleamed in the night.

Help had finally arrived. Still, nobody needed to tell her that if she hadn't shot Balakov, she'd be the one lying dead instead of him. He would've had plenty of time to kill her—or maybe all of them—and quietly disappear.

Wilkie let herself lean against Hix. Then, as if it were the most natural thing in the world, which it might've been considering she'd spent a good many hours on the back of a motorcycle hanging onto him, she wrapped her arms around his waist and left them there while Magdalena finally lit the lamp.

Hix called me sweetheart. The words sang in her heart.

Chapter Twenty-four

The sun shone through the empty window frame in Magdalena's kitchen nook. It's light revealed the previous night's damage in clear detail. Broken doors, broken windows, a smashed chair told of wild rampage. Bullet holes pockmarked the walls and even the floor. Magdalena's flowered china lay in pieces on the floor.

Full to overflowing, the room vibrated under the rumble of male voices. Besides Magdalena, Hix, and Wilkie, what seemed a whole squad of men—most attired in uniforms—wandered in and out. Wilkie didn't know what they all were doing. One, probably the most useful, had found the broom and busied himself sweeping up broken window glass.

Even Magdalena had stopped trying to keep up with everyone. If any of them wanted coffee, he was invited to help himself. She set out a stack of cups and left a full pot on the back of the stove to keep warm. There were plenty of takers, enticed by the rich aroma.

The man in charge had arrived a half-hour ago clutching a satchel. Periodically he would reach into it and withdraw a document, which he read. Silently, to himself. Although he wasn't in uniform, he had taken a chair at the head of the table and was presiding over what had turned into an official investigation.

Or maybe, Wilkie thought, a tremor of fear passing through her, a trial of sorts.

Boothe, the attorney, sat next to him, sweating and pale, but seeming confident. Another man, white-haired, small, with a stern face, perched next to Magdalena and patted her hand every once in a while. Wilkie had no idea who these men were. Except for Boothe, of course.

Hix had taken a stance behind Wilkie. Could be he thought she might faint if this ordeal got to be too much. Could be, she reflected, he was right. An excuse for her to keep in mind if the interview—that's what the man in charge called it—went south.

Boothe seemed to be trying to tell the man in charge something. Gradually, Wilkie realized that, though he wore no uniform, the fellow was the chief of police. He appeared weary as if he'd been up all right. Wilkie saved her sympathy. So had she and Hix and Magdalena—and fought a life or death battle besides.

"Chief Mulholland," Boothe said, setting a hard gaze on Wilkie, "this girl is a thief. She's taken private papers and used them to..."

Wilkie's scornful snort interrupted him. "I most certainly did not." *Jameson is dead,* she told herself. *He'd expect me to put the blame on him. It won't hurt him now.* He'd told her what to do more than once.

Every eye turned to stare at her. Hix put his hands on her shoulders and squeezed. Lightly, so as not to hurt. A warning only.

The man in charge, Thomas Mulholland, pointed his forefinger at her. "You'll have your chance to speak, young lady. You, too, Forry. Until then, both of you keep your mouths shut."

Hix hadn't said anything.

Boothe scowled. "You should jail them, Chief. Right now. Before they have a chance to make up more lies."

The white-haired man caught Mulholland's eye and shook his head, an almost infinitesimal movement. She wouldn't have seen it if she hadn't been paying attention.

"Could be they'd say the same about you, Leonard," Mulholland said.

That's right. He had a first name. Wilkie had almost forgotten.

Leonard Boothe's look of confidence faded

a degree or two. "What do you mean by that? You're not going to give credence to what they're saying, are you? We all know Forry is a convicted felon. And what about the girl? She arrived in town and tried to blackmail me. Me and the firm as a whole. When that didn't work, she stole and murdered right alongside Forry."

The pressure of Hix's hands on her shoulders is all that kept Wilkie silent and in her seat. She didn't know how he stood Boothe talking about him like that without speaking out. But, a felon? She wanted to know the story behind that accusation. *Needed* to know.

The white-haired man had a question for Boothe. "Explain to me, sir, who the dead man is and what he has to do with you. Harry Spooner down at the bank said he worked for him, but here he is with Burke and these other men." He eyed Mulholland. "A bunch of damned hardcases as you must know."

The chief nodded. "Yeah, Leonard. I do know. Where did these men come from? At least some of them got paper out on them. Funny kind of crew for a respectable firm to hire."

Boothe's eyes got a panicked look in them, his gaze darting from man to man. "I... I don't know about that. That's Burke's doing. He hired them. The dead man... I didn't know him. All I know is these two—" he meant Hix and Wilkie—"have left a trail of murder from here to Missoula and back again."

The white-haired man raised a gnarled forefinger. "Who was it they're accused of murdering again?" he asked the chief.

"An elderly rancher by the name of Trench Jackson and his wife; Eldon Venig from Boothe's firm; a woodcutter named Wilmer Spreck; and some Jane Doe in the Missoula hospital."

"Somebody has been busy," the white-haired man said. "That's an impressive list."

"It is, ain't it?"

"And now the man is lying dead in Mrs. Badrac's foyer," Boothe added. He sounded quite self-righteous.

"Yeah, him." Chief Mulholland nodded thoughtfully. "I've got a good many questions about him."

"You'll have to speak to Burke," Boothe said again, quick to shift attention from himself. "I don't know why Bal..." he cut off at the first syllable.

Had the man in charge caught Boothe's slip, Wilkie wondered? She believed the white-haired man had going by the stern look he shot towards Boothe.

"You were saying?" he asked.

The attorney shook his head.

Mulholland's hand slapped the table with a knockout blow. Cups rattled, warning of the potential destruction of the thick crockery. All talk stopped. Even Magdalena gasped.

Wilkie jumped along with most everyone else, even the white-haired man.

"Enough," Mulholland said, staring at Boothe before he turned to the white-haired man. "Judge, let's get on with this. I think we have all we need from Boothe to wind this up for now."

Judge? Wilkie stomach muscles curled around, tying themselves into a knot. Were she and Hix about to be tried and convicted right here? Right now?

The judge's gaze settled on her. "Young lady, you seem to have been the catalyst that started off this crime spree. What have you got to say for yourself?"

"Me?" Wilkie's voice came out in a squeak. She had a sudden thought of Jameson and of how he lay in a coffin bound for Spokane about now. No. She hadn't been the catalyst. That had been a letter.

Lips firming and staring directly at Leonard Boothe, Wilkie reached for her valise. She hadn't let it out of her sight from the moment she returned to the kitchen after the confrontation—

oh, call it what it was — after shooting Balakov dead in Magdalena's foyer.

She twirled the lock, hardly having to look. Opening the valise's flap, she selected a document from inside and handed it to Mulholland. To the man in charge, she meant. The chief of police.

"What's this?" The chief scanned the letter, said "harrumph" as if surprised, and passed it to the judge.

He, after reading it, lay the document, the firm's name prominent in the heading, on the table. "Well, Boothe, seems pretty clear your office initiated first contact with this young lady's—" he turned to Wilkie. "What was he? Your uncle?"

She nodded.

"Letter says you had a job for him." The judge was speaking to Boothe again. "Says the job needed special expertise and secrecy. Says you'll pay three hundred dollars plus expenses if he'll agree to open a Mosler safe and keep quiet about it."

Boothe's eyes flickered side to side as though searching for a way out. "Nonsense. I did no such thing."

The judge's forefinger tapped the page. "This says you did. It has your signature on it."

"A forgery."

"Oh, I think not. Come clean, Leonard. You'll

feel better for it."

Boothe remained silent.

"Three hundred dollars. That's a lordly sum for a locksmith to earn. A year's wages for most folks. Must've been something mighty important to pay that kind of fee," Fred said.

"I didn't. This man, this locksmith—he's nothing but a simple safecracker. A yeggman. A criminal."

White eyebrows rose high on the judge's forehead as he feigned surprise. "A safecracker? A yeggman? A criminal? How would you know?"

Boothe had no answer.

Wilkie reached into the valise and withdrew the pouch containing the gold double eagles he'd given her. "Oh, he paid, all right, after trying to cheat on the bargain. And here's the payment." The incongruity of the pouch bearing the Spooner Bank and Trust of Butte's logo struck her anew.

"I wonder how many Mosler safes you have in Butte," she said.

The judge huffed as though amused by her question.

"This money could've come from anywhere." Boothe sounded a little desperate.

"But it didn't." This time when Wilkie reached into the valise and pulled out a handful of papers, the roomful of people held their collective breath.

And so did she. These were the documents that would prove the attorneys had been stealing their clients' assets. The name *Ilona Banks* clearly headed what appeared to be a financial accounting on the topmost page. A page that bore the firm's letterhead.

But even so, she wondered as she handed more incriminating paperwork to the chief of police if it would be clear enough. Mulholland took a full quarter hour to read everything before rising from his seat and pointing at Boothe. "You're under arrest, Leonard. Embezzlement, conspiracy to defraud, conspiracy to murder. I expect there'll be more charges later on."

Boothe yelped as though struck. "What about them? Forry and his woman?"

Behind her, Hix moved restlessly.

The chief grimaced. "I'll deal with them later. You'd probably better start praying Burke survives the shooting. That'll give you someone else to blame." Pulling his gold-cased pocket watch from a vest pocket, he consulted the time. "Train must be late. Judge, you want to wait a few minutes longer or shall we take this miserable reprobate down to the jail?"

Before the judge could answer, boots clumped down the hall from the front. An elderly man, escorted by a Butte police officer, stepped into the kitchen. A striking white bandage wrapped his head like a helmet. Wilkie gasped aloud, while Hix gave an involuntary shout. "Jackson. You're alive."

"Well, son, I ain't a ghost."

The judge bounded to his feet. Rounding the table, he grabbed the older man's hand as though to shake, changed his mind, and embraced him. "Trench, Trench. First word was that you were dead. You *and* Clara June."

Jackson swiped at his eyes. "Clara June died on me, Emmet. And a couple outlaws did try to kill me. But it wasn't these two." His nod took in Hix and Wilkie. "Far from it. I'm here to clear this young feller's name."

"Mr. Jackson," Wilkie said. "I'm so glad to see Balakov lied. We thought for sure he'd killed you. He told us he had."

"Well, bull-snot, missy. I ain't that easy to kill. Not even for some Bulgarian tough guy."

The judge laughed. "And you always did have a hard head, brother."

Brother? Pure joy bubbled up in Wilkie. Beside her, Hix was close enough she felt a quiver shoot through him. His warm fingers reached for and grasped her cold ones.

Relief, no doubt. With this bogus charge of murder cleared up, the other charges would melt away too. She knew it.

And that's how it happened. As more details of skullduggery came to light, the better the case looked for her and for Hix. The knots in Wilkie's stomach began to unravel.

Magdalena, struck hard by Eldon's perfidy, disappeared into another room to weep, her red-rimmed eyes evident when she returned and turned her investment statements over to Mulholland.

Admitting she'd always favored Eldon, even after she suspected Hix's early troubles stemmed from his cousin's double-dealing, she did her utmost to make amends. Turns out friends in high places can be both a help and a hindrance. Magdalena's friendships proved the strongest and most helpful. With the Jackson brothers backing her, at least Hix—nor Wilkie—were charged with murder. Even so, the chief hauled Hix off to answer to the cattle rustling charges Eldon had saddled him with some years back.

Meanwhile, Boothe and Burke discovered, to their disadvantage, that contacts based solely on monetary terms were liable to collapse.

It was a lesson Wilkie vowed to remember.

***

Two days later, her wound mended enough to allow travel, Wilkie, a heavy heart weighing her down, boarded the train bound for Spokane. They, meaning Chief Mulholland and the judge, hadn't let her see Hix before she left, saying the statement she'd signed might be refused in court if there was any chance of collusion between them.

Collusion? How could there be collusion? They'd gone through the situation together. Of course, their account of events would be the same.

However, not wishing to prolong Hix's time in jail, she did as his lawyer said, feeling all the while as if she'd abandoned him. But his record was about to be expunged. She wouldn't sabotage that for the world.

In Spokane, having been sent general freight delivery, Jameson's coffin awaited her. Everything worked out just as Hix had promised when he put his pals from that rundown saloon to work. Then it was merely a matter of hiring transport to carry his body home, something she managed herself.

The big surprise came when, having left the coffin with the undertaker, she walked through the door of her mother's boarding house and found Millie— the real Millie— in charge.

Millie greeted her with a hug and an unexpected statement. "Your mother is gone," she said. "She left the same day you and Jameson did. I've been running the place. None of the boarders have complained." She made the announcement with a certain amount of pride.

"Mother is gone?" Wilkie repeated.

"Flew the coop." Millie's eyes were flashing dark fire. "She hied off to California with some traveling salesman who offered her a life of luxury."

Wilkie, whose mouth had dropped open wide enough to stick a shoe in, found her voice. "Or so he said."

"Or so he said," Millie agreed, peering behind Wilkie with a puzzled frown. "Wilkie, you look terrible. And where is Jameson?"

Esther had always insisted Millie, being the hired help, call him Mr. Van Slyke. Jameson insisted she call him Jameson, same as Wilkie. That Millie used Jameson's name freely now spoke worlds.

The girls wept then, and again when the undertaker planted the coffin in the little cemetery at the base of the hill overlooking the river that same evening.

Turned out Esther had left a note for Jameson, though none for her. Millie found the note one day while dusting Esther's room. Written on a mere scrap of paper, it had been tucked beneath a hand mirror and almost discarded unread.

Wilkie, casting resentment aside, had no compunction about unfolding and reading the note. The message was short, and nothing like she expected. Mean spirited, for one thing. And shocking, though on second thought, maybe not surprising.

Jameson, she read.

I've had almost twenty years in this pur-gatory, and my penance is finally done. She's all yours. I'm sick of claiming that woman's offspring as my own, and you can go to hell where you belong. By the way, good luck running this crummy boarding house. I almost set it on fire on my way out the door. It would've served you right.

Esther

"What does it say?" Millie asked as she watched Wilkie's expression go from curiosity to shock and lastly, to anger.

"It's..." Legs no longer able to hold her, Wilkie sank down on a chair and handed the note to Millie. They were in the kitchen where Millie was baking some kind of cake.

That woman's offspring? What woman? What offspring? *She's all yours?* Who is all yours? Only one answer made any kind of sense.

Esther had meant her. So who was she?

The question ate at her.

A more pleasant letter came on the twenty-third day after she returned home. Or maybe returned to the boarding house where she sheltered was a more accurate statement. Without Jameson, it didn't feel like home. It felt more like Millie's house. Come to find out that for all Esther's posturing, Millie had been the one truly running the boarding house for several years. And she didn't need help.

With the mundane daily problems out of her hands, Wilkie had nothing much to do. Except mourn for Jameson, rage over the woman she'd been taught to call "mother," puzzle over that cryptic letter, and worry where the funds to support herself, and maybe do a little detective work, were going to come from.

Oh. And miss Hix. And wonder if he ever thought of her. Or if he did, if he thought of her even half as often as she thought of him.

Which meant, when she walked over to the post office on that twenty-third day and found a proper looking letter addressed to Jameson, it made an intriguing break in a dull, lifeless routine.

With Millie standing by and egging her on,

she opened this letter, too.

Millie read it with right along with her. "Look," the Indian girl said. "It's a job proposal."

An honest job proposal—although it took a while for Wilkie to decipher penmanship so outrageously bad it made her laugh out loud. The job concerned a question of inheritance and the lost combination to a dead woman's safe. The apparent heir had tried another locksmith, but he'd been unable to open it without causing damage to the mechanism. The heir was sure the will was inside, and he needed it before the week was out.

Please help, the letter concluded.

"You can do it," Millie said. "You can do this easy."

Excitement thrummed in Wilkie's veins. "Maybe. Do you suppose..." Thinking the proposal over, she lost track of what she meant to say.

"You know you want to." Milly was grinning at her like a dark imp.

A check for traveling expenses had been included. Tempting. A restless need for action poked at her. Could she pull this off on her own?

Why resist the temptation?

Wilkie cashed the check and packed a bag quickly enough to catch the first train headed south.

The next day, having spent hours second-guessing herself and wondering if she'd done the right thing, she got off the train in some podunk little town in southern Idaho where the stationmaster knew the way to Jarvis Pettit's place. It remained only to hire a horse. She had her .32, after all, in her boot. When she reached the gate leading to a big old farmhouse, she transferred it to her pocket.

The place seemed deserted, although a small fuzzy dog came around the corner and barked at her. Well, her and the horse, which shied and generally acted the idiot. Dismounting, she took a deep breath and walked up to the door. Knocked.

Now at last, she was nervous. What would this Jarvis Pettit think? Would he send her away? He'd be a fool if he did. She wasn't Jameson Van Slyke, that's true. Or his daughter. Or maybe not even his niece. But she was Jameson's apprentice, for sure, whether locksmith, safecracker or yeggman.

She knocked again. Someone must have heard her. Lord only knows the dog had given plenty of loud notice. "Hush, you," she told the dog, and he oddly, he obeyed.

Footsteps sounded from inside, a man's stride, walking quickly. She touched the .32 in her pocket as the door opened.

Her heart pounded, faster and faster.

"Hey, Wilkie darlin'." Hix's voice caressed like dark velvet though it might've shook just a little. "Come in. I've got a job for you."

A LOOK AT THE WOMAN WHO BUILT A BRIDGE BY C.K. CRIGGER

Spur Award Winner for Western Romance.

Shay Billings is pleasantly surprised at discovering a new bridge over the river, as it cuts several miles from his trip into town. Ambushed and left for dead, he has even more cause to be grateful when the bridge-builder saves his life. Shay's savior turns out to be a mysterious young woman with extraordinary skills. More importantly, she's a strong ally when he and a few other men are forced to defend themselves and their ranches against a power hungry rich man. Marvin Hammel seems determined to own everything in their small valley, his intention to gobble up not only their homes and their livelihoods, but the water that flows through the land.

January Schutt just wants to be left alone to hide her scars. She's rebuilt the bridge that crosses the river onto her property, and lives like a hermit in a rundown old barn. All that changes when she takes in a wounded Shay Billings. Now she's placed in the middle of a war over water rights. But has she picked the winning side?

AVAILABLE NOW

ABOUT THE AUTHOR

C.K. Crigger was born and raised in North Idaho on the Coeur d'Alene Indian Reservation, and currently lives with her husband, three feisty little dogs and an uppity Persian cat in Spokane Valley, Washington.

Imbued with an abiding love of western traditions and wide-open spaces, Crigger writes of free-spirited people who break from their standard roles.

Her short story, Aldy Neal's Ghost, was a 2007 Spur finalist. Black Crossing, won the 2008 EPIC Award in the historical/western category. Letter of the Law was a 2009 Spur finalist in the audio category. The Woman Who Built a Bridge was the 2019 Spur Award winner for best western romance.